To Love a Spy

ANDREA PICKENS

OLIVERHEBERBOOKS

Prologue

Fog swirled up from the harbor, muffling the slap of the waves against the stone jetties. The damp sea breeze had been growing steadily colder over the last hour, and the clouds scudding across the moon warned of a coming squall.

Turning up the collar of her black silk shirt, Valencia edged back between the bales of cotton.

The man was running late. Very late. But then, she had long ago learned that in her profession, things rarely went according to plan.

Unsheathing a knife from the hidden pocket of her trousers, she slipped silently to the far end of the walkway for another look across the wharves. There was no sign of movement among the moored ships, save for the ghostly flutter of sail canvas. However, the creak of the masts and the thrumming of the wind through the rigging seemed to be getting louder. Or was it just that her nerves were on edge?

Valencia drew a deep breath and forced herself to relax. She wasn't very good at waiting.

Impetuous. That was the word her commander-in-chief had

used to critique her last mission. The oblique criticism still stung. He had, of course, not raised his voice—the blasted man rivaled the Sphinx for stony stoicism. But his sapphirine gaze had betrayed a flicker of disappointment. *Damn his lordly eyes.* It was unfair. She had gotten the job done, and while the explosion of the river barge had been an unforeseen complication, an agent in the field sometimes had to make a split second decision.

Life and death.

Her hand tightened on the knife hilt. No one questioned her courage or skill with weapons. It was her bravado that had put a black mark on her record, and she had been cautioned to keep her daredevil disregard for danger under control.

This time, however, she would give her superior no cause for

complaint ...

The faint scuff of steps drew Valencia from her brooding introspection. Swearing a silent oath, she pulled the hooded mask down over her face and hurried through the pooling shadows to catch up with her quarry. Allowing a distraction—even for an instant—was dangerous. But now, all her senses were on full alert.

Up ahead, she saw him hesitate before darting between the rows of cargo crates. Mingled with the pungent scent of salt and pine tar was a whiff of the man's fear. She quickened her pace, her rope-soiled shoes floating noiselessly over the rough planking. In another few strides, she would be within striking distance. The French informant and his stolen government documents would not be crossing the Channel tonight.

She angled her dagger upward, its razored edge cutting a quicksilver arc in the moonlight. *Another step and ...*

All of a sudden, Valencia caught the deadly gleam of another blade angling out of the gloom.

She whipped around, just in the nick of time to parry the

blow. Knife clashed against knife, the mists muffling the ring of steel.

Snick, snick, snick. Her assailant was strong and quick as a cobra with his thrusts. Yet she, too, was skilled in the art of hand-to-hand combat, having trained with the best swordsman in Europe. Coolly countering the force of the attack, she feinted and probed for an opening. But as she pivoted to slide in under his guard, her foot slipped a fraction.

It took her only a split-second to recover.

Too late, too late.

Pain lanced through her leg.

"Are the English so desperate that they must send a woman to do their dirty work?" Through the slits of her mask, Valencia saw a flash of pearly teeth and the curl of a Death's Head smile. "A grave mistake on their part," said her assailant as his blade cut another slash through flesh and muscle.

A grave mistake. She had been assured that the traitor was alone, but she should have checked behind her back. Twisting, turning, Valencia tried to kick free, but her leg gave way.

As she fell to the ground, she heard a light laugh. "And an even bigger blunder on your part, *cherie*. For now you are going to die."

Through the haze of pain, she saw a last glint of the knife, and then everything went black.

Damn. Damn. Damn. It wasn't supposed to end this way ...

Chapter One
Ten years later

The frigid water cut against her skin, sharp and biting as a blade. Gasping for breath, Valencia shook off the pain and forced her limbs to move. *Stroke, kick, stroke, kick.* The rhythm slowly melted the icy shock and as she fought through the swirling currents, the tension ebbed from her muscles.

Mind over body. It was a lesson learned long ago from an Indian faquir who had taught a special class at her school. Despite its odd name, yoga had proved a powerful force for disciplining both sinew and spirit.

Discipline. Closing her eyes to the sting of the salt, Valencia quickened her pace. As if her former training mattered anymore. But old habits died hard. Every dawn, no matter how rough the seas, she swam across Derrible Bay—a quarter mile out to the jut of rock and a quarter mile back. The physical challenge made her feel whole again—

Don't sink into self-pity, she chided herself, slipping through the waves like a sleek seal. The past was the past. Bitter brooding did naught but put her in a black frame of mind for the rest of the day. Better to simply revel in the surge of strength rippling through her naked arms and legs. The daily exercise kept her body as lean and lithe as in the old days.

After all, it was simply good to be alive.

Her fingers touched the storm-worn stone of the outcropping and she lingered for a moment, watching the first rays of sunlight wash over the horizon. *Red sky at morning, sailors take warning.* The pink glow was deepening to a dark mauve. A storm was brewing somewhere out in the Atlantic—a bad one by the look of it. A prudent ship captain would heed the signs and seek safe harbor for the next few days. The gales at this time of year could be brutal, especially here among the treacherous shoals of the Channels Islands.

Valencia turned and started back to shore. Foul weather was always good for business at her dockside tavern. She had best get into work early and see that Jemmy Welch brought up an extra keg or two of ale. If left to his own devices, the bar man would likely be napping in the back room after enjoying a wee nip of brandy for breakfast.

However, beggars could not be choosy. The town of Maseline was small and an able-bodied man could make more money fishing or farming than working the odd hours for her. Besides, other than a weakness for spirits, Jemmy was an excellent employee. He was trustworthy and always jovial, which balanced her own tendency for introspective brooding. And he didn't mind taking orders from a female.

Most men were loath to admit that a woman might be their equal, either intellectually or physically. It had been rough going for the first few years of business, but the locals no longer questioned her entrepreneurial savvy or her ability to pitch a drunkard out on his ear if he tried to make trouble. Though she was not all that she used to be, she still could hold her own.

For the most part, however, the isle of Sark offered peace and quiet. A haven of tranquility, where the taciturn locals did not ask prying questions. If at times it was *too* tranquil, that was a small price to pay for distancing herself from her former life.

She had once been a Merlin, a highflying member of an elite group of women warriors. As students at Mrs. Merlin's Academy for Extraordinary Young Ladies, she and her comrades-in-arms had engaged in a rigorous program of training, learning the art of spying, swordplay and seduction. Only the very best earned their wings as full-fledged agents.

But for those who won the right to sport a small tattoo of a merlin hawk above their left breast, no assignment was too daunting or too dangerous. Indeed, they were England's ultimate secret weapon, called upon to counter the most diabolical threats to the Crown.

There were times when she missed the training fields, the hell-for-leather riding, the camaraderie of her fellow warriors ...

A last few hard strokes brought back to the rocky beach. Stepping out of the surf, Valencia hurried to towel the salt water from her skin, her gaze as usual avoiding the jagged scar that cut across her thigh. It was not quite so easy to ignore the limp that hobbled her stride. Though a regimen of grueling exercises had made it less pronounced, she was still painfully aware of her own limitations. In the past ...

"To hell with the past," she muttered.

Tugging on her shift, Valencia reached for her woolen gown. Regrets and recriminations were crippling. The trick was to stay one step ahead of such maudlin moods.

She was just tying off the top laces when the crunch of stones underfoot caused her to turn.

"Well, well, wot's we got here?" Two men were closing in on her. The leader—a barrel-chested brute with a mane of matted red hair—dropped his armful of firewood and drew a knife.

"Looks like a tasty tart, Flame." The other man smacked his

lips as he tossed away his sticks. "And we ain't had our breakfast yet."

Finian O'Hanlon, known as 'The Flame' for his explosive temper and burning dislike for the British authorities, was an Irish smuggler who had recently begun to muscle in on the Cornish and Channel Island trade. Neither the local men nor the revenue officials were happy about his presence. The Flame and his crew were said to be ruthless in their pursuit of profit, and rumor had it that the sinking of Will Starling's fishing boat was no accident.

Valencia made no move to flee. The chances of escape were virtually nil, given her bad leg. But a surrender to Fate was not what kept her from running. Sark was her home, its people her neighbors. Will had been a good customer. And a good friend.

"Aye, Seagull, she'll make a nice treat fer us and the laddies back on board." O'Hanlon lunged and caught her arm.

Valencia didn't flinch as his knife kissed up against her throat.

"Looks to be meek as a mouse, don't she? Reckon she's too terrified to twitch a muscle." Seagull laughed. "I hope she's shows a bit more life when I'm swiving her. I like a bit o' fight in my doxies."

"Don't worry, I know plenty 'o ways of warming up a woman." O'Hanlon shoved her roughly toward the narrow footpath that cut through the thickets of gorse and brambles. "Move, missy. And don't be getting any ideas from Seagull. Ye try to kick or scream and I'll slit that lovely neck o' yours."

Valencia allowed herself to be marched to the crest of the rocks. The craggy coastline of the island was dotted with countless hidden inlets and coves, making it nigh on impossible for the revenue patrols to catch a smuggler who knew the ins and outs of the local waters. Flame and his crew were no doubt well aware of the area's advantages.

Sure enough, rounding a jut of windcarved granite, she saw that a dark-hulled ketch was anchored in the narrow spit of water just below, its raked masts hidden from view of the open seas.

"Watch yer step." O'Hanlon tightened his hold on her arm as she stumbled over the uneven scree. "Wouldn't us want te end up wiv damaged goods, now would ye, missie?"

"Heh, heh, heh," grunted Seagull. "She's gonna be a lot worse for wear when we finish taking our pleasure wid her."

"How many of you are there?" asked Valencia.

"Wot's it matter?" retorted Seagull.

"Just curious as to how many arses I have to kick in order to take over the ship," she replied evenly.

Seagull answered with an obscenity.

"Ye got spunk, I'll grant ye that." O'Hanlon's mouth stretched wide to reveal a flash of teeth.

Valencia doubted it was meant as a reassuring smile.

"But if ye know what's good fer ye," continued O'Hanlon, "Ye'll keep a sweet tongue when talking te me, lassie." The blade pressed harder against her flesh. "It's dangerous to make me angry."

That makes two of us, thought Valencia.

The steep path led down to where a dingy was pulled up on the sliver of sand. "Lazy buggers," growled Seagull, slanting a critical eye at the ketch. Spitting into the sea, he fisted the oars. "Looks like Gremlin, Blackie and Cheshire are still sleeping it off."

So, there were five men in all.

Valencia surveyed the deserted deck. It looked to loaded with a full cargo, for an overflow of barrels were stacked in the stern. No doubt the smugglers had decided to take shelter and ride out the coming bad weather, rather than risk crossing the Channel in the teeth of a gale.

"Stow the complaining and row, Seagull." O'Hanlon gave a warning waggle of his knife and smirked. "Don't I always finds us comfort in a storm?"

The Marquess of Lynsley shook the drops of water from his oilskin cloak and entered the Secretary of State for War's private office.

"Forgive me for being late, Bathurst," he murmured, handing it to a young adjutant who discreetly removed both himself and the still-dripping garment from the room. "I came as quickly as I could."

The Secretary of State looked up from a sheaf of military dispatches. "Thank you, Lynsley. My apologies for the filthy conditions, and for calling you back to London on such short notice, but the matter is most urgent."

"So I gathered from your note." After nodding a quick greeting to the other gentlemen at the long table, Lynsley took a seat and opened his document case. The presence of Admiral Cornwallis, commander of the Channel Fleet, and Major Fenimore, General Burrand's top strategist, confirmed that the situation must be grave indeed. "Perhaps you would be so good as to elaborate. The facts were, by necessity, rather sparse."

"Actually, I will let Colonel Whitney explain the problem." The Secretary gestured to the officer seated to his left. "He arrived from Portugal last night, with a personal request from Wellington that we give this top priority."

Lynsley didn't recognize the face, but his uniform identified him as a senior member of the Duke's staff.

"Thank you, milord. As you all undoubtedly know, Wellington has appointed *me* to oversee our intelligence-gathering network throughout the Peninsula, and it was *my* men who discovered the details ..." Whitney made a show of rising as he spoke, and smoothing a hand over the row of medals decorating his chest.

Pompous ass, thought Lynsley as he squared his papers into order. But as usual, he hid his irritation behind a mask of perfunctory politeness. "How good to hear that you are doing your job," he replied dryly. "Please go on."

Whitney hesitated for a fraction before continuing in a slightly less condescending tone. "Er, yes, well, I hardly need explain to you that the recent events in Russia were a grievous blow to Napoleon's aura of invincibility. Word is, his army has suffered huge losses and is in full retreat from Moscow. If our forces strike hard and fast, while morale is low and his chain of command is stretched thin, we may have a chance to end this interminable war ..."

As the colonel droned on, Lynsley surreptitiously studied his own intelligence reports. His official title—Minister to the Secretary of State for War—was a deliberately vague cover for his true responsibilities. Charged with countering foreign espionage and intrigue, he was head of a secret cadre of warriors that dealt with the most dangerous and diabolical threats to England's sovereignty.

As a rule, he usually avoided committee meetings such as this one—the fewer people aware of his real work, the better. But in this case, the latest dispatches from his own informants corroborated what the colonel was saying. The situation was indeed unique. There was finally a chink in the Emperor's armor.

The last page turned with a faint crackle. *Or was there?*

Whitney finished with a flourish. "To sum it up in a nutshell, gentlemen, Boney's forced retreat sends a signal to our faltering Allies that the French are at last vulnerable. However, we recently learned that one of his most dangerous agents—a fellow named Rochambeau—has made a diabolical discovery. One that may cause our advantage to go up in flames."

The other men around the table straightened in their chairs.

Lynsley looked up as well. His most recent report from the Peninsula had made mention of a disquieting incident in the city of Cordoba. So far, the information had not been confirmed. But if Rochambeau was involved, that was bad news indeed.

"Kindly dispel with the theatrics, colonel," he said. "And report the facts."

Whitney gave an aggrieved sniff, clearly enjoying the captive audience. However, on meeting the marquess's stony stare, he swallowed any retort and continued. "For some time, our army intelligence network in southern Spain had been hearing rumors concerning an elderly Arab scholar who special-ized in the study of ancient science. It was said that he had unearthed some long lost treatise on the art of explosives." He drew a deep breath. "One that apparently detailed discoveries made by the Turks, using innovations developed in China. Which, as you all undoubtedly know, was where gunpowder was first created—"

"Cut to the chase, man," growled Admiral Cornwallis. "None of us need a lecture in military history."

"In this case, background information is important," replied Whitney through gritted teeth. "For it explains why Wellesley dispatched me to Whitehall with such urgency. But as you wish me to get to the point—it is this! After experi-menting with the information he discovered, the scientist succeeded in creating a ... a diabolical secret weapon. Not only is the explosive power far beyond anything we currently possess, but we have also been told that the resulting flames cannot be extinguished by water alone. My understanding is that it's like the ancient Greek Fire, but with a modern twist."

The colonel's voice rose a notch. "If true, just imagine what it would do to our Royal Navy. Such a substance could turn the tide of war in Napoleon's favor and allow the French to invade our shores."

Cornwallis paled.

Fenimore looked more skeptical. "A diabolical secret weapon? Surely you are exaggerating."

"I am not," said Whitney stiffly. "Furthermore, we know that the formula, and a small sample of the stuff are on their way to Paris as we speak, carried by Rochambeau."

"Why can't we get a copy of the bloody formula, too?" demanded the Admiral. "Fight fire with fire is what I say."

"Impossible," said Whitney curtly. "The scholar was murdered and his laboratory destroyed by the Frenchman, including all the ancient manuscripts. There is no other copy. Just the original laboratory journal."

"Which will be locked right and tight in the French military headquarters," muttered Cornwallis. "And guarded by a horde of Hussars."

"On the contrary, that is the one glimmer of good news we have." Looking somewhat less defensive, Whitney was quick to continue. "Apparently the journal is written in some arcane code, and Rochambeau is unwilling to let the military take a crack at deciphering the formula and thus steal all the glory for the discovery. Instead, he means to keep the notes and sample a secret until he can personally hand them over to the Emperor. So, chances are that for the next few weeks, the material will be in his private residence, not be locked away in a Ministry vault." He cracked his knuckles. "If we could get our hands on it and spirit it out of the country ..."

"And if pigs could fly," murmured Fenimore.

The colonel shot him a quelling look, then held the pause a moment longer. "Once again, gentlemen, I ask you to consider the consequences if Napoleon is allowed to develop this for military use!"

Lynsley's mood turned more brooding as the others began to pepper the colonel with more questions. Steepling his fingers, he stared meditatively at the recent reports sent out from his own operatives across the Channel. They all confirmed that with Wellington on the offensive in Spain and Napoleon fighting his way through the eastern Europe, the French were at long last vulnerable.

Vulnerable.

But by some strange twist of fate, his own forces were also not at full strength.

Of all the cursed luck ...

As if echoing his sentiments, Admiral Cornwallis let loose with a volley of expletives. "Damn it," he added. "We simply *must* find a way to get at that weapon. From what you say, Whitney, it may spell the difference between a quick, decisive victory and allowing the Little Corsican to rise, like a phoenix, from the ashes of Moscow."

"Eloquently put, Sir William," said Fenimore. His brow arched in question, he looked to the Lord Bathurst.

The Secretary looked to Lynsley. "What about the Merlins?"

Lynsley blew out his cheeks. He had known that this question was coming. "I am sorry to say that their ranks are somewhat depleted at the moment. In truth, I have no one whom I consider ready to take on an assignment of this magnitude."

The ensuing silence was broken by the clinking of the colonel's medals. Crossing his arms with a sneering huff, the officer muttered "women" under his breath.

The marquess was tempted to reach across the polished oak and stuff the gaudy bits of brass down the man's throat. Though he rarely betrayed any hint of emotion, the gratuitous insult struck a raw nerve.

"Perhaps if you pulled your head from out of your arse, you would see the light, Whitney," he snapped. "This is a new century and the old world order is crumbling. Those who can't accept radical new concepts—such as women being the equals of men when it comes to brains and bravery—will be left in the dust."

Assuming an even more offensive drawl, Lynsley went on to rattle off several incidents where his Merlins had saved the day for England and her allies.

The Secretary, always the consummate diplomat, interceded before the colonel could reply. "Now, Thomas, no one is questioning the courage or competence of your, er, troops. We were merely, er, hoping ..."

"That the girls could put aside their knitting and cooking long enough to pull your cods out of the fire?" he said sharply. "By the by, I see in my notes that it was one of Colonel Whitney's cavalry patrols that let Rochambeau slip through their fingers in the first place."

The officer had the grace to flush. "Yes, but if the Royal Navy had intercepted the schooner—"

"Let us not bicker on who is to blame, gentlemen," interrupted Bathurst. "We are, after all, on the same side."

Lynsley leaned back, feeling their gazes once again shift to him.

Damn.

He supposed it was up to him to come up with a plan of action. Though God only knew what it might be. Sighing, he took a moment to pack up his papers. "Let us meet back here at the end of the day. By then I will have some ideas put together for you."

The colonel did not look pleased at the delay. However the

Secretary hustled him through the parting protocols and out of the office before any further fireworks could erupt.

"Do try to come up with something, Thomas," murmured Bathurst as he watched the Admiral and Major Fenimore follow in Whitney's wake. "Knightley is breathing down my neck to make a move—any move."

"Even if the slightest slip would prove fatal?"

Bathurst made a wry face. "That is what comes from being so bloody good at what you do. The Crown expects miracles from the Merlins."

"No matter than I am merely a flesh and blood man, not a magician?" said Lynsley somewhat waspishly.

The Secretary regarded him with some concern. "Is something troubling you? I don't think I've ever seen you so ... out of sorts."

"Forgive me," muttered Lynsley. "Men like Whitney, who are ruled by arrogance rather than intelligence, are particularly annoying. Especially when the women they so disparage are expected to ride to their rescue."

"I am sorry to put you in such a damnably difficult position. But I have no choice."

"I know, Henry." He ran a hand through his hair. "I'll come up with something."

The Secretary gave a ghost of a smile. "You always do."

You always do.

The drumbeat of his steps seemed a mocking echo of the words as Lynsley traversed the warren of Whitehall corridors leading down to his own suite of offices. Despite his avowal to Bathurst, he was not feeling overly sanguine about the chances of cobbling together a successful plan. A mission of this magnitude required months of meticulous planning. Proper reconnaissance, lines of supply, safe houses, support staff ... And even then, there were a myriad of things that could go wrong.

It would take an act of God to pull off a miracle at this late moment.

Slouching into his desk chair, he absently picked up the sheaf of documents on his blotter. Numerous people owed him numerous favors, but even if he called in—

His eyes fell on the top paper. After reading the scrawled message, he tapped thoughtfully at his chin.

Perhaps he did have a guardian angel after all.

It would take a good deal of luck, as well as divine intervention, but if he moved fast, the idea just might be turned into the answer to his prayers.

Chapter Two

"I don't see that I have any choice, Charlotte." As he spoke, Lynsley looked around the headmistress's office. How long had Mrs. Merlin's Academy for Extraordinary Young Ladies been in existence? Had it really been two decades?

Time flies, he thought with a wry grimace. Lord, he had been barely older than the current students of the Master Class when he had come up with the idea of a secret school for spies—female spies.

Yes, he had been young—and too brimming with hubris and optimism to conceive of how impossible the idea was. His lips curled up at the corners. Perhaps that was why it had, against all odds, succeeded. He had simply refused to accept 'no' as an answer, despite all the rational arguments against it.

He rubbed at his brow, suddenly aware of the grey hairs beginning to tinge his temples.

Mrs. Merlin sighed as she served him a helping of tea and strawberry tarts. "So you say, Thomas. And yet, sometimes I wonder ..."

"Wonder what?" he asked.

"Whether you are secretly craving a return to action."

His smile became a touch more pronounced. "You think I'm too old for the game?"

"Too valuable," replied the headmistress with her usual pragmatism. "Surely there must be an alternative to risking yourself in such a dangerous mission."

"If you have a suggestion, I am open to hearing it."

For a moment, Mrs. Merlin's face was half obscured by the steam rising up from the teapot. With her delicate features and dove-gray hair drawn back in a simple chignon, the elderly lady looked frail as a feather. But Lynsley knew her far too well to be deceived by appearances. The headmistress of Mrs. Merlin's Academy for Extraordinary Young Ladies was still sharp enough to show her pupils a thing or two about handling a sword or a pistol. Even now, he could see the point of a poniard poking out from beneath her lace cuff.

"We might consider Verona," mused Mrs. Merlin. "She has both the skills and the nerve to succeed in a mission like this."

"I am all too familiar with her cockiness and her courage." Lynsley sighed, and then shook his head. "But no, even though she's the best we have, she's not ready to match wits with an experienced killer like Rochambert. I can't in good conscience give her the order."

"Then perhaps you should simply tell the Secretary to look elsewhere for help," said the headmistress. "Some things are impossible, even for us. As we teach our girls, there are times when it is best to back away and wait for a more opportune moment."

"I made a stab at saying no," he replied wryly. "But Bathurst is under extreme pressure from the government to do something about the situation, no matter the risks. He's supported me many times in the past when I was under fire. I can hardly refuse to return the favor."

"He won't thank you if you end up in a French prison." Mrs. Merlin brushed a bit of powdered sugar from her lip. "Or worse."

"Thank you for the vote of confidence," murmured Lynsley dryly.

She fixed him with a searching stare. "All jesting aside, Thomas. Do you truly believe you can succeed?"

"Despite what you think, I am not yet in my dotage. In my younger days, I was not half bad at this sort of thing."

She rose without comment and moved to her desk. He heard a drawer slide open, followed by the rustle of paper and the scrape of a penknife. "Perhaps the key question to ask is whether you believe that this weapon actually exists. A substance that combines an explosive power beyond our wildest imagination with a fire that can't be extinguished by water? It seems ... unthinkable."

"I asked the same question of my scientific consultant. As it happens, Lady Merton met El-Halabi several years ago when he was in Cambridge for a symposium on Medieval manuscripts. Based on her research, she is of the opinion that such a thing is theoretically possible."

"Then we must take the threat seriously. Lady Merton's expertise in chemistry is unimpeachable, despite her sex."

"Yes, it is," said Lynsley softly.

Mrs. Merlin looked grim. "So, you mean to go through with this, come hell or high water?"

He regarded the gilt framed portrait of Francis Walsingham, England's first spymaster for a long moment before answer. "We have a duty to do what we are asked, no matter how dangerous or daunting, Charlotte. I won't send an unfledged Merlin on a mission like this. So I had better do the job myself."

Pierre Rochambeau was the most dangerous agent the

French had. Lynsley had reason to know his deadly skill all too well. One of his Merlins ...

He did not like to dwell on his failures. It was hard enough to send his women into danger. The guilt he felt when a mission went wrong tore at his insides. It was no wonder, he supposed, that sleep was often elusive.

A fresh sheet of foolscap slapped down on the desk blotter, rousing him from such dark musings. "When do they want you to leave?" asked the headmistress.

"As soon as possible. I am aiming for tonight, on the midnight tide," he replied. "A coastal cutter is waiting at Southampton to take me across the Channel."

"You are going alone?"

"Yes."

"Hmmph." Mrs. Merlin adjusted her gold-rimmed spectacles. "Well, then, we haven't any time to waste. Give me an overview of the situation. If I can't dissuade you, I can at least try to help you come up with a viable strategy for success."

Lynsley gave an inward smile. Now he knew how the Academy students felt on being subjected to the headmistress's intense scrutiny. A good many of the Merlins had sat in his place, answering both her questions and his.

Had they also experienced the small flutter of exhilaration on knowing they would soon be flying into action? Perhaps Mrs. Merlin was right. Perhaps he did miss the thrum of his pulse pounding wildly through his veins, the challenge of the unknown. He had been sitting behind a desk for more years than he cared to count.

A regimented routine. To tell the truth, his life of late *had* been feeling a bit flat.

"I mean to keep it simple," he replied. "I plan to land in St. Pierre Eglise—"

"Why such a small town as St. Pierre Eglise, when the

larger ports of Calaise or Dieppe are so much closer?" interrupted Mrs. Merlin.

"In his latest report, the head of my Normandy network informed me that an American envoy from President Madison is visiting relatives near the city before heading on to meet with French officials in the capital. I have already sent word for our operatives to invite the man for a more prolonged stay in the area." He smiled faintly. "Masquerading as Mr. Tobias Payne Tremaine, I shall be welcome in the salons and mansions of the *haute monde*."

"So far, so good. It's unlikely the French are familiar with Tremaine's face. He's a new appointment to Mr. Madison's diplomatic corps, if I remember correctly."

"Your memory, as always, is sharp as a tack," replied Lynsley.

Mrs. Merlin tapped a pen to her chin. "What about the American officials in Paris?"

"The entire delegation is presently on a trip to the south of France for talks on the Barbary pirate problem."

Mrs. Merlin added a few lines to her notes. "Very good. So once you are in Paris, what then?"

Lynsley shrugged. "From there I shall just have to play it by ear. The agent holding the weapon is a man who enjoys the finer things in life when he is not on assignment—wine, women, witty conversation. He will be moving in the highest circles of Parisian society, savoring all the sumptuous pleasures that the City of Light has to offer.

"Have you any ally in the city?" she asked.

"I've one or two names, but whether they are trustworthy is another matter. For all practical purposes, I shall assume I am on my own if things go awry."

"We always give our Merlins a plan of escape," she said softly.

"There simply isn't time, Charlotte. This is a unique opportunity. We can't afford to let it slip through our fingers." The marquess uncrossed his legs and rose. "Think of the countless lives that will be saved, not only by keeping such a weapon from being turned on our sailors, but also by bringing this war to a quick end."

Candlelight glinted off her glass lenses as Mrs. Merlin added a few more lines to her notes.

Good Lord, was that a telltale glitter of tears clinging to her lashes?

He glanced away for a moment. Duty and discipline were basic principles of the Academy's code of honor. Emotion was left unspoken.

Perhaps the flicker was merely a quirk of the flames, for when she set down her pen and looked up, her eyes reflected naught but a steely composure. "Do try to make sure that one of those lives is your own, Thomas."

"I will. I've no desire to stick my spoon in the wall just yet."

"Well then, you had best be off." The headmistress waved a curt dismissal.

His hand was on the door latch when she added, "*Bonne chance, mon vieux.*"

Lynsley turned. "*Merci.*"

"Hold her arms and lift up her skirts," ordered O'Hanlon.

Valencia let herself go limp as Seagull dragged her to the ship's rail.

"Ready fer some heat, sweeting." The Flame waggled his hips as he set aside his knife and started to unbuckle the leather belt around his middle.

Steady, steady.

Ignoring the clammy touch of Seagull's hand on her thigh,

Valencia concentrated on gauging the roll of ship. Timing would be everything. She was a bit rusty in some of the maneuvers, but hopefully it wouldn't throw her off too badly.

As the sea ebbed, she shifted her feet ever so slightly.

O'Hanlon's pants were down around his knees—that would slow him up a step. Seagull began a leering laugh ...

Rolling with the next wave, Valencia threw her weight into him. His grip loosened for an instant, allowing her to smash an elbow into his throat.

"Arrrgh!" He doubled over with a rasping gurgle.

Spinning around in the same whirlwind movement, she slammed a fist into his gut, dropping him to the deck.

Still fumbling with his pants, O'Hanlon snatched up a marlinspike from a pile of rope. "Why, you little bitch," he snarled, refastening his front flap "I was going to leave you alive, but now you'll not be fit for crab bait when I finish having my way with you."

"Don't bet on it," she replied.

Steel winked in the sunlight as he jabbed out a series of slashes and feints. Valencia measured his movements as she managed to evade the weapon. He was quick as a snake, which came as no surprise. A man in his line of work would likely have a number of back alley tricks to try—she didn't imagine that he was going to fight fair.

But neither was she.

Dropping back, she shuffled sideways.

A laugh, low and nasty, sounded. "I've got ye cornered, now."

He was right—another step would bring her back up against the forecastle hatchway. With the tangle of rigging straight ahead, all angles of escape were cut off. There was nowhere to go but …

Glancing up, Valencia spotted one of the main shrouds snugged tight around a cleat. She leapt up, grabbed the rigging ax from its bracket and hacked through the rope in one fell swoop.

Whoomph! The furled sail and spars dropped like a stone. Catching the tail end of the rope as it whipped through the air, Valencia flew up in a blur of skirts. She swung across the deck, just out of reach of O'Hanlon's slashing spike, and grabbed another line in midair. Tucking into a tight somersault, she landed lightly on deck behind him.

Bellowing with impotent rage, the smuggler whipped around and slashed yet again with his spike. He was a fraction too late—the steel cut harmlessly through the air.

Valencia timed her slide perfectly and countered with swift sidearm chop to his wrist.

A howl punctuated the crack of the snapping bone.

Then he sunk to the deck not far from the fallen Seagull. The slap of the sea against the ship's hull did not quite drown their mewling moans.

Valencia rubbed at her hand and winced. *Damn.* Along with yoga, Chinese martial arts had been part of her basic school training. But apparently she was out of practice.

If the angle wasn't quite right on that blow, it hurt like hell.

Moving on, she ducked around to the ship's wheel and drew the brace of pistols holstered by the mizzenmast. Once she tied up O'Hanlon, Seagull and the sleeping crew, she would make up a few gunpowder flares. The signal of smoke and sparks would soon bring help. *Let Captain Taft of the Revenue Service decide what to do with the bilge rats.*

"Don't move," she snapped at Seagull, who was just beginning to crawl to his knees. "Or I'll put a bullet between your eyes." She cocked both hammers. "And in case you are wondering, I can shoot the wick off a candle at thirty paces."

"Who the devil *are* you?" groaned O'Hanlon.

"Me?" She shrugged. "Why, I'm just a simple tavern keeper."

Captain Taft of the British Revenue Service cutter *Bulldog* whistled softly as he surveyed the trussed-up prisoners. "The Flame and his crew caught red-handed? I shall ask my superiors that you be given a medal. Maybe two."

Valencia grinned. "You go ahead and take the credit. I'd much rather have the cargo of French brandy as my reward, if you don't mind."

Taft laughed. "You've certainly earned it. I think I can be convinced to turn a blind eye to its transfer."

"Excellent. And in the spirit of comradely cooperation, you and your crew will drink for free tonight."

"You may end up with the worst of the bargain, Mrs Kestrel …"

Given that widows were accorded more more freedom from the strictures of society than unmarried misses, Valencia had thought it wise to assume a conveniently dead husband when she chose to take up residence on the island. With the war raging on the Continent, nobody had ever thought to question her assertion.

"Considering the weather, we will not be sailing our usual patrols," continued Taft. He chuckled, and then cleared his throat. "Er, might I ask inquire just how you came to best a gang of the roughest smugglers in these waters?"

"Actually, I'd rather you didn't ask," she replied.

His brows quirked up. "According to O'Hanlon's account, he was not battling an innkeeper but a Death's Head Hussar."

"You know the Irish—they are wont to exaggerate."

Taft gave a pointed look at the smuggler's splinted arm and bruised face but tactfully dropped the subject. "My men will be taking the boat around to Maseline harbor now. May we offer you a ride?"

"Thank you, but no. Just give me a row to shore, if you please. I would rather walk back to town."

The dingy dropped her on the strand. Valencia watched the sailors pull back to the smuggler's cutter and climb aboard. The crack of canvas, loud as gunshots, rang out as the sails caught in the wind and the vessel headed for the opening between the rocks.

She turned, but found herself in no hurry to head for the steep path leading back up to the crest of the cliffs. Her gaze lingered on the freshening seas and the wheeling gulls. Their raucous cries and freewheeling antics drew a harried sigh from her lips.

How exhilarating it was to spread wings and fly.

Flexing her hands, Valencia was aware of the thrum in her blood. Her pulse was still racing from the excitement.

Admit it. She made a face. She missed the challenge, the thrill, the danger. It made her feel so ... alive.

And that her spur-of-the-moment plan had succeeded gave her a measure of satisfaction. *Pride?* Perhaps. Though after all these years she should no longer feel she had anything to prove. Still, there were many a night when she lay awake brooding over a confrontation that had not gone so well.

Her last mission as a Merlin had been one of the few failures of her elite group.

Valencia kicked at a pebble. Had she made a fatal mistake that night? Or had her opponent simply been better than she was? Over and over she had relived the events in her head ... the mists rising up from the harbor, the pungent smells of oakum and pine tar, the whisper of footsteps over the salt soaked jetty ...

She had been quick with her knife. But not quick enough. Only the fortuitous arrival of a harbor foot patrol had kept the French agent from administering the *coup de grace*.

Her superior had not blamed her for letting her target get away, though others were not so forgiving. She had heard whispers that Whitehall was furious with the failure. But ultimately the question of blame became moot. Physical injury had made it impossible for her to continue in active service.

It was, for all involved, seen as a blessing in disguise—everyone saved face.

Her jaw tightened. Except for her, of course. Offered a less demanding job, she had handed in her wings and stormed out of the Academy office.

Angry, disillusioned, she had vowed never to look back.

Still, the memories were hard to forget. The years of training at the Academy, the camaraderie with her sisters-in-arms. Her class had been the very first, and the struggles to master the demanding curriculum and the daunting skepticism of the government had not been easy.

Valencia caught herself unconsciously rubbing at the tiny tattoo above her left breast. It had left an indelible mark on her, no matter how much she wished to deny it.

A glance up showed that the skies were fast darkening to the same ink-black shade. Gusts buffeted the nearby rocks, the swirling currents whipping the waves to a froth of whitecaps. Looking west, she felt the sting of the salt spray against her cheeks. A gale was brewing. And it was only going to get worse. God help any ship caught in the teeth of this storm. Tonight was not the night to challenge the elements.

Sometimes discretion was the better part of valor. It was a lesson that she ought to have taken to heart earlier in life.

But live and learn.

Throwing her hood up over her windsnarled hair, Valencia turned away from the water's edge and headed for home.

The hull gave another wild lurch.

"You had best go below, sir," cried the captain, trying to make himself heard above the howling wind.

Lynsley clung to the mast as waves washed over the deck. "There must be something I can do to lend a hand," he shouted back.

A flash of lightening showed the officer's salt-streaked face was grey with exhaustion. Crippled by a broken rudder, the ship had been fighting the storm for what seemed like an eternity. Somehow the crew had managed to climb aloft and reef the sails, but even under reduced canvas, the ship could make no headway the raging seas.

"You can try to help me hold the course steady," croaked the captain through cracked lips.

Lynsley clawed his way to the ship's wheel. Despite his oilskin cloak, he was soaked to the bone by the frigid seawater and lashing rain, and his hands were stiff as blocks of ice.

"What bearing?" he asked, trying to make out the markings of the compass in the swirling darkness. The flying spray had long since extinguished the binnacle light.

A rope snapped overhead and the whipping end nearly knocked off his head.

"Just try to keep the bow headed into the wind," gasped the captain. Another flash of storm-blurred light gave a glimpse of the fellow's hands, which were raw and bloodied from fighting the fury of the waves. "God only knows where we are now. I don't think we've drifted far enough south to fear running aground on the shoals of Cap D'Antifer."

"Ah, well, that's a relief. For a moment I was worried," said Lynsley dryly as he gripped the slippery spokes.

The captain gave a harried laugh. "Sorry, sir. I would have had you across before the blow hit if not for the damn rudder pin snapping."

"Life is full of unexpected surprises," replied Lynsley. "Bad luck can strike at any time."

"Aye, sir. If we can just weather the next—" The captain's words were cut off by a clap of thunder.

And then by the crack of the mainmast.

The deck pitched to a near perpendicular angle, throwing Lynsley hard against the aft hatchway. All around, he heard the sound of splintering wood and snapping rigging.

As the next wave slammed into the ship, Lynsley felt himself slipping, sliding.

Bloody hell. The lee rail was already buried in a roiling wash of water. In another moment ...

A wall of water rose up, black as Hades. He had one last thought before being sucked under.

Mrs. Merlin was going to be madder than a wet hen.

Chapter Three

The worst of the storm had blown itself out by dawn. From the crest of the cliff, Valencia surveyed the gunmetal grey seas and decided it was safe enough to venture a swim in the shallow part of the bay. The wind had died down to a stiff breeze, and as she picked her way down to the strand, it seemed almost calm.

Ebb and flow. The forces of nature had their own immutable rhythm. Only a fool tried to challenge such elemental truths. Sometimes the prudent course of action was to hunker down in a snug shelter with a good book and a glass of fine French brandy.

Her lips quirked as she shifted her hold on a jug of spirits. She rarely drank, but this was a particularly good vintage, and its warmth had been most welcome last night. After her swim, she would leave it as a gift for Harry Holcroft, the elderly farmer who often shared his catch of rabbits with her.

Valencia's smile faded as she spotted a splintered spar and scrap of canvas floating in the surf. *Why were men so reckless?* The Channel coast was notoriously treacherous at this time of year. What reason was worth risking a life for, she wondered grimly. Any captain worth his salt should have known better than to challenge the storm.

More wreckage littered the beach. She stepped over a tangle of rigging and swore softly. "Damn fools," she began—and then broke into a run.

The body had washed ashore at the far end of the crescent cove and was lying face down on the smooth stones.

Valencia crouched down and took gentle hold of the man's sodden coat. There was no movement, no sign of life as her fingers felt for a pulse. His flesh was cold as marble.

Poor devil. It would take a miracle for him to have survived the storm. Gritting her teeth for the worst, she slowly turned him over.

And nearly swooned in shock.

Despite the muddled bruises and tangled hair, the face confronting her was all too familiar. A ghost from another life, come back to haunt her.

Valencia bit back an oath. As if her own thoughts were not disturbing enough.

The man suddenly stirred, a whispered sigh slipping from his salt cracked lips, along with retching sound that brought up a spill of salt water.

"Hell and damnation." This time she said it aloud.

Of all the cursed luck. There were countless coves and rocky beaches along the jagged coastline of her island. And yet, by some perverse twist of fate, the Marquess of Lynsley had landed here.

Forcing her to come face to face with her past.

Waves of crimson buffeted his body. His hands, his face, his clothing were wet with burning blood. He tried to move his feet, but the swirling currents held him down. The cry for help was growing fainter. Too late, too late. Her voice was lost in a scream ...

"Milord?"

The dream ended as always—engulfing him in a wrenching feeling of helplessness. But as Lynsley slowly opened his eyes, he thought for a moment that he was hallucinating. *Were his past sins now coming back to plague him in consciousness as well as sleep?* The Bournemouth mission had been the worst of his failings. He should have anticipated the trouble. He should have aborted the attack. He should have ...

"Awake, are you?"

Her voice was not quite as he remembered it. A note of cynicism overshadowed the confidence of old, giving it a harder edge. *How many years had it been?* Nine? Ten?

No doubt they had both changed past recognition.

"Here, you had better try to drink something," added Valencia.

"Thank you," he murmured, after a swallow of the hot broth. "Where am I?"

"The isle of Sark," she said brusquely. "Near Maseline. I assume your ship foundered in the storm."

"Yes." Lynsley closed his eyes, recalling the fury of the wind whipping through the rigging. "We would have weathered it, but the rudder pin snapped and we were at the mercy of the wind and waves."

"The captain should never have chanced a journey with such a gale blowing in."

"It was not the man's fault," he replied. "The matter was most urgent. If anyone is to blame, it is I."

Valencia didn't answer. Turning away, she began to fuss with a tray on the bedside table. He heard the clink of cutlery and the rattle of earthenware dishes. "Can you manage a bite of porridge?" she asked. "I've brought hot water and can make some tea as well, if you like."

"Tea would be most welcome."

The flickering candlelight illuminated her profile as she worked. *Valencia.* The Spanish name had a sinuous, sultry sound that suited her looks. She was still breathtakingly beautiful. Her hair, lustrous as polished ebony, fell in shimmering waves over her shoulders. If anything, the years had strengthened the line of her cheekbones, the arch of her neck. There was a new depth to her seagreen gaze, and the ripple of shadows beneath the surface only added to the allure of mystery.

A man could drown in such eyes ...

Lowering his lashes, Lynsley found himself wondering if she had ever married. Many men must have asked.

But then, perhaps she did have a husband and a gaggle of children sitting in the next room. He knew nothing about her life since that stormy afternoon at the Academy when she had refused a desk assignment and handed in her resignation.

Bloody hell. He had bungled that meeting badly. He should have sensed her vulnerability and done better at softening the blow. It was yet another shortcoming, one he had recognized only too late.

He had tried to track her down, but ironically, her training had allowed her to disappear without a trace.

"Do you live here alone?" Lynsley finally asked. A quick glance around the small bedchamber revealed nothing to indicate the presence of a man in her life.

"That is really no concern of yours, Lord Lynsley," she replied coolly.

" I was not trying to pry, Valencia. I merely wish to know that you are ... well."

"I don't need a man to take care of me." Her chin took on a

martial jut. "Wasn't that one of the very first lessons you had drummed into us at the Academy?"

Heaving a small sigh, the marquess abandoned any further attempt to make small talk. He didn't have the strength to engage in a bout of verbal fencing. His mind was still muzzy, his body weakened by surging shivers of hot and cold.

Glass clinked against metal. "I've mixed a draught to bring down the fever," she said. "You should try and get some rest."

She was right. He could not afford any weakness of the flesh —or feelings—to upset his plans. Swallowing the medicine in silence, he let himself drift into sleep. On waking, he must be ready to move on.

Valencia reached out to smooth the tangled hair from the marquess's brow. His flesh was still a touch feverish, but the labored rasp had eased from his breathing. It was a good sign. Inflammation of the lungs was a real danger after such an ordeal.

Her hand lingered for a moment, tracing the jut of his cheekbone, the line of his jaw ...

She drew her fingers away as if burned and set to making up a cold compress. She would *not* allow his reappearance in her life, however shocking, to upset her hard-won peace of mind. Fate had thrown them together.

But thankfully, Duty would quickly draw them apart.

Duty. As she wrung out the felt and folded it over his forehead, she couldn't help wondering what had brought him to be sailing the Channel in a raging gale. Not a holiday, that was for sure. The marquess was all business and no pleasure.

Finished with the task, Valencia took up the candle and withdrew from the darkened bedchamber. The parlor was filled with the pale, pearlescent light of dawn, but rather than lighten her spirits, she found herself feeling as if a black cloud was hanging over her head.

Bloody hell. She looked around the snug cottage. White-washed walls, cheery chintzes, soft wool rugs, wooden beams polished to the patina of aged sherry—she had painstakingly crafted every detail. It was a cozy, comfortable space. It was her world, her home. She would *not* let the Marquess of Lynsley darken the one place she felt safe.

Wandering into the kitchen, she lit the stove and set the kettle on the hob. *Tea.* Valencia allowed a reluctant smile. Along with Mrs. Merlin's famed strawberry tarts, it was served to sooth taut nerves during critical meetings at the Academy. The head-mistress claimed that sustenance helped one to think clearly in times of stress.

She took a seat by the window and sipped the strong, fragrant brew. Perhaps there was some measure of truth in the idea. Somehow, she did feel marginally more relaxed. The warmth of her own hand-picked pottery, the smell of fresh-cut herbs from her garden hanging over the work table, the soft whistling of the still-boiling water was comforting.

Lord Lynsley had asked obliquely about a husband. Well, she didn't need a man in her life to be happy. Her chin rose a fraction. It wasn't that she hadn't been asked. A number of proposals had come her way. Despite her physical flaw, the opposite sex still seemed to find her ... attractive.

Catching a glimpse of her own reflection in the leaded glass, she studied her features. To her own eye, her mouth was a little too wide, her nose a trifle too long for true beauty. But men seemed to find the thick, curling tumble of her tresses alluring, even though their color was black as a raven's wing, rather than a sweet, shimmering gold.

Light and dark.

She was after all, a creature of shadows.

Perhaps that was why she had chosen to live alone. Oh, there had been the occasional discreet affairs. Trained in the swashbuckling skills of a man's world, she saw no reason why she couldn't play by the same rules as they did. But she had never let anyone come too close.

And that wasn't about to change.

Swirling the dregs of her drink, Valencia set the cup aside. She didn't need a gypsy's skill at reading tea leaves to predict that the Marquess of Lynsley would soon be just another memory.

Lynsley awoke feeling ready to analyze the situation with some measure of his usual clear-headed logic. It had been shock as well as exhaustion that had dulled his wits on first regaining consciousness from his watery ordeal. Seeing Valencia had been like seeing a ghost of his past shortcomings.

Or sins.

God only knew if he had been right to ask so much of the young orphan girls whom he chose for admission into Mrs. Merlin's Academy.

But any thought of penance would have to be put off until some later time.

Right now, he had a mission to accomplish and nothing must distract him. Already precious time had been wasted.

Wincing, the marquess slowly sat up and flexed his limbs to assess the damage. No broken bones, he decided, just a welter of bumps and bruises. He would be moving rather gingerly for the next few days.

But move he must.

Damn. Already an obstacle stood in his way. His portmanteau had, of course, been lost at sea. He would need fresh clothing and enough funds to arrange a crossing to the coast of

Normandy. Out of old habit, he had taken the precaution of sewing some gold coins into the lining of his coat. Had they survived the storm?

Gritting his teeth, Lynsley swung his legs to the floor, wondering where to start looking ...

"You ought not try to rise, sir," came a chiding voice from the shadowed doorway. "If there is something you need, I shall fetch it for you."

"I need my clothes, to begin with." Aware that the flannel nightshirt barely covered his calves, Lynsley hitched the blanket over his legs. "And directions to the closest fishing harbor."

"Anxious to be on your way?" Her voice was sharp, sarcastic. "I am sorry to hear my humble hospitality is not to your liking, milord."

"Whatever my feelings, they are irrelevant," he replied. "As you know, a mission takes precedence over all else."

Flint struck steel and a candle flared to life. "Your clothes are in tatters and you—you are in no condition to be up and about."

"I've faced far worse in the past. I'll manage," said Lynsley calmly. The light flickered over her frown, leaving her eyes wreathed in darkness. "Though in this instance, time is of the essence, so I don't mind admitting that I could use your help."

Valencia gave a bitter laugh. "Why you?" she asked abruptly.

He didn't answer for a moment. "There was no one else ready." A glimmer of a smile played on his lips. "Over the last year, I've lost my three best Merlins."

"Dead?" she demanded.

"Married," he replied softly.

"It must have been a sore blow to discover that they loved a mere mortal more than their duty," she snapped.

Lynsley closed his eyes. "You didn't used to be so cynical, Valencia."

"I didn't used to be crippled either."

For a moment, the only sound in the bedchamber was the smoky hiss of the peat fire. Then she seemed to regret her harshness and expelled a sharp sigh. "That was unfair."

"Not really," replied the marquess. "But I cannot change the past. Neither of us can."

There was an awkward silence, as she mixed a spoonful of dark powder into a glass of water. "A draught of willowbark will help ease the aches and pains."

"Perhaps you would rather make it hemlock," he said dryly.

Her lips twitched but Valencia didn't reply. Instead she asked, "Who are you after?"

Truth or lies? Deception was often the difference between life and death during a mission. Lynsley hesitated a fraction before making his decision.

"Pierre Rochambert."

The spoon slipped from her fingers and fell to the floor.

He reached down and retrieved it from the rug.

"Pierre Rochambert." Slowly swiping the pewter against her sleeve, Valencia finished her stirring, then carefully set it aside.

"Yes." He tried to catch a glimpse of her face, but she had already turned away, hiding behind the ebony veil of her hair. Glass clinked against glass, the brittle sounds followed by the scrape of metal as she put away the box of medicines.

Lynsley heard her draw in a harsh breath, then let it out ever so slowly.

"Very well. I'll help." Her eyes met his. "But only on one condition."

"And what is that?"

"I go with you."

The demand took Lynsley completely by surprise. He had

been expecting her to ask for a promise to respect her privacy and forget all about this chance encounter. Using the swirl of shadows to mask his expression, he replied, "Revenge is not a good motive for a mission. The risks are great enough without emotion coming into play."

"That is the deal. Take it or leave, milord."

"Valencia—"

"However, I should warn you that without my vouching, you won't get far," she added with deliberate nonchalance. "The locals are wary of strangers, and you're not carrying enough gold to overcome their suspicions."

An oath slipped from Lynsley's lips. Naturally, she would know all the standard tricks of the trade. "That's blackmail," he growled.

"But of course. It's part of our basic training at the Academy," she replied evenly.

"You've been taught *too* well," he muttered.

Sparks glinted in her gaze as she turned away. A mere reflection of the candleflame, he wondered. Or the stirring of some inner fire?

"I haven't forgotten the lessons of the past, sir," came a low whisper.

"Would that you recalled the ones regarding obeying a direct order," he said with a harried sigh.

Valencia's shoulders stiffened. "I am no longer under your command."

"Then let me phrase it as a request," he said. "Let me handle this on my own."

She shook her head. "Sorry, but I can't."

Lynsley swore again. "Bloody hell! Don't you see that such a reckless, obstinate attitude jeopardizes the chances—"

A low laugh caused him to cut off his ire.

"Sorry," she said again, a half smile softening the sardonic set of her mouth. "But an outburst of emotion from the unflappable Lord Lynsley is something of a shock." The twitch of her lips stilled. "You know, among the Merlins you were known as 'The Sphinx' because your expression was always an enigma. Indeed, it appeared carved out of stone. None of us could ever guess at what you were *really* thinking."

"I imagine you have some inkling of my thoughts right now," he replied tersely.

"Yes—you wish me to Hades. But you have to admit, sir, that we are both creatures of the Underworld, at home in the swirl of murk and shadows."

"But as you just said, it is no longer your world," he reminded her. "You can't have it both ways, Valencia."

"No, not if I am bound by your rules, milord. However, I no longer feel I have to play fair."

"Damn it, this isn't a game," he growled.

Valencia turned, the sudden swoosh of wool stirring the tension between them as she jerked her skirts up. Holding the candle close to her bared leg, she let out a harsh sigh. "I've lived with that knowledge for ten years."

The scar, an angry red slash of puckered flesh, started just above her left knee and cut the length of her thigh. The full impact was obscured by the delicate lace of her drawers. But Lynsley recalled the surgeon's report, describing in gristly detail the damage the Frenchman's knife had done to muscle and sinew.

He looked away.

"Not a pretty sight, is it, milord?" The cloth fell back place.

"I ..." His throat tightened. *What could he say?*

"I don't want your pity, Lord Lynsley," she said roughly. "I want a chance—"

"For what? Revenge? Redemption?"

"Perhaps a little of both," she said with a wry sigh.

"Valencia, please reconsider."

"No, sir. And that's flat." Her face was once again a mask of martial resolve. "We go together, or the mission is off."

He drew in a long breath and held it pent up until his lungs threatened to burst. *Duty. Desire.* Did he really have a choice? "Then I have no alternative but to accept your terms. However, I, too, have a condition."

Her sable lashes fluttered in the gloom. "Which is?"

"You must agree that I am in command. For any chance of success, a mission of this nature must be run with military precision. If I cannot depend on your following orders without question, I won't put your life—or mine—at risk."

Valencia didn't answer right away.

"Yes or no. Black and white—in this there are no subtle shades of grey," he added.

"Very well, sir. I accept your conditions." She snapped off a mock salute before pulling up a chair.

"So, what's the plan of attack?"

Chapter Four

It *was* a dirty trick, admitted Valencia as she watched the whisper of candlelight play across Lynsley's features. She had placed him in an impossible position—either way he turned, he was forced to compromise his rigid notions of honor. She had counted on the fact that duty to country would overshadow his personal ethics. But on seeing the conflict in his eyes before he looked away, she couldn't help feeling a bit guilty.

All is fair in love and war. The old adage sprung to mind, yet strangely enough, it made her even more uncomfortable. Was it wise to step back into the fray? She had carved out a quiet niche for herself on this out of the way island. Why risk reopening old wounds?

It was a question she couldn't really answer.

"Might I have a bite to eat while we talk?" The marquess massaged at his temples. His hair was longer now than in the past, and touched with silver at the temples. "I am going to need my strength if I am to be battling both you and Rochambert."

"I won't be a distraction, sir. You have my word."

"Hmmph." His grunt was impossible to interpret.

Valencia let it pass. "I've some cold mutton and cheese in

the larder, along with a loaf of freshly baked bread." She paused for a fraction. "Sorry, no strawberry tarts."

His lips twitched.

"How is Mrs. Merlin?" she asked hesitantly.

"Her hair is a bit greyer, and her glasses a bit thicker, but the old bird is as sharp as ever," he replied. "She can still shoot a hole through a shilling at twenty paces."

"I am glad to hear it." She cleared her throat. "I'll be back in a moment with a tray."

"No, I'll come with you." Lynsley rose, awkwardly wrapping the blanket around his middle. "Might I have my trousers back? Now that we have finished negotiations, there is no need to hold them hostage."

"They have been reduced to rags, I'm afraid. However, I should be able to find something suitable in one of my trunks. Over the years I've accumulated an assortment of men's clothing from the various shipwrecks and smugglers that have washed up on these shores."

"But not a man to go with them?"

Valencia felt a flush come to her cheeks. "That isn't really any of your business, sir."

"On the contrary. It *is* my business to know the background of my soldiers. Whether you have a loved one waiting for you at home may affect your judgment when push comes to shove."

He was right, of course. "Very well sir. The answer is no, I have no husband, no current lover."

Lynsley nodded gravely.

"If there are no further questions, sir, I will go find you something to wear." Valencia moved to the doorway and turned for her own rooms. "The kitchen is to the right, and at the end of the passageway."

Damn the man, she fumed as she threw open the truck and began to rummage through the cast-off garments. Somehow, she always felt like a scruffy schoolgirl in his presence. Awkward and unsure, while he always appeared so calm and in command.

Of course the dratted man had an air of aristocratic authority about him. He was a privileged patrician, born to a life of wealth and rank. While she was an orphan, a lone child forced to grow up fast in the muck and violence of the stews of St. Giles.

She paused for a moment, recalling that fateful encounter. Their paths had crossed when she had tried to pick his pocket. She had nearly succeeded—she was one of the most skilled dippers in the area, despite her tender age—but at the last moment the marquess had caught her hand. She had fought like the very devil to free herself from his grip. Even then, she had been very good with a blade. Lynsley still bore the traces of her wrath on his knuckles. Yet rather than haul her off to the nearest magistrate, he offered her a place in a newly formed school with an odd-sounding name.

Mrs. Merlin's Academy for Extraordinary Young Ladies. She hadn't had any idea what an Academy was, but any place seemed better than the filth and poverty of the London slums. Besides, she had always had an adventurous streak. And the elegant gentleman had a nice smile and kindly blue eyes that seemed to see straight through to her soul.

Valencia bit her lip. She must have been ten or eleven at the time, though her true age was anyone's guess. Now she had just turned one and thirty. *A woman of the world.* On countless occasions, she had proven herself to be resilient, resourceful and tougher than Toledo steel.

So why were her hands trembling as she smoothed the wrinkles from a pair of rough wool pants? Merlins were meant to be fearless. And she was said to have been the most fearless of them all.

"I have *not* lost my nerve," she whispered to herself. She had failed once to prove her mettle. It wouldn't happen again.

Grabbing up a thick knitted jumper and work shoes to go along with the trousers, Valencia slammed the trunk shut. From now on, she would keep any misgivings locked away.

It was time to fly.

The slate tiles were chill against his bare feet as he shuffled down the hallway. Lynsley shivered slightly, acutely aware that beneath the borrowed blanket and nightshirt he was wearing only his drawers. No wonder he felt so strangely vulnerable. So stripped of all his defenses.

Bloody hell. Had he made yet another mistake with her? She had suffered enough on account of his miscalculations. He had no right to draw her back into danger. Duty? It was too easy an excuse. The real reason was far more complex, but damn if he could explain it, even to himself.

Taking up the flint and steel, Lynsley struck a spark to the lone taper by the pantry and watched a flame flicker into life. He ought to have doused her demand on the spot. Instead he had been oddly indecisive—something quite out of character for him.

But then, he hadn't been himself lately.

Grimacing, Lynsley opened the larder. There was no going back—the deal was done. He would just have to make the best of it.

And try to make sure that neither of them got burned to a crisp.

"You have a nice nest," said Lynsley as she entered the kitchen.

He had stirred the coals to life in the stove and set a kettle on the hob.

"It has none of the elegant amenities of your mansion on Grosvenor Square, milord." Even to her own ears, the reply sounded waspish. "And as you see, the service is sadly lacking."

The marquess smiled and continued to cut the meat into neat slices. "It is my sister who lives in the family townhouse. I prefer smaller quarters in a less visible part of Town."

"You have a sister?"

His brow quirked. "I am human. Or like Jove, did you think I had stepped fully formed from Zeus's forehead?"

"I—I never thought ... that is, I hadn't ever imagined you with family," she stammered. To cover her confusion, she quickly asked, "What of you, sir—are you married?"

"No," he answered softly.

"Why not?" she pressed. "As an exalted member of the nobility, aren't you expected to set up a nursery and sire an heir?"

He deflected the question with a shrug. "I have a younger brother who has three lively boys. I should not be ashamed to pass on the title to one of them."

"Surely there is a *cher ami* tucked away in a snug little house on the outskirts of Mayfair." Valencia knew she was being impertinent, but didn't care.

Lynsley smiled. "My work is a hard enough mistress."

The curl of his mouth sent a strange little shiver skating along her spine.

His face was leaner than it has been ten years ago, and a crinkling of fine lines was etched around his eyes. There was, however, the same piercing intensity to their ice blue color. Cool and clear as faceted gemstones.

Oddly enough it was now a rush of heat prickling along her flesh.

His features had a chiseled austerity, a sculpted strength—long, straight nose, prominent cheekbones, squared chin. It was the sinuous shape of his lips that softened the planes and kept him from looking too forbidding. Whether he knew it or not, the Marquess of Lynsley had a sinfully attractive smile.

"Indeed," she finally replied, relieved to hear that her voice was not as fluttery as her insides. Embarrassed that he might have caught her staring, she slapped the clothing down on the work table. "These ought to be a decent fit. You can change in the pantry while I finish laying out the bread and cheese."

He handed over the knife. "Thank you. I shall not be unhappy to shed this nightshirt. It itches like the devil."

"No doubt you are used to wearing only the finest silk to bed."

"Actually, I sleep in the nude."

Valencia felt her face flame. "Touché, sir."

His fingertips grazed lightly against her wrist. "I would rather we were not always at daggers drawn. God knows you have reason to be angry with me, but if we are to work together, you must try to set it aside for the duration of the mission."

"Yes, sir," she said.

"That was not an order, Valencia. It was a ... suggestion." He turned for the pantry. "I hope you will take it to heart."

Bloody hell. She took a savage swipe at the loaf of bread. The marquess must now think she was an aging shrew as well as a woebegone warrior. She gave a small sniff, but the sting of salt on her lashes was like a slap in the face. Merlins didn't cry, she chastised herself. If she was going to succumb to self-pity here in her own cottage, she might as well surrender her wings here and now.

Duty. Discipline. She had not yet forgotten the lessons drummed into her at the Academy. The marquess would find no further fault with her attitude.

"If that cheddar was Rochambert, he would have died a thousand deaths." Lynsley looked almost boyish, dressed in simple fisherman's clothes with his tousled brown hair curling around his ears. In the candlelight, the burnished gold highlights far outshone the strands of silver.

His body was still lean and lithe, she had noted earlier. And though he had developed a deliberate slouch over the years to disguise his true height and the breadth of his shoulders, she found it hard to believe that most people accepted his cover as a deskbound bureaucrat, a titled toff who did nothing more strenuous than push pens around on his blotter.

"I look forward to slicing his liver into foie gras," she said lightly. "And serving it with a sauce of champagne and champignons."

"You are making my mouth water." He sat down on the stool next to her and dug into plate of the cold mutton and mint jelly. "It seems you have added cooking to your arsenal of skills. That is rosemary flavoring the roasted meat, is it not?"

"I learned out of necessity," she answered, feeling absurdly pleased by the simple praise. "I have an herb garden out back, and a small orchard of apples and pears."

"Mmmm." He topped a slice of cheese with a dollop of her spiced chutney.

"Would you care for a glass of cognac?"

"Don't tell me you also make wine?" he murmured.

"I assure you, this is far superior to any homemade brew, sir." Valencia fetched a bottle from her stillroom and poured him a measure.

"This would put the cellars at White's to blush," he said after a small sip, "Smuggled?"

"Of course." She nibbled at a morsel of bread. "Are you going to have me arrested?"

"No. I am going to have you refill my glass."

Taking up her knife, Valencia pretended to eat while watching him out of the corner of her eye. There was an odd sort of domesticity to the scene. Against all reason, the marquess did not seem out of place in her tiny kitchen. The kettle was whistling softly on the stove, the lamp cast a mellow glow over the pine table. Anyone looking in through the mullioned window would take them for an old married couple ...

"Ought we not be having a council of war, milord?" she demanded abruptly.

The spell was broken. He finished the last bite of mutton, then leaned back and sighed. "Yes, let us get down to business. First of all, we need transport to France."

"I take it you have a rendezvous point in mind."

He nodded. "St. Pierre Eglise."

"Leave that to me," said Valencia. "It will be easy to arrange. Then what?"

"The head of our operations in Normandy sent word that an American envoy from Washington is visiting relatives in Valognes before going on to Paris for talks on trade between the two countries." Lynsley tugged at his cuff. "I do hope Tobias Tremaine and I are of the same size, as I will have to borrow his clothing as well as his persona."

"Does Mr. Tremaine have a wife?" she inquired.

"I am not sure. This was rather a spur of the moment decision, so I am somewhat lacking in background information. It will, of course, be easy enough to find out."

"You did not used to take such risks, milord."

"In this case, I was given little choice."

Valencia studied the grain of the tabletop for a moment. "And from there it is on to Paris?"

"Precisely."

"What are we after?" She lifted her gaze "Aside from Pierre Rochambert's head on a platter."

"Put aside your emotions, Valencia. Our mission is far more important than taking revenge on one of the Emperor's assassins. If you cannot accept that, tell me now and I will find my way back to London."

"I understand, sir. My attempt at humor was ill-advised."

Lynsley's expression softened a touch. "I am merely asking you to understand that I am deadly serious about our ultimate goal. Nothing must interfere with our ability to think and act dispassionately. A great many lives may be saved if we do our job correctly." He allowed a quirk of his lips. "As for humor, it is always an invaluable weapon in keeping things in perspective."

Repressing a smile, she nodded. It struck her as slightly ironic that the inscrutable Lord Lynsley was lecturing her on humor. She could recall several instances in the distant past when her overexuberant spirits during Academy field maneuvers had earned her serious demerits. In fact, it was the marquess himself who had meted out a month of mucking the stables as punishment for placing a stink bomb in the artillery master's gun box.

In the past, she had been carefree to a fault. Unlike now.

"Our goal?" she murmured, shaking off such reveries.

"To steal a coded scientific formula, along with a sample of the chemical concoction. We have recently learned that the French have gotten their hands on an ancient manuscript that spells out the makings of an explosive new substance—a potent weapon of destruction that ignites a fire resistant to water."

Valencia's eyes widened. "Good Lord, " she whispered. "But that means our Navy would be—"

"Helpless in the face of such a threat." finished Lynsley. "Indeed. So now you understand why I could not say no when Bathurst asked me to handle the mission."

What she also understood was how difficult and dangerous a mission this was going to be. He had yet to spell out the specifics but she had no illusions that gaining access to such a vital document was going to be easy.

Not with Pierre Rochambert standing guard over it.

That Lynsley had chosen to undertake the task himself, rather than send one of the woman warriors under his command made her regret her earlier sarcasm. Not that his action surprised her. Valencia swallowed hard. Deep down, she had always sensed he was a man of great compassion, as well as a man of honor and integrity.

"Having second thoughts?" he inquired softly. "I would not blame you in the least if you wish to reconsider."

"On the contrary, I am even more determined to see this through." She shot a glance at the clock atop her cupboard. "There are still several hours until the tide turns. Get some more rest, sir. I will go arrange our transportation."

"Perhaps I should go with you—"

"Not necessary," she said brusquely. "In fact. I would rather handle the initial negotiations by myself."

He lifted a brow. "You have contacts with the, er, right sort of people to sail to France without asking any questions."

A smile spread over her face. "Lord Lynsley, as I own the only tavern in Maseline Harbor, I know every vessel and every sailor on this island, including those who would sail up the River Styx if the price was right. You will have your boat, sir. But it may cost you dear."

His lips twitched. "May I start a tab? I assure you, I am good for the blunt."

"Whitehall can also bloody well pay my expenses for hiring someone to run the place while I am away."

"Agreed," replied the marquess.

"I'll be back shortly. Be ready to shove off."

· · ·

Valencia returned within the hour, having found her friend both willing and sober.

"It's all arranged," she murmured to Lynsley, who was stretched out on her sofa.

One eye opened in an instant, its clear, calm blue color caught in the flicker of moonlight. She doubted he been sleeping, though he looked remarkably refreshed for a man who had been fished from the violent seas only a day before.

"Excellent," he murmured. "When do we shove off?"

"Now," she replied. "There's no time to waste. We have to meet our man in one of the south coves. It's a half mile walk from here."

He rose, wincing slightly.

"Will you manage?"

"A little stiffness is all—the ravages of old age." he replied with a wry smile. "It will wear off in a trice."

"I'll just be a moment." Ducking into her bedchamber, Valencia changed into a dark shirt and trousers.

Lynsley eyed the outfit as she reappeared and threw a black cloak over her shoulders. "Kept the old uniform?" he murmured.

"It comes in handy at times," she said. Heading for the kitchen, she quickly filled a small canvas bag with food and drink. "Follow me."

Beneath a dappling of pale moonlight they threaded through the woods behind her cottage, and found the narrow path skirting the cliffs. Valencia was grateful that Lynsley seemed content to travel in silence.

Everything had happened so quickly—she had yet to sort out her conflicting emotions. A part of her warned that she was a fool to be stepping back into the past. She had cobbled together a comfortable life for herself. Why risk losing all she had worked for?

And yet, a part of her was bubbling with excitement at the prospect of heading into battle.

The way became steeper, and she gave up trying to make sense of her decision. She would not think of the past or the future. Only the present.

"Watch this section of rocks, sir. The footing is treacherous." Her own limp forced her to slow as she traversed the loose scree.

Behind her, the marquess moved with a cat-like stealth. Whatever his official duties, he clearly didn't spend all his time behind a desk, she mused.

As they came closer to the small crescent beach, she signaled for him to stop and then scanned the surrounding rocks. Spotting a dark shape deep in the mizzled shadows of the cliffs, Valencia hurried down the last few steps. Despite his fondness for French brandy, Jack Durfee could always be counted on in a pinch.

Pebbles crunched underfoot as the fisherman and part-time smuggler stepped out from the shelter of the outcropping. In the scudding light, he looked to be cut from a solid block of granite, though like the stones, there were a few rough edges.

His voice for a start, which sounded like the jangling of rusty anchor chains.

Valencia answered his greeting, then gestured at Lynsley. "This is my friend, Tom."

"In a spot 'o trouble, are ye now, Tommy?" Jack gave a throaty chuckle. "Don't worry mon. If anyone can steer ye clear o' the revenue men and Home Fleet, it's me."

Lynsley did not bat an eye as a beefy hand clapped him on the shoulder. Returning the man's grin, the marquess answered in the guttural slang of the Southwark slums.

Lud, thought Valencia. If the highborn heiresses of Mayfair could see him now—the polished, poised Lord Lynsley trading off-color quips with a fisherman who smelled of spirits and dead mackerel. No doubt they would all fall into a dead faint.

"I got wot ye asked for, Miss Val." Jack passed over a small burlap sack. "It will cost something extra, though."

She nodded. A quick glance inside showed the two naval pistols were the latest models.

"I threw in the power and bullets at no extra charge."

"Thank you. I hope you did not run into any difficulty with Captain Taft and his men," she said.

"Heh, heh, heh." Jack's laugh grew louder. "The crew is four sheets to the wind in yer tavern. The captain gave them a night's liberty as reward fer catching O'Hanlon and his men."

"Then maybe I shall be able to afford your exorbitant price," she replied dryly.

"We all heard it's you who deserve the credit," he added.

"Don't believe everything you hear, Jack. The account has likely become much exaggerated." Valencia turned to the dingy floating in the surf. "Come on, we don't want to miss the tide."

"Right-o, Madam Val."

She heard the rasp of another chuckle rise above the splashing water.

"She's ain't yer usual female, eh, Tommy?" went on her friend. "'Tis a rare one could make the men of these waters take orders, but not many 'o us would dare disobey."

"Aye," murmured Lynsley. "She is definitely a force to be reckoned with."

Chapter Five

"Your note said to expect you two days ago." The door opened a crack. "I was beginning to think the plan had been called off."

Lynsley shaded his eyes from the beam of the lantern. "A spot of bad weather slowed me down. Sorry to be late."

The head of his network in Normandy motioned for the marquess to step inside the abandoned shepherd's shelter. As Valencia materialized from the mists, his brow shot up. "I was under the impression you were coming alone."

"Change of plans, Jalet. Due to the storm, I had to improvise," replied Lynsley. "Any trouble on your end?"

"No, everything went smoothly on this end. Our men had no trouble in waylaying the American consul's coach on a deserted stretch of road outside of Cherbourg," said Jalet. "Mr. Tremaine and his wife are now our guests at an isolated farmhouse near here, though I daresay they are none too happy about the change in their travel plans." His mouth twitched faintly. "The accommodations are not quite as luxurious as those of the Mansion de Magret in Paris."

"I'm afraid they will have to accept our hospitality for a fortnight longer, before boarding a schooner for Jamaica, courtesy of His Majesty's Royal Navy. By the time they return to Washington and register an official complaint, our mission will have served its purpose."

Jalet looked curious, but knew better than to ask any questions. "I've a hay cart waiting in the lane to take you to our guests. From there, the traveling coach is ready to depart whenever you are ready. I assume you are anxious to make up for lost time."

"Correct." Lynsley slanted a sidelong look at Valencia, wondering if he was setting too grueling a pace for her. Her face was drawn, and the shadow smudged beneath her eyes looked drawn in with charcoal. Quite likely she hadn't slept since hauling him back from the dead.

She was already moving for the opening in the stones. "What are we waiting for? Let's go."

He would have to keep an eye on her and watch that she did not push herself too hard. Quite likely she would hike to hell and back on her bad leg if she thought it would bring her a measure of redemption. She had no need to prove anything to him.

But to herself ...

Lynsley set his mouth in a grim line and hoped he had not made a grave mistake. Not that she had allowed him any choice. The mission demanded that he risk whatever was necessary to have a chance at success.

"Right. We have lost time to make up for."

A bumpy ride over the winding track brought them to a whitewashed stone house and adjoining barns, set amid several acres of hayfields and apple orchards. Surrounding on all sides by rolling forestland, it was indeed far off the beaten path and unlikely to attract prying eyes.

"A good choice," remarked Valencia, as she removed her

cloak and shook the straw from her hair. The sun had now risen above the trees, showing a wisp of smoke curling up from the chimney. "I do hope we are in time for breakfast. I'm famished."

Jalet grinned in Gallic appreciation as he caught a first look at her face and figure. "I shall have our cook make up a hearty repast, *mademoiselle*. Fresh eggs, smoked ham, warm baguettes and our famous Normandy cider."

Lynsley felt his own stomach growl. "By all means, let us dine first, and then we shall greet our American guests."

"Mr. and Mrs. Tremaine are not early risers, sir," said Jalet. "But I shall inform them that their presence is requested in the parlor."

They made quick work of the excellent meal while Jalet went off to arrange the interview. Lynsley was glad to see that a touch of color had returned to Valencia's cheeks as she finished the last bite of buttered baguette and pushed back her plate.

"What do you intend to tell the consul?" she asked.

"Oh, I shall be very diplomatic," he replied. "I shall—"

A stentorian shout penetrated through stone and solid oak, indicating that Mr. Tremaine was in a different frame of mind.

"It is an outrage that you demand we come downstairs at the ungodly hour! Once again, I *demand* to speak to the person who has perpetrated this vile kidnapping!"

"Americans tend to be rather grouchy before they have had their morning coffee." The marquess rose. "Ready?"

"Wouldn't miss it for the world," she replied. "I am curious to see you in action, sir."

"Let the despicable dastard show his face," continued the American in a loud bellow. "I should like to know who dares attack a diplomat here in France on official government business."

Lynsley threw open the parlor door. "That would be me."

His appearance elicited a gasp from the consul's wife, a

rather horse-faced lady with auburn hair and pale skin. Seeing Valencia in trousers and brandishing a pistol, she went several shades whiter and fell silent.

Lynsley didn't blame the lady for looking afraid for her life. With his three day stubble, matted hair and coarse clothing, he no doubt resembled a cutthroat pirate.

Her husband, however, refused to be intimidated. "Release us at once, you rogue! I am a representative of the American government, and President Madison will be *most* displeased to hear of this incident."

"If I were you, I would endeavor to speak a touch more civilly to my captors." Lynsley smiled, but made a show of drawing the pistol from his waistband and checking the priming. "You are hardly in a position to be making threats."

"D-d-do moderate your voice, Tobias," stammered his wife. "I-I am sure this man will be willing to discuss the matter reasonably."

"Hmmph!" Tremaine scowled. "I suppose you want a ransom?"

"Not at all, sir," said Lynsley.

"Then what?"

"Why don't you take off your coat, sir," replied Lynsley politely. "You are looking a trifle warm."

The American looked about to retort when his wife whispered, "Please, do as he says, Tobias."

"Allow me to take it for you." Lynsley held out his hand. "Quality fabric," he remarked, rubbing the superfine wool between his fingers. "And excellent tailoring." He set down his pistol and stripped off his knitted jumper. Slipping the garment over his ragged linen shirt, he smoothed at the lapels. "The sleeves are a touch short, but that can be mended."

Dagget sputtered in outrage. "You mean to take my *coat*, sirrah?"

"And your hat." Lynsley took up the elegant high crown beaver from the sideboard and tipped it low over one eye. "And the rest of your wardrobe as well. However, I shall be a gentleman and leave you your wife."

The lady gave a little shriek.

"By god, you are no gentleman!" shouted Tremaine.

"Actually, he is," said Valencia. "The Marquess of Carabas," she added with a straight face, using the name of the make-believe hero in the fable 'Puss In Boots.'"

The consul's wife squinted in confusion through her lorgnette. "The man does not look like a titled—"

"The man's only title is that of a scurrilous thief!" Tremaine shook his fist. "I will see you hung for this, you scoundrel!"

"The only cravat I will be wearing is one of your freshly starched lengths of linen. Good day, Mr. Tremaine." Lynsley inclined a courtly bow. "And you, madam. I regret to inform you that a good deal of your clothing will also be leaving with us. Your belongings will be returned ... eventually. In the meantime, enjoy your stay in rural France. I do apologize that you will miss Paris. Perhaps next time."

Retreating with a jaunty salute, he closed the door on a string of invectives. "A bit hot under the collar, isn't he?"

Valencia regarded him with an odd stare.

"Come, while I gather up Mr. Tremaine's credentials and clothing you must also pick out a wardrobe." Turning for the stairs, he ran a hand over his bristly chin. "The coach and horses won't be ready to leave for an hour or two, so in the meantime, I've ordered hot water to be brought up to both bedchambers. I don't know about you, but for me, a bath would be most welcome."

. . .

"Aye," replied Valencia dryly as she fell in step behind him. "Perhaps when the layers of dirt and salt are washed away, Mrs. Tremaine would recognize the true nobility of your lordly person."

"I devoutly hope not." Lynsley wrinkled his nose. "Do I smell as bad as I look?"

"Worse." She choked down a laugh as they hurried down the corridor. "That was really rather naughty of you ,sir."

He grinned. "I daresay it was."

This whimsical side of the solemn and serious Lord Lynsley was a real revelation. "You are truly finding all of this fun," she said, slanting a sidelong look at his stubbled profile.

"Guilty as charged." He did not look at all repentant.

"You've barely escaped death by drowning, you've nearly instigated another war with our former colonies, and you'll be shot as spy if you make one slip in Paris." She shook her head. "Most men would not find that remotely amusing."

"One man's poison is another man's pleasure," he answered with a faint smile.

Why *did* the marquess do what he did?

Valencia had often puzzled over the question. Not for money, that was for sure. His family fortune was said to be one of the largest in all of England. He could well afford to live a leisured life of pampered indulgence. Any whim, any desire satisfied at the snap of his fingers.

He did not appear to crave personal prestige or power either. By all accounts she had heard, Lynsley shunned attention, going out of his way to see that credit for his successes went to others.

She frowned. It was one thing for her, a penniless orphan, to accept such risks. She had learned at an early age that violence and deceit was a sordid reality of life. The Academy had given her a chance to fight against tyranny and injustice. Lynsley, on the other hand, had surely been shielded from any hardship by virtue of his wealth and rank.

The Marquess of Mystery, she thought wryly. Whatever his reasons, he kept them very private.

On entering Mrs. Tremaine's bedchamber, Valencia quickly nudged such musings aside. The present challenge must take precedence over speculation on the marquess's motivations.

From the adjoining room, she heard Lynsley directing Jalet's men to begin packing up one of the trunks. The marquess was fortunate in that he and the consul were close to the same size and build. It was going to be trickier for her. Tremaine's wife was shorter and stouter—and quite a bit more well-endowed in the chest.

Valencia made a face as she surveyed the dresses hanging in the painted armoire. "I may have to stick to trousers," she muttered to herself, fingering the frothings of silk and lace. Her willowy figure—slim as a rapier, and just as flat—seemed better suited to boy's garments than fancy ballgowns, she admitted with just a touch of regret.

Turning around, she found Lynsley regarding her with an oddly inscrutable look. It was gone in an instant, replaced by a purely pragmatic glance at the wardrobe. He moved to her side and quickly sorted through the garments.

Calling to Jalet, he asked, "Is there a local girl you can trust who is skilled with a needle and thread? It would be helpful if she could serve as a lady's maid for part of the trip. I have sent word to London for one of my own people, but she and my valet won't be meeting us until Caen."

"As it happens, the owners of this place have a daughter who will be perfect for the job," replied his agent. "I shall send her up directly and she can alter one of the traveling dresses while *mademoiselle* bathes."

"She may have to be a magician," quipped Valencia.

The marquess was already inspecting a seagreen gown of watered silk. "The hem of this one can be let down, and the bodice can be pinched in at the seams—a good two inches on either side should do the trick."

She flushed slightly to think he had been measuring her chest against the American lady's buxom bosom.

And quite accurately, she admitted.

"You appear to have a great deal of experience in sizing up women," she muttered as Jalet headed for the stairs.

"In our line of work, one must have a sharp eye for detail," he responded blandly.

She couldn't argue with that. Tossing her cloak and pistol on the dressing table, she loosened the top fastening of her shirt. "I trust that scrutiny does not require you to remain here while I bathe."

Lynsley let the sarcasm go over his head. He draped the dress over his arm with a small nod. "I'll have the girl get to work on this. The hot water is here now. You need not rush. It will take some time for her to finish."

Once she was alone, Valencia stripped off her salt-stiff garments and sunk into the suds with a sigh of relief. Steam curled up from the copper tub, redolent with the fragrance of the lavender soap. The warmth was soothing against her weary limbs. But beneath the soft caress, she was aware of a more uncomfortable heat.

Damn the man. Water sloshed over the sides as she tipped a pitcher of water over her head. Lynsley still aroused a tempest of conflicting emotions within her. *Hot and cold, fire and ice.* She had thought herself finally free of emotional extremes. Age had tempered her disillusionment, rubbed the rough edges off her doubts and her anger.

Or so she had thought.

Holding her breath, she sunk beneath the surface. No, she

would *not* let him bring out the worst in her. Whatever her other faults, she would not allow him to think she had lost every last vestige of professionalism. Hell, she was still a Merlin in spirit if not in name.

And a Merlin did not snap like an ill-tempered shrew.

Especially as the marquess had meant nothing personal by his comment on her bosom. He had merely been expressing a practical observation. Valencia's mouth quirked wryly as she rinsed the last of the soap from her hair. The marquess might just as well have been looking at melons or oranges.

A dispassionate devotion to duty.

She must match his discipline.

A long soak steeped some of the tension from her muscles. Feeling somewhat better for no longer reeking of dead crabs and rotting seaweed, she stepped from the tub and slowly toweled the water from her skin. *Discipline*, she repeated to herself, avoiding a glance at the jagged scar cutting across her thigh. She was here to settle an old score with Rochambert, not carp at Lynsley.

Not even in the deepest depths of despair had she ever thought he had deliberately meant to hurt her.

That she had been fallible, fragile was her fault, not his. *So why was it so bloody hard to forgive and forget the past?*

"*Pardon, mademoiselle,* but I have finished the alterations on your gown." A tentative voice sounded from the other side of the bathing screen. "Would you care to try it on now, in case there are any last-minute changes to make?"

Time to slip into her battledress, like a knight donning armor. Time to make herself impervious to pain.

"Yes, thank you."

The rest of the hour passed in a flurry of activity. With Marie-Claire's help, Valencia sorted through the rest of Mrs. Tremaine's staggering assortment of clothing and chose a small trunkful of essentials. Lynsley had looked in just long enough to say that once they arrived in Paris, a more fitting selection of styles and colors could be ordered.

Whether he approved of the seagreen silk was impossible to discern—he did not seem to notice her change from trousers to skirts.

After seeing the luggage and temporary servants safely stowed in the baggage coach, Lynsley handed Valencia into the consul's private barouche. Freshly shaved and attired in the American's expensive clothes, he certainly looked like a distinguished diplomat, right down to the gold rimmed spectacles, which accentuated the patrician line of his nose.

"Bon voyage," called Jalet as he signaled the coachman to spring the horses. "And *bonne chance.*"

Valencia slumped against squabs, gingerly drawing the soft wool lap robe over her knees. She hadn't realized how exhausted she was until now. Since fishing the marquess out of the sea, she hadn't had more than a few hours of sleep ...

"Is you leg hurting you?" asked Lynsley quietly as he took the seat opposite her.

She gave a small shrug. "It sometimes acts up after a bout of prolonged exercise, but it's nothing to be concerned about. It won't slow me down, if that's what you mean."

He shifted to the oposite seat, then suddenly reached down and took her foot in his hands.

"Sir!" she squeaked as he slid off her slipper and began to massage her toes.

"From now on, you must call me Thomas." His fingers moved lightly against her flesh, kneading her sole with long, lithe strokes. "After all, we are supposed to be an old married couple."

She closed her eyes and leaned back. Lud, it was a heavenly sensation. Heat prickled along the length of her leg as he deepened his efforts. Slowly but surely, the throbbing pain in her thigh melted away under the sensual play of pressure. His well-tended hands were strong and capable. *Hard and soft.* Strangely enough, it did not feel like a contradiction.

Just a moment longer, she promised herself. Then she would tell him to stop.

A frisson of guilt tickled at her conscience—a whisper of warning that she should not be finding his touch so seductive. She shouldn't allow such intimacy. The masquerade was just that—a sham, and she had best not get too comfortable with it.

"Mmmm." Somehow her intended command came out as a drowsy purr. She gave a feline stretch and snuggled a bit deeper into the soft leather. Another turn of the carriage wheels, that was all. Then she would rouse from her naughty indulgence ...

Valencia awoke some time later to find her head on Lynsley's chest and his coat wrapped around her shoulders.

"Oh!" Flustered, she tried to pull away.

"I don't bite," murmured the marquess, keeping her snugged in the crook of his arm. "Or do I still have a whiff of dead flounder and fluke clinging to my person?"

She drew a breath for a tart reply, only to find herself distracted by the subtle spice of bay rum melded with a distinctly masculine scent, impossible to describe—save to say it was *Him.*

"Mr. Tremaine's cologne is actually quite pleasant," she managed to reply. "No hint of fish or rotting cabbage. Apparently the Americans are not quite the primitive savages our newspapers describe."

Lynsley chuckled, his breath stirring the strands of hair by her ear. "Civility does not make for front page copy. The public wants to read about murder, scandal and disasters. Not necessarily in that order."

Her lips twitched. The marquess possessed just the dry sort of humor she liked. "I'm afraid I can't argue with you on that."

"That would be a first," he murmured.

"I *did* give you a hard time during my school days, didn't I," she mused. "Though to be truthful, all of us girls were frightened of you ..."

His brows shot up in surprise.

"Of disappointing you, that is," she quickly added. "We knew how much you believed in us, and we never wanted to let you down. Even though the Academy is sequestered from the outside world, it was well-known that people thought you were crazy to put your trust in a band of rag-tag orphans from the London stews.

Lynsley made a wry face. "That is putting it politely."

Valencia smiled, then suddenly felt compelled to ask, "Why did you do it, sir? Found the Academy, I mean."

When he didn't answer right away, she thought he meant to ignore the question. But after a stretch of silence, he responded.

"Sometimes one has to step outside the boundaries of conformity to achieve real change." Though his expression remained impassive, his voice seemed to warm to the subject. "I read a book on Hasan-I-Sabah, a Muslim caliph who raised a secret society of warriors at his mountain citadels. His men were known for their deadly skills and fanatic loyalty. The caliph used them only in times of dire danger to his rule, and legend had it they never failed on a mission. The very name *Hashishim*—or Assassins —was enough to strike terror in the heart of the Master's enemy."

He paused. "It got me to thinking ..."

"For a staid aristocrat, you have some very revolutionary ideas. It's a wonder they didn't march you off to Bedlam."

"More than one Minister was sorely tempted to have me committed," he replied with a wry smile. "But in the end, I convinced the government to give us an old estate that was being used as cavalry pastures. I pay all the operating expenses out of my own pocket, and Mrs. Merlin oversees the day-to-day administration."

"No wonder part of our basic training stressed that we should never be afraid of taking a bold initiative if we were sure we were right. Even if it meant risking a few demerits."

Lynsley smiled. "You were never afraid of challenging me, that's for sure."

Recalling some of her youthful transgressions, Valencia couldn't help but grimace. "I was a rebellious little hellion at times, wasn't I? Considering how often I provoked a clash of wills, I'm surprised you didn't drum me out of the service."

He considered her words for a moment before answering, "You had a hair-trigger temper and a certain streak of stubbornness. But they were far overshadowed by your indomitable courage and code of honor. You held yourself to a higher standard that I ever did." Shadows fell across his face as the carriage wheels bumped over the rutted road. The scudding shapes clouded his eyes, concealing all but a flicker of brooding introspection.

Was he, too, second-guessing those past decisions? she wondered.

"I always believed that in the moment of truth, you would do the right thing," he finished.

Right. Or wrong. There was no room for error. In their world, life came down to split-second decisions.

"Sorry to have let you down, " she snapped.

So much for her recent resolve to remain even-tempered. The reminder, however oblique, of her shortcoming was like setting a match to tinder.

The old anger flared to flames inside her.

"God knows, it isn't often that the Almighty Lord Lynsley makes an error in judgment," she added.

His arm tightened around her. "You didn't let me down, Valencia," he replied, ignoring her sarcasm. "If anything, it is the other way around."

Her eyes widened in surprise.

"I should have anticipated that an agent as experienced as Rochambert would have doubled back to make sure that his man was not being followed," he said softly. "I should have sent in reinforcements."

"*I* should have been more alert. I was careless and overconfident. I let down my guard."

"Valencia ..."

She finally freed herself from his arms and slid across the seat. "Please, I thought we had agreed not rehash the past. We have enough to worry about in our future." Smoothing at her skirts, she was horrified to see her hands were trembling. Fisting the folds of the blanket, she yanked it over her legs, hoping to cover her weakness with a flurry of fury.

"Damn it, I don't need you to remind me that my last mission ended in a woeful dereliction of duty. It will *not* happen again."

She had forgotten how breathtakingly blue his eyes looked in a certain shade of light. Like slivers of aquamarine, reflecting a myriad of subtle facets—pure, polished, perfect.

And piercing as razored steel.

Lynsley held her gaze for an instant longer before reaching over for the extra blanket folded on the seat. "It looks like we are in for a spot of rain. You may need this to ward off the chill."

"Thank you," she muttered, uncomfortably aware of how ungracious she sounded. "Now, if you don't mind, I am going to try to get some sleep. We have a long road ahead of us."

Chapter Six

Lynsley peered out the windowpane as the coach rumbled over the cobblestones. The setting sun shimmered off the slow-moving current of the Seine, and in the distance, the soaring stone spires of Notre Dame cathedral shone pure as polished alabaster against the pale pink skies. *The City of Light.* There was an aura of enchantment about Paris. Like a supremely sensual woman, its sinuous streets, its pungent perfumes, its sultry sounds seduced the senses.

A promise of pleasure.

And pain.

As if he needed any reminder of the dangers. He must remain impervious to her charms.

A glance at Valencia showed her face pressed up against the glass, watching with undisguised enchantment as they approached the Pont Neuf. Her presence only added to the awareness that he was walking on a razor's edge. The slightest slip would be deadly.

After the first flare of conflict, the rest of the journey from Normandy had passed without further fireworks. He and Valencia had been scrupulously polite to each other, but a subtle tension crackled beneath every exchange. Rather than allow it to distract him, he must find a way to turn it to his advantage.

A beautiful young wife, at odds with her older husband. Pierre Rochambert was a notorious womanizer and might very well find such a scenario tempting.

As for his own feelings about using Valencia as bait ...

His personal emotions were irrelevant in light of the mission. Duty demanded dispassionate decisions. He, of all people, knew that was the cardinal rule of espionage.

Leaning back, Lynsley resumed reading over Tremaine's documents.

"Anything else I should know?" asked Valencia.

"Not at the moment," he replied, not looking up from the papers. "A elegant residence has been leased for us off rue St. Germaine. Perkins and Bailin will have us settled in by evening."

In the port city of Caen, the rendezvous with the two agents sent from London had gone off without a hitch. His usual team of valet and lady's maid was on assignment elsewhere, but given McAllister's distinctive Scottish accent, the pair he had chosen was better suited for the job. Both were Americans by birth, and their knowledge of the country and its customs would be invaluable in maintaining the masquerade, especially for Valencia.

"Tomorrow I shall present my credentials to the Emperor's Foreign Ministry," continued Lynsley. "And then we shall make a show of strolling the boulevards and visiting the fashionable shops. You must order a number of gowns and accessories—a diplomat's wife would be eager to appear dressed in the latest styles."

"Shopping," she muttered with considerably less enthusiasm than most females.

His lips twitched. "It's quite crucial to our charade."

"Of course." She tugged at the fringe of her shawl. "Speaking of our charade, sir, how can you be sure that you won't be recognized as an imposter by the other American diplomats?"

"The American delegation is currently away in the south of France, for talks on how to deal with the Barbary pirates."

She looked surprised. "How is it that you always seem to know so much about all that goes on in the world?"

"It's my business to be informed."

She considered his reply for a moment. "Still, it's more than likely that there are other Americans here in Paris who are acquainted with the real Tobias Tremaine."

"Yes, you have a point," agreed the marquess. "I have been thinking about that problem."

He rubbed at his jaw. Growing out his side whiskers had already subtlely altered the shape of his face. And his hair was several shades lighter, thank to the potions and chemicals brought from London by his valet.

"I have some expertise in the art of disguise," he went on. "But given all the other variables in this assignment, I'd rather not have to worry about assuming another man's appearance every day." Taking up the top document, Lynsley passed it to her.

Valencia read it over slowly. "How did you manage this without Whitehall's resources at your fingertips?"

"My skills at forgery are fairly well honed," he replied. "Bailin brought along the basic tools of the trade. I always like to be prepared."

She took another look at the thick parchment. "So, we are now Mr. and Mrs. Thomas Daggett."

"I am not overly fond of the name Tobias," he murmured. "The actual Thomas Daggett is a wealthy merchant from the state of Connecticut who has handled some minor trade matters for the American government last year. I've created an additional document, which explains that a sudden illness prevented Tremaine from making the voyage. We won't be here long enough for any inquiry to be made, should someone question the substitution."

"Ah." Her tone was neutral. "And what, pray tell, is the moniker I should go by?"

"Whatever you like. The real Mrs. Daggett is named Elizabeth, but a man may call his wife by a pet name."

"Then let us stick as close to the truth as possible," she said. "I shall introduce myself as Valencia, saying I prefer to go by my middle name, as it is more interesting than plain Elizabeth."

She traced a finger over the thick wax seals and ribbons affixed to the document. His special mixtures of solvent and glue had allowed him to transfer the originals to the forgery without leaving a trace of the tampering.

"My grandmother was Spanish," she continued, embellishing the explanation. "She lived on the Caribbean island of Hispanola when she met my grandfather, a rich American ship captain. A touch of Latin blood will explain my fiery temperament."

"Excellent," said Lynsley. "To play a role effectively, one must create a convincing persona."

A tinge of color ridged her cheekbones. "I haven't forgotten my basic training, sir. The art of deception is one of the first lessons we learn at the Academy."

Damn. She seemed determined to read criticism into every word or gesture he made. "Then I need not remind you that from here on in, you must call me Thomas, not sir."

She allowed a tight smile. "Ah, but as a much younger bride, I am still rather in awe of you, and your august government position."

"Touché." Lynsley gave a wry chuckle. "Shall I assume a cane and a senile shuffle?"

A flash of humor lit in her eyes. "The spectacles are enough of a concession to age. By the by, are they real?"

"No, my sight is still sharp enough without magnifying lenses," he replied, looking over the top of the gold wire frames. "At the risk of ruffling your feathers again, *querida*, let me remind you to keep your own eyes open at all times. So far, we haven't really been tested. That is about to change."

"Is all in order, madam?"

Valencia swept another look around the bedchamber, taking in the sumptuous furnishings and decorative *objets d'art*. Despite their revolutionary fervor, Parisians still loved their decadent pleasures, she observed with a sardonic smile. The opulent damask draperies, the gilt-trimmed furniture, the carved canopied bed—all of it would have been right at home in the splendor of the Sun King's palace.

"Yes. Thank you, Perkins," she replied. "Though I fear my meager wardrobe looks rather lost in that armoire." Indeed, the painted piece looked bigger than her cottage, and the handful of gowns purloined from Mrs. Daggett hung like woeful waifs in its shadows.

How fitting, thought Valencia, seeing as she was an urchin invading a world of pomp and privilege.

"That will soon be rectified, madam," replied her maid. "Mr. Daggett says we are to make a shopping expedition on the morrow, and begin ordering a more fitting array of items for a diplomat's wife. Evening gowns, day dresses, bonnets, fans, gloves ..."

A sigh slipped from Valencia's lips, along with a low oath, as the maid continued rattling off the list of essentials. *Damn*. One would think they were equipping a bloody army, rather than one lone foot soldier.

It had been a long time since she had studied the fashions of the *beau monde*. Her knowledge of styles was sadly out of date. The one saving grace was that an American was expected to have no fashion sense.

Perhaps she could ask Lynsley.

After all, the marquess moved within the highest circle of Society in London. No doubt his prodigious knowledge included keeping *au courant* with the latest looks for ladies.

She fingered the ruffled bodice of her borrowed carriage dress. Indeed, the odds were, he was intimately familiar with every little thing that a wealthy lady wore. He was rich, he was titled, he was handsome. Gentlemen of his rank had their pick of unhappy wives to dally with, along with their expensive mistresses ...

Valencia shut the armoire door with a tad more force than was necessary. Lynsley's love life was none of her concern.

"How the devil am I to decide whether mutton sleeves or bouffant sleeves are currently in vogue?" she added under her breath.

Perkins cleared her throat with a discreet cough. "If I may make a suggestion, madam."

"You need not stand on ceremony with me when we are in private," she replied. "I prefer plain speaking."

"Very good, madam." The maid certainly appeared a no-nonsense woman. She was a rail-thin and middle-aged, with angular features that would never be called pretty. Her mouse brown hair was scraped back in a tight bun, its unremarkable color reflected in the taupe and grey shades of her dress.

In short, a figure easy to overlook, which was no doubt by design. Valencia didn't miss the alertness in the woman's hazel eyes.

"As part of my job, I am expected to keep up with all the latest fashion trends," went on Perkins. "I shall be happy to offer advice, but there is an even easier way to conquer the problem."

Valencia raised a questioning brow.

"We need only learn who is the most exclusive *modiste* in town, and then ask her to outfit you for making the rounds of the *haute monde*," explained the maid. With her shop's reputation at stake, the woman will personally oversee every stitch of the way, from the choice of fabric and style, right down to the last ribbon and flounce."

"An excellent plan of attack, Perkins." Valencia gave herself a mental kick for not thinking of it herself. "Thank you."

"Yes, madam." The maid allowed a faint smile to soften the set of her mouth. It was gone in an instant, replaced by a rigid correctness. "Shall I help you unlace your gown?"

"No. I shall manage on my own tonight."

"Very good, madam." Bobbing a curtsy, Perkins let herself out of the room.

Valencia took a seat at the dressing table and began to brush out her hair. The exchange had been a disquieting reminder that her Academy skills had grown dull from disuse, especially those having to do with playing the part of a grand lady. She sighed, and the sudden flare of the candlelight caught the flicker of doubt on her face.

Did she still have the mettle to be a Merlin?

Averting her gaze from the looking glass, she tugged the bristles through her hair. In the past, no challenge had been too daunting ...

Her chin rose, her spine stiffened as her fingers touched the tiny tattoo above her breast. "I can still rise to the occasion," she whispered.

Crossing the carpet, Valencia undressed and slipped into the silk wrapper that Perkins had laid out on the bed. Though tired from the long day of travel, she found herself too restless to turn down the coverlet just yet. Instead, she drifted around the large room, pausing to inspect the Limoges figurines on the sidetable and the ormolu clock on the mantel.

Her steps slowed as she came to the paneled door that connected her set of rooms to Lynsley's suite. Pressing her palms to the polished oak, she went very still. For a moment there was naught but the sound of her own breathing, and then she heard a whisper of movement.

Listening hard, Valencia could just make out the light tread of bare feet on the Aubusson carpet.

So, like her, the marquess had not yet retired for the night.

Was he also naked beneath a robe of thin silk? Perhaps he was headed toward the hearth, intent on enjoying a last glass of port before seeking his bed. Earlier in the day, she had caught a glimpse of an upholstered armchair in his room, perfect for stretching his legs out toward the fire ...

Her cheeks began to burn.

Don't go there, Valencia warned herself. What strange flight of fancy had her thoughts straying to such intimate images of Lord Lynsley at leisure?

For God's sake, the man was a paragon of propriety—he probably slept in his starched shirt and faultlessly folded cravat.

And yet, his quip from her cottage kept echoing in the back of her mind.

I sleep in the nude.

The words were teasing. Tantalizing. She squeezed her eyes shut, but could not keep an enticing image from taking shape. She had seen enough of his body to know that the chiseled contours of his chest were all muscle, and the sleek stretch of his shoulders tapered to a lean waist and ...

A nice arse.

Bloody hell. Valencia was tempted to pound her forehead

against the door until something cracked—preferably her own rebellious imagination, rather than the oak. Maybe a few solid smacks would knock some sense through her skull. To entertain such erotic thoughts, even for an instant, was the kiss of death. There was only one reason she had come to Paris, and it was *not* to fantasize about Lynsley's lordly charms.

She backed away, cursing her own weakness of the flesh. It had been a long time—apparently far too long a time—since she had enjoyed any intimacies with a man. The enforced closeness with a virile specimen of the opposite sex was stirring the strangest desires.

But a Merlin must always be disciplined and dispassionate. Come morning, she would martial her wayward longings and keep her thoughts in line.

The next morning, after an early morning stroll through the narrow streets of their quartier, Lynsley attired himself in Mr. Tremaine's most elegant set of clothing and came down to breakfast.

"Just toast and coffee," he informed the servant standing by the sideboard.

The American government had arranged for the mansion to come staffed with local servants. A cook, two footmen and three maids, according to his valet. Bailin could be counted on to keep a close eye on household. Still, they would all have to be discreet in their discussions. Despite the fact that France and America were allies, the Parisian authorities had likely planted an informant to listen for any interesting information.

On second thought, he would have Bailin see to hiring a new staff. They, too, would likely be bribed, but not for a while.

As he sat down, he noted that Valencia's place was untouched. The trip had been tiring and the afternoon was going to be a whirlwind of activity, what with dress fittings and numerous stops to choose a stylish array of accessories. It was good that she was catching up on her sleep.

As for his own slumber, he had passed a fitful night. Strange dreams, and the prickling sensation of being watched. But that was only natural. Nerves were always stretched taut at the start of a mission. Their arrival in Paris meant that the real challenge was just beginning.

Signaling to the footman, Lynsley called for his valet. "Bailin," he said loudly. "Have the carriage brought around. I mean to present myself to the Minister of American Affairs and Commerce this morning. Leave word for my wife that I shall return in time for her shopping excursion."

"Very good, sir." The valet held out an ebony walking stick and high crown beaver hat. "Shall I arrange a visit to a tailor for you as well, sir, in order to replace the trunk of clothing lost during the voyage."

"Yes," he replied. That should explain their lack of luggage to curious eyes. "I shall need more than what I possess right now to make the proper impression on our hosts."

It was only a short ride from his residence to the French Ministry. Lynsley stepped smartly from this carriage and marched up the steps, ignoring the shouts of the startled guards. Americans were, after all, were known to be unintimidated by pomp and protocol.

"Monsieur! *S'il vous plait* ..."

Deciding that the man who emerged from the front office looked important enough to notice, Lynsley came to a halt. "Daggett," he announced brusquely, waving his credentials in front of the fellow's nose. "Representing President Madison. I assume you are expecting me. Indeed, I would have been here days ago, but the roads in Normandy are even worse than the cart tracks of Connecticut. Are they always that bad?"

"Er, yes, monsieur. That is, no, monsieur." Flustered, the man eyed the packet of papers as if it were a rattlesnake.

"Well, don't just stand there, sir. Inform Mr. Levalier that I am here, and ready to begin our talks.

"Er ..."

Lynsley repeated the request in execrable French.

"No need to shout, Monsieur Daggett. I understand English."

"Then what is the problem?" demanded Lynsley.

"Monsieur Levalier is presently in a meeting with a minister from the Palais de Justice. If you would care to wait in my office, I shall tell his

secretary—"

"I don't care for it at all," he interrupted. "But I suppose I shall have to cool my heels for the present." Lynsley allowed himself to be ushered into a small, wood-paneled room and promptly assumed the chair behind the desk. "Now, run along. I haven't got all day."

"*Oui*, monsieur," muttered the man as he shut the door with a snap.

Lynsley allowed a twitch of his lips. Mr. Daggett was fast on his way to earning a reputation for boorish behavior. A fact that suited his purposes nicely. No one would wonder that his lovely young wife found Frenchmen considerably more charming.

His smile quickly thinned to a grim line. If only he could find a way to avoid involving Valencia in this dangerous deception. But no amount of pacing the previous night had led him to an alternative plan. Rochambert had a weakness for beautiful women. And so, duty demanded that he exploit the advantage—no matter his own personal feelings on the matter.

Loath though he was to admit it, Valencia was going to be a powerful weapon against the Frenchman. Her sultry looks, her shapely body gave him an edge in the deadly game of cat and mouse. She would serve as a distraction.

Drawing a deep breath, he forced his jaw to unclench. *A distraction.* Such things did not usually concern him. Over the years, he had learned how to discipline both mind and body to the rigorous demands of his job. The sense of single-minded purpose had become second nature.

Until now.

Strangely enough, this mission had stirred a more primal passion. One that might be far more dangerous than gunpowder or steel.

Perhaps Mrs. Merlin had been right to warn him about allowing an assignment to become too personal. It was, after all, one of the first tenets they drummed into their students. Emotion was the greatest enemy of all.

"Monsieur Daggett."

Sharpening his scowl, Lynsley looked up.

"Monsieur Levalier will see you now." Apparently the first administrator had had quite enough of the obnoxious American, for it was a young clerk who stood nervously in the doorway. "Please follow me."

"Hmmph. It's about time."

Backing up quickly, the clerk led the way down the marbled corridor and up a flight of stairs.

"Ah, Monsieur Daggett." Levalier rose from his massive desk and came forward to greet him. "Pardon, pardon for making you wait, sir. Allow me to offer you some refreshments. The perhaps you would care to present yourself to our Foreign Office and receive an official greetings."

Lynsley gave a brusque bow. "I prefer not to stand on ceremony, sir. I've already been delayed in my travels. If you don't mind, I should rather get down to business."

"But of course." Levalier gestured for him to have a seat.

Everything about the minister was soft—his fleshy hands, his silky voice, his pomaded curls, his superfine coat. Everything save for his razored smile.

Lynsley reminded himself not to underestimate the man. Napoleon was known for choosing men based on their ability, not their birth.

"Seeing as all looks to be in perfect order, there is no reason to waste your time in formalities," went on Levalier. He refolded the Lynsley's documents without a second glance. "I shall have my secretary take care of all the perfunctory paperwork."

"Excellent," replied Lynsley. "President Madison is anxious to reach an accord on the trade of goods between our two countries."

"As is the Emperor, Monsieur Dagget.," said the minister.

"Speaking of which, how goes his Eastern campaign? I heard rumblings in Caen that the Imperial army was in full retreat from Russia. Is it true that he is headed back to Paris?"

Levalier's smile turned a tad pinched. "War often requires a shift in strategy. Our Emperor is a master tactician. I assure you, there is nothing to worry about."

"I devoutly hope not. But can't you do something about the Peninsula? The British are becoming a cursed nuisance, especially that pesky fellow, Wellesley."

"Marmont will deal with Wellesley," said the minister tightly. "One sometimes suffers small setbacks in the course of a campaign." He paused. "Has your capital recovered from the British invasion? We heard that the redcoat forces torched much of the city, including your White House."

"Bloody British," muttered Lynsley. "The sooner this interminable war is over, the better."

"Indeed, indeed." Levalier recovered his composure. "It soon will be."

Deciding that he had been irritating enough for the moment, Lynsley polished his spectacles on his sleeve and then took several sheets of paper from his coat pocket. "I have made a short list of the topics my government would like to discuss—"

Levalier interrupted him with a low laugh. "My dear Monsieur Daggett, much as I admire your work ethic, it will be at least a few days before we can begin our discussions."

"Why the delay?" he grumbled.

"I must arrange the schedule with my other colleagues, and that will take time." He gave a Gallic shrug. "What is your hurry? You are in Paris, *non*? Why not enjoy all of the sumptuous splendors that our city offers."

"Hmmph," Lynsley pulled a face. "My wife will no doubt be delighted to do as you say. She talks of nothing but French fashion and fripperies."

"We Parisians are renowned for our sense of style."

"And my wife is renowned for her ability to spend money like a drunken sailor." He flicked a mote of dust from his sleeve. "I suppose that is the price one pays for marrying a bewitching beauty. Still, it is not always easy to keep her amused."

As he had hoped, Levalier looked intrigued by the mention of an attractive lady. "Well, we must see to it that your wife— and you—are not bored during your stay here. There is a party tonight at Monsieur Dubouffet's mansion off rue de Rivoli. The *crème de la crème* of Paris will be there. I hope you will join us."

"Thank you. I daresay we shall," said Lynsley after a brief hesitation.

"I look forward to meeting Madame Daggett. She sounds like a lady who can bring a man to his knees."

"That she can," murmured the marquess. "That she can."

Chapter Seven

"Turn." Madame Violette tapped the tip of her scissors to the table. "Now the other way." A pause. "Lift your arms."

Stripped to her shift, Valencia felt like a filly on sale at Tattersall's famous horse market. "Ouch," she muttered, as the team of seamstresses continued their poking and prodding into every inch of her flesh.

How did highborn ladies put up with such embarrassing indignities? she wondered. Perhaps because they had been trained since birth to accept their role as brood mares for the blooded stallions of the *ton. Demure and docile.* She gave an inward wince. That was likely the sort of female Lynsley would eventually marry. Duty would demand that he sire an heir. And the marquess was not a man to ignore his responsibilities.

Indeed, Valencia found it strange that he had put off breeding. By now, most men of his age and title would have bowed to tradition and set up a nursery. As a peer of the realm, he would be expected to make a match based on bloodlines, land and money. *Privilege begat privilege.*

For her, it was a world far more foreign than France.

"That is enough, madame." With a wave of her pattern card, the modiste signaled that she had finished putting Valencia through her paces. "You may relax for a moment."

Valencia flexed her shoulders. Why her thoughts kept spurring to intimate musing on the marquess was puzzling. And provoking.

"With a bit of lift here, and here ..." Madame Violette's measuring stick touched under Valencia's breasts. "We will have every lady in Paris green with envy." The modiste pursed her lips. "Speaking of which, you must promise me to burn that puce gown. From now on, you are to wear only shades of emerald, seafoam or indigo blue."

Staring down at her chest, Valencia made a face. "I'm afraid I'm not giving you much to work with."

"You don't need melons to make a man's mouth water," said Madame Violette with an earthy laugh. "Trust me, when I am done with you, *cherie*, the opposite sex will be begging to taste your fruit."

The seamstresses tittered.

"Pardon, may I feel your peaches?" whispered one of them.

"Oooh, I should like to suck the juice from your oranges."

Valencia blushed at the ribald chatter. Though why she should be embarrassed by the frank mention of sex was puzzling. It must be the thoughts of Lynsley that had her in such a strange mood.

After all, she had come to Paris fully intending to wield her body as a weapon. Seduction was a standard part of the Academy's arsenal, and she had been trained by an expert on how manipulate male lust. A former courtesan to the King of Spain had taught the class on all the little tricks of the trade. And according to her it was child's play to gain the upper hand in the battle of the sexes as most men could be coaxed into thinking with a different part of their anatomy instead of their brains.

But not Lynsley. If ever a man were in control of his mind and his body it was the marquess.

"That's enough, girls." The snap of the tapemeasure cut through the laughter. "Let us get down to work."

Arms folded, Lynsley leaned against the doorway and watched the modiste adjust the last bit of pattern cloth.

"Alors, that will do, Madame Daggett," said the woman through a mouthful of pins. "If only all my clients were so easy to work with. Your form is *magnifique.*"

He was in complete agreement. The scanty scraps of muslin displayed Valencia's leggy height and sleek curves in exquisite detail.

"Am I dismissed?" she asked plaintively.

"*Oui,* you may get dressed now." A sniff expressed the dressmaker's opinion of the offending garments. "But remember, you must promise me to burn that hideous gown once your new wardrobe is delivered."

Valencia stepped down from the block, as if seeking to escape the guillotine blade, and hurried to the dressing room.

"Your wife possesses a unique beauty." Spotting Lynsley in the doorway, Madame Violette sketched a quick curtsey. "Normally I would have said '*non*' to such a rush job, but it is not often that I have such a mannequin with which to work."

"Thank you for making the exception." Lynsley repressed a smile. His purse had most likely been as persuasive as Valencia's beauty. The woman was the most sought-after *modiste* in Paris and knew her worth.

"No need to thank me, sir," replied Madame Violette with a crafty grin. "When your wife appears in public in my new designs, my workshop will be busy for weeks filling the new orders."

Valencia appeared from behind the curtain. "I think I would rather face the sabers of Marshall Soult's cavalry than any more of your pins," she announced, smoothing at the tie of her sash.

Madame Violette contrived to look injured. "A few little pricks here and there are a small price to pay for the sake of artistic perfection. And your husband agrees with me."

She turned sharply, noticing his presence for the first time. "Oh, I did not see you come in."

Lynsley nodded a greeting. "I finished early at the tailor and thought I would stop by to escort you home."

"How thoughtful." Valencia smiled, but hesitated a fraction before accepting his arm.

Would she ever be comfortable in his presence? Or would she always see him as a forbidding figure of authority, he wondered. *Aloof. Untouchable.* He had only himself to blame, he supposed. He had always taken great pains to keep a formal distance between himself and the students. But even in those first years, his relationship with Valencia had been ... different.

"Sir?"

Roused from his momentary reveries, Lynsley looked up from the display of fashionable accessories to find her eying him with a quizzical look.

"If you can't tear yourself away from the painted fans, I can wait for you outside." She waved a hand in front of her cheeks. "All these silks and satins have made my head spin. I'm afraid I need a breath of fresh air."

He took a moment to choose a lovely double vellum leaf with carved ivory sticks. The gouache painting depicted a classical scene from Greek mythology. Diana the Huntress.

"Please add that to our purchases," he said, handing it one of the shop girls.

Valencia's expression turned even more odd as they exited the atelier.

"What?" he murmured.

"Nothing. It's just that ..." She pulled a face. "I don't think I've ever had a man pick out something so frivolous as a fan for me."

"Surely you've received gifts from the opposite sex."

"Flowers. The occasional box of sweetmeats." Her lips twitched in amusement. "And Jeb Gervin gives me a jugged hare every Christmas."

Dead rabbits? Lynsley reversed direction in mid-step. "Come, let us stroll down the street a bit before returning to the carriage. The shops along the rue de Rivoli are said to be quite chic."

"Bosh," she huffed under her breath. "I've seen quite enough fancy fripperies."

But despite her reluctance, Valencia was soon perusing the various windows displays with undisguised enjoyment. "Look at the exquisite workmanship," she exclaimed, leaning in to study a toy troop of mounted Hussars. "Every detail is authentic, right down to the red braid and forest green color of their coats."

Most ladies of his acquaintance would not be waxing enthusiastic over painted lead soldiers. But instead of smiling, Lynsley suddenly felt as if his chest were circled in steel. Because of *his* Academy, war was a way of life for the Merlins. Valencia had been allowed precious little chance to enjoy the softer side of being a woman.

Before she could object, Lynsley turned abruptly and marched her through the door of the adjoining jewelry shop. A bell tinkled discreetly, its muted tone echoed by the rich black velvet lining the glass cases. In contrast, the sparkling gemstones and polished gold gleamed with a hard-edged brilliance.

He heard Valencia suck in her breath.

"We must keep up appearances," he murmured. "As the

wife of a distinguished diplomat, you will be expected to display a suitable reflection of his wealth and prestige."

"But—"

He pointed to a double strand necklace of pearls highlighted by a teardrop emerald pendant. "We will see that," he announced in a loud voice to the sales clerk who was hovering close by.

"With pleasure, monsieur." The man presented the piece with a low bow.

Removing his gloves, the marquess unfastened the clasp. "Bend your head, my dear." The gold was cool and smooth against his fingers, yet heat prickled through him as he touched the downy wisps of hair at the nape of her neck.

She shivered.

"Now turn around. Ah, as I thought—it matches your eyes to perfection." Lynsley held up a looking glass. "Do you like it?"

"I—I ..." Valencia fingered her throat.

"We will take it." He indicated a pair of matching pearl and emerald ear bobs. "Those as well."

"Don't be absurd!" she hissed in his ear. "Good Lord, they are far too expensive!"

"I can afford it." He paid for the purchases and tucked the beribboned package into his pocket.

"Don't worry, I shall return them to you as soon as we return home," she muttered they returned to the street. "You may then give them to a *cher amie*, so that your blunt won't have been entirely wasted."

The hell he would.

A sigh trailed after her words. "Surely we are finished for the day."

"Not quite." A small sign, handpainted in pastel colors, marked the tiny shop next door as a *parfumerie*. As Lynsley led the way inside, he was enveloped in a heady swirl of scents, ranging from light florals to lush spices. The effect was enticing, intoxicating.

Sheer silk draperies filtered the sunlight, giving the vast assortment of vials and bottles a hazy, painterly cast. Pale golds blended into topaz yellows, lavenders deepened to amethyst purples.

"*Bonjour*." The proprietress emerged from a tiny store room. With her chestnut hair, brick red gown and olive skin, she reminded the marquess of a *marron glace*—a sugared sweetmeat. The impression was heightened by the woman's Mediterranean accent. Her words had the syrupy softness of the south of France. "I am Mademoiselle Aix, owner of this establishment. Are you looking for something special?"

"Yes," replied Lynsley. "Something unique for the lady." Ignoring Valencia's soft snort, he went on. "Something individual—something that is made for her and her alone."

"Ah, *oui*. A fragrance so distinct that even in utter darkness a man would recognize her by scent alone."

He nodded. The woman had grasped the essence of his meaning.

"You have come to the right place, monsieur." Mademoiselle Aix fixed them with an appraising stare. "I must say, I don't see many English customers these days."

"We are American," answered Lynsley casually.

The woman's brow lifted a fraction. "*Pardon*. I am not often wrong in my assessment of people." Her eyes lingered on him a touch longer before shifting to Valencia. "Does madame have a favorite scent to begin with?"

"I haven't given it much thought," muttered Valencia. "Verbena, I suppose."

"*Non*, it is far too light for you." The proprietress beckoned them to follow her to the back of the shop. "A soupcon of lemon is all very well for a top note, but for a lady of your sultry looks, we must layer it with something more complex."

Valencia hung back. "Is this really necessary?" she asked him in a low voice. "Perfume is surely an extravagance—"

"You are meant to be a sensuous creature, remember?" he replied. His thigh grazed hers as he pressed her forward. "Men like Rochambert respond sexually to the primal senses of touch, sight, and smell."

Her eyes widened a fraction.

"Come, madame, we shall start by sampling some Oriental scents." Mademoiselle Aix assembled a handful of tiny bottles from her cedarwood shelves. "Ylang ylang, ginger, lotus, patchouli." The clink of glass stirred up a hint of sweetness in the air. "Hold out your hand."

Valencia slowly turned back her cuff.

The proprietress dabbed one of the crystal stoppers to the inside of her wrist.

She lifted it slowly to her face and inhaled. "Mmmm."

Mademoiselle Aix caught her cuff. "Oh, we have just begun, madame." She added several more touches, then rubbed them into the skin. "Pepper, cinnamon, and just a hint of vanilla. Now try again."

As Lynsley watched her nostrils flare, his breath stilled.

Another sniff and Valencia's wariness slowly melted into a liquid smile. "I never knew perfume could be so nuanced." Smoothing back the lace from her skin, she turned and held her wrist close to his nose. "You have far more experience in this than I do. What do you think?"

"I think it ..."

A perfume to drive a man mad with longing. Closing his eyes, he envisoned her naked, with pearlescent drops of the scent trickling between her bare breasts.

"I think it suits you," he finished gruffly.

"Really?" Was there a whiff of mischief in her manner? She gave another breezy wave, her fingers nearly touching his cheek. "You don't find it too strong?"

"My perfumes are never overpowering," said Mademoiselle Aix. She flicked a few droplets over Valencia's silky topcurls. "They should be subtle, yet seductive, drawing a man's attention without him quite knowing why."

Lynsley had to quell the urge to bury his face in her hair.

"Mix up a bottle—a large bottle—and send it to our residence," he said after willing his jaw to unclench.

"With pleasure." The proprietress began to collect her samples. "I will make up something for you too, monsieur. Something clean and manly."

"And mysterious," added Valencia as she met the other woman's gaze. The fringe of her lashes shadowed her eyes.

Dark and inscrutable as midnight sin. For one delirious instant, Lynsley imagined allowing his self-control to shatter, along with all the crystal bottles, as he lay her across the counter and covered her body with his.

"So, the gentleman hides something beneath those very sober shades of charcoal grey?" The proprietress cocked her head. "Yes, I think you are right, madame."

Years of practice allowed him to resume a mask of bland formality. "Like many women, my wife has a vivid imagination."

"Your wife does not appear to be a woman with a weakness for fantasy." Mademoiselle Aix tapped a painted nail to his lapel. "I would guess that she possesses a strength of character that is quite rare. But then, I think you know that, eh?"

"Why do you think I married her?" Lynsley handed over a wad of banknotes and murmured an address. "Can you have it delivered it by the end of the day?"

"But of course." The proprietress tucked the francs into her bodice. "Anything else? Bath salts, perhaps, or my special massage oil for invigorating tired muscles?"

"Maybe another time." Already unsettled by the strange lapse in self-control, he thought it best to escape before Mademoiselle Aix could embellish on the idea of limbs glistening with a satin sheen. "Come, my dear. The hour is growing late and we must not be late for our evening engagement."

"Enjoy your stay in Paris," called Madame Aix. "It is a city to stir all the senses."

Chapter Eight

Shadows danced across the walls, the black and white patterns mimicking the sinuous swirl of the colored silks. Laughter, bright and brittle as cut glass, echoed off the crystal chandeliers. Candles flared as the waltz spun to a crescendo.

Valencia slanted a glance at the dancefloor, feeling as though a thousand little tongues of fire were lapping against her flesh. She had forgotten the heat and the heady thrum of excitement that pulsed through the ballrooms of the *haute monde*. English or French, it was all the same. Power and privilege had a language all its own.

"Would you care for another glass of champagne?" murmured Lynsley, his own glass barely touched.

She demurred, fearing any more wine would go straight to her head. The heat of the ballroom was already having an intoxicating effect, intensifying the smoky spice of the cheroots and the sultry sweetness of the lush perfumes, including her own. Feminine florals and spice mingled with an earthier, masculine musk.

The effect was exotic, enticing.

It had been a long time since she had drunk it all in.

"A prudent course," he agreed, edging around the refreshment table. After passing an arrangement of potted palms, the marquess drew her into a shadowed alcove, from which they could observe the other guests. "You have merely to sparkle and laugh often. Everyone will assume your effervescence is due to the champagne."

Valencia nodded, aware of what role she was to play. Even at the height of her powers, she had been more of a huntress than a temptress. She hoped the lack of practice in her seduction skills would not be too glaringly evident. Breaking up tavern fights did not require much poise or polish.

"I am looking for Levalier," said Lynsley as he paused to scan the crowd. "He will be our entrée into society. Not only he is hoping to make an advantageous trade agreement for his country with me, but he has the look of man who likes beautiful women. I've told him about you, and he is quite anxious to make your acquaintance."

She watched the dancing, grateful that her maid was a wizard with a curling iron and hairpins. Her raven-dark hair, which she usually wore in a simple plait, was gathered in a stylish topknot and fell in a graceful tumble of ringlets. A threading of tiny seed pearls added lustrous highlights, complementing the costly necklace at her throat. Compared to the other ladies, she decided that she didn't appear a country crow

...

Angling her gaze, she saw that Lynsley was studying her profile. "You are looking very lovely tonight," he murmured.

"Your operatives are quite good at their jobs," she replied obliquely.

His face remained expressionless.

"And I was fortunate that Madame Violette had a ballgown

made up for a client who decided that the color did not suit," she continued. "It required little alteration to meet Madame's exacting standards."

Lynsley's gaze flicked from her face to her bodice and back again. "The fit is perfect. As is the color. I trust that the *modiste* suggested a palette of sea greens and smoky jades to complement your eyes."

To her surprise, a flush began to steal up from her bosom to her bare shoulders.

Damn. She must remember that his praise was not personal. She was merely a means to an end.

"Far too many shades, if you ask me," replied Valencia with a light laugh. "As I said, it was *not* a pleasant experience to be poked with pins for hours on end."

The marquess smiled. "I am sure you endured far worse from Da Rimini in your fencing classes."

"*Il Lupino* would draw blood if he was in a foul mood." She sighed. "How is the wily old wolf?"

"Getting a bit long in the tooth, though his blade still carries a wicked bite," said Lynsley. "These days, he has an assistant who handles many of the daily duties."

"Another Italian?"

His lips twitched. "*Si.*"

"God help the girls. I am not sure that is the sort of swordsmanship the students should be exposed to. Perhaps you ought to hire a German. Or a monk. The Jesuits have a tradition of martial—"

Lynsley placed a hand on her arm, cutting off their banter. "Do you see the man entering the ballroom? The one with the oiled sidewhiskers and brocade waistcoat? That is Levalier."

Before she could respond, the marquess drew her out of the shadows and called loudly to a passing servant for more champagne. "The stage is set. Time to assume our roles," he added in a soft whisper.

Valencia felt a surge of excitement. She had not realized just how much she had missed the glittering lights, the action, the challenge of putting on a perfect performance. She had spent years learning her lines.

She must trust that she knew them by heart.

"Ah, Monsieur Dagget! There you are!" Levalier made his way through the crowd, accompanied by another man.

"And this must be your wife." Inclining a flourishing bow, he took her hand and brought it to his lips. "*Enchante*, madame. Your husband's praise did not do you justice."

"*Merci, monsieur*," she answered.

"Allow me to introduce Mr. Levalier, my dear," said Lynsley. "He is the gentleman with whom I am to negotiate a trade agreement for our country."

"La, do not allow your talks to go *too* smoothly, monsieur." she said with a coy smile. "I am hoping for a long stay here in Paris."

"*Bon!*" He turned to his companion and winked. "You heard the lady, Jean-Michel. We must make things just a little hard on her husband."

Lynsley's lips took on a sardonic curl. "You must be Noilly, from the Maritime Ministry," he said brusquely. "Have we set a time to meet?"

"All business and no pleasure, Monsieur Daggett?" Levalier exaggerated a sigh. "Come, you are in Paris, sir. It would be a shame not to sample some of its sumptuous delights."

"Really, Thomas. Mr. Levalier is right," said Valencia. It was the first time she had used his given name, but it came out smoothly enough. "You must learn to relax and show some ... *joie de vivre*."

"Precisely, madame. I see you already understand the Gallic spirit."

"You speak our language as well?" asked Noilly.

"Just a little schoolgirl French," she replied. "But I look forward to learning much more while I am here."

"Your accent is delightful, and as for your vocabulary, I am sure we can see to it that your knowledge of our language is greatly expanded. Indeed ..." Levalier offered her his arm. "While Noilly discusses the schedule of talks with your husband, allow me to begin introducing you to our circle of friends."

"Why, thank you." She set her glove on his sleeve. "I would like that very much."

Lynsley drained his glass. "See that you don't lead my wife astray, Levalier."

What a consummate actor, thought Valencia. His voice held an edge of possessiveness.

The minister made a face, a gesture she didn't miss.

"A jealous husband?" he asked. Softly as they moved away

She shrugged. "He may be American but he has very English notions about how a wife should behave."

Levalier chuckled. "And *Les Anglaise* can be so very strict about such things."

"True," she replied. "They tend to have no sense of adventure."

His eyes took on a speculative gleam.

Deciding not to push her flirtations too far, Valencia quickly changed the subject. "How is it that Parisians always appear so fashionable?"

"Perhaps it is because we have a flair for the dramatic." He laughed. "Even during the tumultuous days of the Revolution, before Napoleon took command, Paris was always on the cutting edge of style."

She raised a brow.

"Take, for example, the styles during the days when the *Directoires* were in change. They were quite outrageous," said Levalier. "Vestal dresses, high waisted Minerva tunics, curled wigs in every color of the rainbow—purple was a particular favorite of Therese Tallien. Some of the ladies wore fabrics so transparent that nothing was left to the imagination. Many went barefoot, with golden rings flashing on each of their toes."

"Surely you exaggerate."

"*Mais non*, I assure you I don't." He led her along the colonnaded length of the ballroom and paused beneath one of the arches. "Our former empress, Josephine, and her friends Therese Tallien and Juliette Recamier were legendary for their daring sense of dress. Indeed, one evening Madame Tallien wagered a man that her entire outfit, including her bracelets and boots, weighed less than two six-franc gold coins."

"And how did they resolve the bet?" asked Valencia. "There would appear to be some difficulties in coming to an accurate measure."

"Not really. She called for a scale and stripped." Levalier bared his teeth in a smile. "And won."

"They sound like females who were not afraid to flaunt their individuality," mused Valencia.

"Ah. An interesting way of seeing it, Madame Daggett." Levalier took a sip of his wine. "So you believe a lady should be allowed a certain amount of freedom?"

"Like you, sir, we Americans fought a war to break away from the strictures of the past." She leaned in closer. "Why should men get to have all the fun?"

The minister wet his lips. "Why, indeed?"

Valencia turned her attention to the movements taking form on the ballroom floor. "Dancing appears quite fashionable as well."

"*Oui*, Parisians love to dance. It is more than a fashion, it is an obsession. Right after the Terror, there were balls everywhere—in former convents, in the Elysee Palace. Even in the graveyards. In St. Sulpice cemetery, the people laid boards over the headstones and danced until dawn." He gave a glance at the waltzing couples. "Perhaps you would care to take a turn in the next set, madame?"

"I would rather see some of the other rooms," she replied. "I don't move very well on the dance floor."

"Forgive me if I have touched on a sore subject." He gave a delicate cough. "I could not help but note that your leg appears to trouble you."

"An old riding accident," said Valencia. "I hardly notice it anymore. However, some people are put off by a limp."

"Rest assured, it does nothing to diminish your loveliness."

She tapped her fan lightly against his arm. "La, I see the Gallic reputation for gallantry has not been exaggerated."

He gave a mock grimace. "It is impossible to speak too highly of your charms, madame."

The exchange of pleasantries continued as they moved from the ballroom to the adjoining salon. Keeping a smile on her face, Valencia pretended to give the minister her full attention. Her eyes, however, were making a surreptitious study of her surroundings.

Liberte. Egalite. Fraternite. As far as she could see, the grand slogan of the Revolution had effected little change in human nature. Hereditary titles might have been abolished, but the rich and powerful still set themselves above the masses. The sparkle of precious jewels, the rustle of lush silks, the bubbling of costly champagne—the haute monde of Paris lived very well indeed.

Her gaze lingered on a gilt framed paining on the far wall. "A Da Vinci?" she remarked.

"Yes. Our host served for a time in Lombardy, where he

oversaw the talks which worked out the financial settlements involved in ending the armed conflict."

"And when he returned, he brought back a collection of art," she said dryly.

"The spoils of war," said Levalier with a small smile. "It is a fact of life. And I like to think that we French are pragmatic as well as poetic."

"A practical combination." Valencia looked to a circle of men and women gathered near the marble fireplace. "But let us not talk of this interminable war, sir. It is so very depressing, and I wish to enjoy my stay here in your splendid city."

"But of course. A lady should not be subject to such a topic. Come, I will introduce you to some of my friends, who will see that you never have a dull moment in Paris."

Levalier drew her into the center of the group and made a show of announcing her arrival. "While I discuss affairs of state with the lady's illustrious husband, I am counting on you, *mes amis*, to show Mrs. Daggett all the pleasures of Paris."

Valencia carefully noted each name as the gentlemen bowed over her hand. *Dumont, Hillaire, Mersault* ... Not that she needed any introduction to the man she and Lynsley sought. She would recognize Pierre Rochambert the instant those amber-gold eyes turned her way.

The ladies were not quite as effusive in their welcome. Still, she soon had a number of invitations for the next few days. Tea at the Pavilion of Hanover on boulevard des Italiennes, a stroll in the Tulleries gardens, shopping in rue St. Honore, a visit to the Louvre Museum.

"And you and your husband must come to the Comedie Francaise on Thursday evening," said Madame Gervaise, a petite blonde who had been introduced as the wife of merchant. A very wealthy merchant, judging by the size of the sapphire nestle in her cleavage. "We have a box, and the great Joseph Talma is performing."

"Thank you," she murmured. "I adore the theatre."

"And you must come as my guests to a small supper afterward," added Monsieur Mersault. "My friend Rochambert keeps the best chef in town and his entertainments are known for the sumptuous spread of delicacies."

The champagne was like a thousand little swordpoints prickling against her tongue at the mention of their quarry's name. Valencia swallowed her excitement and smiled. "What a treat! How could Thomas and I say no."

Lynsley slanted a look to the archway at the far end of the ballroom. Valencia had been gone for some time. There was no cause for concern, he reminded himself. It was not as if he were letting a lamb loose among wolves. She was trained to deal with dangerous predators.

Yet he couldn't help remembering that for all her formidable skills, she had fallen prey to a vicious attack. Not for any weakness on her part. The marquess felt his jaw tighten. *The fault was his.* He should have anticipated the trap. He should have had someone watching her back.

"An interesting suggestion, Mr. Noilly, and one that we will certainly discuss in greater detail once Levalier sets a time for our talks," he said abruptly. "But now, if you will excuse me, I think I shall go find my wife."

Circling around the perimeter of the ballroom floor, Lynsley was aware of the curious stares following his movement. A subtle reminder of just how delicate a dance he and Valencia must perform here in Paris. They must be in perfect harmony to pull it off—the slightest misstep and their demise would be swift and sure.

He paused for a moment to watch the kaleidoscope blur of colors crescendo into the last spinning figures of the waltz, then slipped into the shadowed corridor.

In the side salon, several gentlemen surrounded Valencia, The wine had brought a rosy glow to her cheeks, and the fire-gold candlelight caught the brilliance of her emerald eyes. She looked ... magnificent. No wonder the men appeared to be hanging on her every word.

"Ah, here you are, my dear," he murmured, bringing his hand to rest at the small of her back.

She stiffened slightly at his touch, then relaxed.

"Alas, it seems Monsieur Daggett has come to claim his lovely wife," said Levalier, exaggerating a sigh. "Must you take her away so soon? The night is still young."

"It was a long and tiring trip from Normandy," replied Lynsley. "I am sure she is a trifle fatigued."

"As you see, sirs, my husband seems to feel he must look out for me, though in truth I am not so fragile as he seems to think." Valencia regarded him through the sable fringe of her lashes. He couldn't tell whether she was amused or annoyed. "Really, Thomas, you will give these gentlemen the wrong impression."

"Who could blame your husband for being a bit protective?" murmured Dumont. "I, too, would wish to see to your well-being, Madame Daggett."

Valencia favored the man with a coy smile. "How very reassuring to know that I am surrounded by such gallant chevaliers."

The Frenchmen exchanged smug looks. No doubt imagining that the cabbage-mannered American would soon be a cuckolded dolt, thought Lynsley. He had no trouble assuming a slight scowl.

"But perhaps you are right, Thomas," she went on. "I suppose it would be best to take an early leave tonight, seeing as I have accepted a number of invitations for us the coming week." A whisper of silk sounded as she shifted a step closer to him. "Including a visit to the *Comedie Francais*—and you know how I *adore* the theatre. Monsieur Mersault was also kind enough to ask us to a supper engagement afterward. His friend is a noted connoisseur of fine wine and superb cuisine, so I took the liberty of saying yes. It sounded like an evening too good to miss."

Despite her air of nonchalance, Lynsley sensed the quickening of her pulse as she placed her hand on his sleeve. "Indeed?" he drawled, feigning a look of indifference. "I shall leave our social schedule to you, my dear. I trust you to choose whatever pleases you, and I shall follow along."

"How very amiable of you," observed Levalier.

Lynsley smiled. "In marriage, one learns quickly that there are certain battles a man never wins."

"It seems the same truths hold sway on either side of the Atlantic," said Hillaire with a chuckle.

"*Bon soir*, Madame Daggett." Levalier pressed a kiss to her glove. "I look forward to seeing a great deal of you in the coming weeks."

As the minister's gaze met his, Lynsley fixed him with a cool stare before taking leave of the group with a curt nod. He waited until they were in the privacy of their coach before remarking, "I take it you have something of interest to report."

"Yes." Wrapping her shawl a bit tighter around her shoulders, Valencia leaned back again the squabs. " Our host for the apres-theatre supper will be Pierre Rochambert."

The low flicker of the carriage lamp did not reach her face. Through the wisps of smoke and shadow he saw only the ghostly shimmer of her bare shoulders and throat. Pale and perfect as porcelain.

And oh so vulnerable.

Damn. The marquess turned his gaze to the glass panes, and took a moment to watch the muddle of lights roll by. "Good work," he replied evenly, once he had forced the clench of his jaw to relax. "I had not expected to make such quick progress."

"You don't sound overly happy about it." Her voice was muffled by the gloom.

"On the contrary. Every moment we spend in Paris is fraught with danger. The sooner we get the job done, the better."

Chapter Nine

Despite his assertion, the marquess seemed in no hurry to make any clandestine forays to further their efforts. Indeed, to Valencia, the next few days passed in a dizzying whirl of mundane activity. Bonnets, gloves, silks, lace—the shopping seemed endless, as did the stream of invitations from the hostesses of the *haute monde*.

Between the two, Valencia barely saw Lynsley, save for a briefing at breakfast to go over the daily schedule. His ministry talks had started in earnest, leaving him little time for strategy sessions with her.

Damn. If the dratted man thought to leave her stranded in the opulent salons while he seized the chances to learn more about their quarry, he was in for a rude awakening.

After returning home from an evening concert at the residence of Madame. De Vergennes, Valencia found her mood growing more discordant by the moment. Lynsley had once again announced that he was engaged to dine with the gentlemen from the Ministry, and while she had no real reason to doubt his word, she couldn't help wondering whether he was leaving her in the dark.

Turning her gaze from the night sky, she tightened the sash of her wrapper and moved away from the window. The clock on the mantel showed it close to midnight. Tomorrow evening they were due to meet Rochambert face to face. Surely Lynsley would want to discuss their plan of attack.

And yet, he had passed by her door a half hour earlier without so much as slowing his step. Tiptoeing closer to the door connecting their suites, Valencia listened for any sound. If she heard a snore, she just might burst in and shake him out of his comfortable slumber. Her own nerves were so on edge that sleep seemed impossible.

"Ahem." A soft cough and the clink of glass announced that the marquess was still up.

Valencia hesitated for a moment, then snapped the brass latch open. *To hell with waiting and wondering.* Lynsley had no right to treat her as if she were not an equal in this mission.

"Any new information I should know?" she asked, masking her misgivings with a brusque question.

Lynsley looked up from his notes. He, too, was dressed in naught but a silk robe, his bare feet stretched out to the banked embers of the bedchamber fire. "None to speak of," he answered. He lifted his brandy glass to his lips. "If you are having trouble sleeping, feel free to help yourself to a drink." There was a tray of decanters on a sideboard by his chair. "The sherry is excellent, but you may find the armagnac a bit strong for your taste."

"I've owned a tavern for a number of years, sir." She marched straight for the spirits, refusing to retreat in the face of his icy calm. Did nothing ruffle the man's composure? He was always so cool, so collected.

While she, with her limping step and prickly moods, always felt so awkward, so unsure in front of him.

"Trust me," she added. "I can drink any man under the table."

"No need to prove it tonight," he answered. Both his voice and his expression remained perfectly neutral. "We both must keep a clear head for tomorrow."

"As to that, sir." Valencia paused beside his chair, fighting to keep her smoldering anger from flaring into flames. "Don't you think we ought to be discussing our strategy for confronting Rochambert?"

"Actually, the last thing I want is to confront the man at this point."

"Then what have you in mind?" she demanded.

Lynsley shrugged. "If I think of anything specific, you will be the first to know. Otherwise we will just have to play it by ear."

She bit her lip, wondering if he was holding something back. Not that she had any hope of forcing him into a verbal slip. When it came to dueling with words, the marquess was the master.

Still, the idea that he was toying with her piqued her pride. "I trust ..." Seeing the back of his collar was twisted, she reached out to smooth the fabric. Her fingers slid lightly over the folds, tangling with the curling strands of his hair.

The sudden sensation—a tantalizing tickle of silk on silk— sent a strange tingling through her.

"Lud, your muscles are tied in knots," she said, feeling him tense beneath her hand. Without really thinking, she began to massage the back of his neck.

"The meeting went on for hours." His voice took on a sharper edge. "I will unwind in a moment."

"Sit still and lean forward," she ordered, drawing her hands out from the ridge of his spine. The sloping stretch of his shoulders was broader than she had imagined, and the contours more chiseled. Intrigued, she deepened her touch, exploring the subtleties of his shape. "Try to relax."

Valencia heard his breath rasp in and out. Increasing the tempo of her strokes, she worked her fingertips in slow, circling paths. Beneath the silk dressing gown, she could feel the warmth of his body and sculpted strength of the slabbed muscle.

Her pulse began to quicken. There was something acutely intimate about his closeness, and the faint thud of his heartbeat against her palms. She leaned a bit closer, inhaling the subtle spice of Madame Aix's cologne mingled with his own male scent.

"That's enough," he growled, shifting abruptly and trying to brush off her touch.

"Lud, why are you so snappish tonight, Thomas?" She deliberately used his given name, the first time she had done so in private. After all, she was no longer a young fledgling, in awe of her superior. "You are acting like a bear with a thorn in his arse."

Swearing softly, Lynsley shifted the papers in his lap.

Good Lord, was that a telltale twitch?

Was it possible that the stone-faced Lord Lynsley was not impervious to normal masculine desire?

Cocking her head, she regarded him with a curious stare. "Are you in an ill-tempered mood because you haven't had sex for a while? In our Academy class on seduction, *La Paloma* said that men get awfully edgy if they go too long without it."

Lynsley's shoulder muscles went rigid as steel beneath her lingering hand.

"Thank you for the lecture on male biology," he said through gritted teeth. "But I assure you, as the head of the school, I am quite familiar with the curriculum. And if I need any further elucidation on the subject, I shall ask."

Apparently she had touched a sore spot.

"Seeing as you don't have a wife, you must seek sexual release elsewhere. Since you claim you have no *cher amie* in London, you must have a bawdy house that you favor," she persisted, taking a rather perverse delight in seeing him squirm. "I've heard that Cupid's Cave is highly favored by gentlemen of the *ton*."

"My personal life is not a subject that I discuss with anyone," he snapped.

"It doesn't seem to me that you have much of one," she replied. "From what we heard at school, you are married to your job. Why is that? Why have you never taken a wife?"

He rose abruptly. "You are out of line, Valencia. Way out of line. Kindly return to your own quarters." His voice was carefully controlled. "I have work to do."

She was about to retort when a spark of the fire flared up, throwing his profile in harsh contrast. She had never seen him look so tense, so tired—his face was drawn so taut it seemed his cheekbones might slice through the flesh.

Suddenly ashamed of herself and her childish taunts, she dropped her chin. "Yes, sir," she whispered, and retreated without another word.

Bloody hell. Against his better judgment, Lynsley poured himself another brandy and downed it in one gulp. To his dismay, he saw his hands were shaking.

He must get a grip on his emotions. He had spent years perfecting his iron-fisted control over mind and body. Only to have it come perilously close to cracking into a thousand tiny shards at the touch of Valencia's hands.

She had been naked beneath the sashed wrapper. The shape of her breasts had been tantalizing apparent though the cream-colored silk, and the lamplight had silhouetted the sinuous curves of her hips.

He pressed his brow to the cool marble of the mantelpiece, hoping to quell the rising heat in his blood. Fire crackled through his limbs, its burn far more potent than any French brandy. Had she any idea how mesmerizing she was with her ebony hair tumbled around her shoulders and her emerald eyes alight with anger.

And curse him for a damnable fool, he had reacted with pure, animal lust to her touch.

Admit it! whispered one of the demons who had taken possession of his reason. For one mad moment he had wondered what she would have said if he had suggested that she satisfy his primal needs.

Valencia, her glorious body twined with his.

The idea was ...

Impossible.

Setting the glass aside, Lynsley stared at his palm. He had been gripping it so tightly that the pattern of the cut crystal was imprinted on his flesh. Damn the woman for having such a powerful effect on him. Ten years should have been long enough to drown out the spark of elemental attraction. But the thunder and lightning of that ill-fated Atlantic gale was nothing in comparison to the storm of emotion now raging in his head.

Duty must never give way to desire. It was one of the cardinal rules that the Academy drummed into its students. He had better heed his own teachings, else risk seeing this mission go up in smoke.

No, he would not—could not—fail. For her sake, as well as for that of his country. He couldn't live with himself if Valencia were hurt again because of a weakness on his part.

Letting the dressing gown slide from his shoulders, Lynsley raised his arms over his head and arched back into a deep stretch. *Balance.* Yoga was all about keeping mind and body in perfect harmony. He must quell the dissonant voices that threatened his equilibrium. Control the strange impulses coursing through his flesh. And most of all, he must maintain a distance, a detachment from her.

The job was already far too personal.

The next evening saw the curtain rise on their first move to meet Pierre Rochambert. Arriving at the *Comedie Francaise,* Valencia forgot for the moment her personal musing on the marquess. The stylish crowd and ornate architecture were fascinating, and like the thespians backstage, she felt a thrill of anticipation, now that the moment for playing her own role was at hand.

"The Emperor is a great lover of the theatre, Madame Daggett," confided Madame Gervaise the wife of their host. "And he adores Corneille's plays. I do hope you enjoy tonight's performance of *Cinna.*"

"I am sure I shall be enthralled," she replied.

"Monsieur Talma is our most brilliant actor, Madame Daggett," added Madame Gervaise. "He is the Emperor's favorite."

"And so is Mademoiselle George," added Mersault dryly. "Indeed, when she made her debut in Paris in '02, she was often called upon to give private performances backstage."

Valencia raised her lorgnette and surveyed the surrounding theatre boxes, which were fast filling up. "And does the current Empress see that as a comedy or a tragedy?'

He gave a Gallic shrug. "Paris is not very prudish about such things," he replied. "We French have a certain ... *joie de vivre.*"

"Yes, I am beginning to see just how much people in Paris

enjoy life." Valencia slanted a look at Lynsley who appeared to be paying no attention to her *tete a tete* with the minister.

"And what of you, Madame Daggett?" asked Mersault in a conspiratorial whisper. "Do you enjoy life?"

"Very much." Valencia lowered her voice to a matching murmur. "Though New Haven is rather dull." She paused. "It is so provincial, even for America. And seeing as its college was founded to teach the clergy, the city is quite straitlaced."

"Ah, my condolences." He winked. "We shall have to make sure that you enjoy your stay here. Paris is anything but provincial."

Fluttering her fan, Valencia turned her profile to the lamplight, aware that the man's gaze was caressing her face, her bosom ...

A smile drew her lips upward. It was rather nice to be the subject of such obvious admiration, even though the Frenchman would likely be flirting with anyone wearing skirts. Flowery words, florid sentiments—the fisherman and farmers who frequented her tavern were not much given to poetry.

Mersault edged his chair closer. "Tell me, does your husband permit you to explore our city on your own?"

"Thomas?" She gave a tiny toss of her curls. "I have my ways of getting him to accede to my wishes."

"I am sure you do," he replied with a throaty chuckle.

"Pray, do share your *bon mots* with the rest of us, Mersault," said Lynsley rather loudly.

"I was merely pointing out some of the notable people in attendance to your wife, Monsieur Daggett." The Frenchman's words came out smooth as butter. "There, in the second tier, is General Penaud, commandant of the Imperial Guard, who is notorious for his insatiable appetite for Breton oysters and beautiful women."

"Does everyone misbehave in this city?" growled Lynsley.

As yet, his manner was not overtly upset, but the tone implied trouble could be brewing if his wife were too attentive to other men.

"It is an unfortunate weakness of us Parisians, monsieur," answered Mersault.

Levalier gave a slight cough. "Let us not give Monsieur Daggett the wrong impression of our city, Gaston," he murmured, then quickly changed the subject. "Do you attend the theatre often at home, monsieur?"

"New Haven has little to offer in way of theatrics," replied the marquess stiffly, his gaze lingering on Valencia just an instant before returning to the stage.

"Jean-Louis tells me your city is known for its institution of higher learning," said Levalier's wife.

Lynsley gave a gruff nod. "Yes, Yale College is considered one of America's finest. My father, Naphtali Daggett was appointed to the first professorship, and later served as its president. When the British raided the city during our War of Independence, he fought with a company of students despite his advanced age and was taken prisoner during the fighting. The beating he received from his captors cut short his life. He died the next year from his injuries."

"Then you have personal reason to feel no love for the Redcoats," remarked Mersault.

"Indeed. Nothing would give me greater pleasure than to see your Emperor boil the Lobsterbacks in oil. In New England, we steam them in seaweed and serve them with melted butter."

Levalier laughed. "Speaking of cuisine, sir, I should like to hear more of your own trading business. You deal in spice from the Caribbean?"

"Nutmeg and mace from Grenada, along with cacao from Mexico. Of late, though, I have been dealing with a merchant in Martinique for a special type of sugar." Lynsley proceed to explain the merits of soil and climate for each of the Leeward Islands in excruciating detail.

Valencia repressed a smile as she watched the faces of the Frenchmen grow glazed with boredom. Was there any subject that the marquess could not discourse on with intelligence? His breadth of knowledge was remarkable. A fact which was helping him play the role of a prig to perfection.

Prig. Reminded of the previous night, she felt a faint tinge of color steal to her face. She *had* been out of line. Outrageously so. She had no right to provoke him, to pry into his personal life. But somehow, her temper had got the better of her.

She had not apologized. She had felt too awkward and unsure to broach the subject. And Lynsley, drawing no doubt on centuries of good breeding, had acted as though the incident had never occurred. Just like a consummate gentleman.

No—just like a patient schoolmaster overlooking the transgression of an unruly student.

Slanting a look at him from under her lashes, Valencia wondered if he would ever see her as naught but an errant fledgling. A blot on the Academy record book.

She had given him precious little reason to respect her judgment. From the earliest days at the school, her temper seemed to get the better of her in his presence.

Trouble. She had been naught but trouble.

The soft swoosh of the rising curtain reminded her that the mission must take center stage. Focusing her eyes straight ahead, Valencia resolved that her own mordant musings would from now on remain hidden in the wings.

"Madames et monsieurs ..."

The play passed pleasantly enough, with each act drawing enthusiastic applause from the audience. However, she listened with only half an ear, intent on rehearsing her own lines for the coming supper engagement. She would prove to the marquess that she, too, could play the role she had been trained for without a slip.

"Did you enjoy the acting, Mrs. Daggett?" inquired Mersault as the curtain dropped on the final scene.

"Very much," she murmured.

"Well, prepare yourself for another treat. Supper will be another feast for the senses."

Folding her fan, she slapped it lightly against his sleeve. "You are whetting my appetite, sir."

"You are in Paris, madame. A city that offers pleasures for every palate. I promise you won't be disappointed."

"How gratifying to hear it, Mr. Mersault." Lynsley moved between them. "Like our previous president, Mr. Jefferson, I am quite fond of your country's claret. You must recommend a wine merchant so I may order some cases to take home."

"No doubt you will also wish to order some champagne as well, Monsieur Daggett."

"On the whole, I find the stuff too frivolous for my taste," said Lynsley gruffly. Taking Valencia's arm, he turned away. "Come, my dear. The carriage will be waiting."

It wasn't until the wheels started to roll over the cobblestones that the marquess spoke again. "Just a reminder, Valencia." He had made no mention of the coming challenge until now. "Don't do anything rash."

Her chin rose a notch. "Is that an order?" she asked.

"Yes," he replied calmly. "As a matter of fact, it is."

In spite of her resolve to remain detached, she bristled. "And suppose I disobey?" She knew she shouldn't seek to stir up trouble, but that air of calm and logic kept goading her to challenge his authority.

"Then I shall be forced to take steps to ensure your insubordination doesn't compromise the mission."

"Should I take that as a threat, Thomas?"

"No. It is merely a statement of fact. But I trust it won't come to that. You gave me your word, and I have faith in your integrity, Valencia. And your sense of honor."

Damn. He had her neatly boxed in.

"Very clever," she muttered.

A glimmer of a smile curled on his lips. "How else would I survive a school full of strong-willed females?"

"By locking us in a dungeon?" she quipped.

"The thought had occurred to me on several occasions," replied Lynsley.

"Most likely all of them included me."

Valencia thought back on her days as the top Merlin. She had been brimming with youthful hubris, sure that she was invincible. How very naïve such self-confidence must have seemed to him.

"There have been others who have come close to matching your spirit," said Lynsley.

"But none so stubborn as to defy your every lecture on common sense." Her lips quivered, unsure whether to form a smile or a scowl.

"Perhaps I learned a few lessons," replied Lynsley.

The admission surprised her. "Such as?"

He didn't answer right away, but leaned back against the squabs, as if deep in thought.

Lynsley was not only a master of the rhetorical, she realized. He was a master at withdrawing into the shadows. To a place where his inner self was hidden. And no one else was allowed to follow.

Valencia bit her lip as she slanted a look at the shroud of darkness hiding his face. Had anyone ever penetrated his defenses?

"Confine you flirtations to Mersault tonight," he finally said. "Let us not show too obvious an interest in Rochambert."

"I haven't forgotten all the lessons from the past," she said.

"Good, for those who do not recall history are doomed to repeat it."

A hint of wry humor? Or an oblique warning? With Lynsley it was not ever easy to discern his true meaning. "Seeing as I am reminded every day of what damage Rochambert is capable of," she replied. "I am no more keen that you are to have him gain the upper hand."

Chapter Ten

Rochambert's tastes ran to the extravagant, noted Lynsley as he entered the mansion's foyer. The fluted marble columns and checkered floor tiles still retained their Louis XIV polish. All around was an air of pomp. Of privilege. The gleam of the gilded moldings and ornate furniture seemed to wink in subtle mockery at the Revolution's ideals of egalitarian principles.

A noble sentiment on paper, but in reality, some people appeared more equal than others. Napoleon clearly believed in rewarding those who served him well.

"An impressive place, *non?*" murmured Levalier.

"Quite," replied the marquess. "Your friend must be a very important man here in Paris."

"Let us just say he has the complete confidence of the Emperor, who values his services."

"A trusted advisor is apparently worth his weight in gold to your leader," observed Lynsley dryly.

Levalier chuckled. "I am glad to see that Americans have a sense of humor, monsieur. You are not at all like *les Anglaise,* who are insufferably stiff and starchy."

"They think that they rule the world," he said with a straight face.

"*Oui*, but when Napoleon sits on the throne in Buckingham Palace they will be put in their place."

"A nation of shopkeepers," said Lynsley, repeating one of Napoleon's famous tirades against England.

"Who lack any sense of style or taste." Levalier plucked two glasses of champagne from a passing footman's silver tray. "But enough talk of the enemy. Come, I have some friends I want you to meet."

For the moment, Valencia kept to the company of the other ladies, using the trillings of trivial talk to survey the surrounding company. From across the room, she watched Lynsley move among the Ministry gentlemen, his conservative dark navy coat at odds with the flamboyant colors and exaggerated styling favored by the Frenchmen.

The longish sidewhiskers had altered the shape of his face, making all of his features appear elongated to a sharper edge. The marquess had also assumed a more rigid bearing. He looked taller, broader, and a good deal more arrogant than his usual self. Indeed, everything about his mannerisms appeared more aggressive.

Valencia found herself marveling at his skill to slip into a role. The changes were subtle yet extremely effective. The Marquess of Lynsley took pains to blend into the woodwork. Mr. Thomas Daggett did not.

A clandestine agent must be a chameleon. A master of deception, making it impossible to tell truth from lies ...

Her attention was suddenly claimed by the approach of M. Mersault and a golden-haired gentleman whose scimitar smile cut a chill down her spine.

"Madame Daggett, allow me to present you to our host, Pierre Rochambert."

"Thank you for including me and my husband in your soiree, Monsieur," she murmured as Rochambert lifted her glove to his lips. "Your mansion is quite impressive. The furnishings are exquisite, and what a magnificent collection of art."

"I consider myself a connoisseur of beauty, madame," he replied. "So I am delighted to welcome you into my home."

Forcing her insides to unclench, Valencia acknowledged the compliment with a light laugh.

"What do you do, Monsieur Rochambert?" she asked. "Besides collect exquisite art."

The two men exchanged glances. "I help the Emperor eliminate niggling little problems of state that arise from time to time," answered Rochambert.

"Pierre is being much too modest," said Mersault. "He is an invaluable asset in the fight against tyranny."

Valencia's only reaction was a petulant purse of her lips. "La, I shall be very happy when this interminable war is over. You gentlemen seem to talk of nothing else."

"You are quite right to chastise us, madame," said Rochambert. "Ladies have no interest in bullets and blades." His brow waggled. "Tell me, what does interest you?"

"Fashion," she replied coyly. "And all of the things that adds to life's pleasure."

"What about flowers?" asked Mersault. "The former Empress created magnificent rose gardens at Malmaison. They are well worth a visit"

"I love the colors and perfumes of roses, but alas, our harsh New England winters make it hard to keep such plants."

"Surely a hothouse would keep them safe," observed Mersault.

She made a face. "My husband considers such things an unnecessary extravagance."

Rochambert took a sip of his wine. "A husband ought to indulge his wife's fancies."

"American men have much to learn from their Continental counterparts. Perhaps a bit of your Gallic gallantry will rub off on this trip." Valencia exaggerated a pout. "Thomas is terribly serious. And he is quite determined to do well on this trip. You see, this is his first diplomatic mission for President Madison."

"An honor, to be sure. I am sure that he merited it," said Rochambert smoothly.

She shrugged. "No doubt. He certainly spends enough of his time on it. When he is not engaged in talks with you and your ministers, Monsieur Mersault, he is studying an endless array of papers."

Mersault chuckled. "In my experience, ladies are no more fond of documents than they are of weapons. We shall have to see that you are not bored to death, eh, Pierre?"

"*Oui*—but of course," replied Rochambert with a smooth smile. As his gaze slid from the peak of her curling topknot to the plunging décolletage of her new Parisian gown, his brow furrowed ever so slightly. "Have we met before?' he asked slowly.

"Have you ever been to Charleston, monsieur? Or Boston?" asked Valencia.

"*Non*, I have traveled extensively across Europe but never to the New World."

"I did not think so." She let her words hang for a moment in the air before adding, "I would remember it very well had we encountered each other in the past."

His lips parted, revealing a peek of pearly teeth. "So should I. Strange, there is something familiar about you."

She batted her lashes. "Perhaps it is my Mediterranean blood.

"Spanish?" he asked.

"La, however did you guess?" she teased.

Rochambert laughed. "Your name, to begin with."

"Yes, my grandmother was from the city of Valencia. My mother thought it pretty enough to use as my middle name. I've always disliked Elizabeth—it sounds so stiff and formal." She took a sip of her champagne. "Actually, Thomas prefers it as well. He thinks it has an exotic ring."

"Ah." Rochambert eyed her from over the rim of his wineglass." So your husband likes exotic things?"

Valencia made a coy face and fluttered her lashes. "Really now, monsieur, you cannot expect me to reveal my husband's deepest, darkest secrets to a stranger, can you?"

His nostrils flared slightly as he drew in a breath. Did he scent a challenge? Men like Rochambert were predators at heart. They couldn't resist the thrill of the hunt.

"Then I shall have to make sure we become better acquainted," he replied softly.

Valencia didn't reply, leaving it to his imagination to interpret the arch of her brow.

Time to disengage from the enemy.

Lynsley was right. A frontal assault against a man of Rochambert's cunning and guile would never work. To have any chance at victory, they must keep him off guard. She would give the marquess no reason to accuse her of disobeying orders.

Snapping her fan open, she turned and tapped one of the passing Hussar officers on the sleeve. "Ah, there you are, Capitain Parquand. You simply *must* finish telling me about the exhibit of Spanish paintings at the Palais de Luxumburg."

Rochambert was forced to make room for the young man to bow over her hand.

"Pray, excuse me, monsieur," she said, taking care that their eyes did not quite meet.

"Until later, Madame Daggett," he murmured.

She didn't look back, but sensed his gaze following her for several moments.

Yes, until later, Monsieur Rochambert.

"Your wife is a most charming creature, Monsieur Daggett," observed Levalier, tipping his glass in salute.

"Indeed, she is a lady of rare beauty," agreed Noilly. "And you, sir, are a gentleman of rare courage to bring her with you to Paris," he added with a sly wink.

"Hmmph." Lynsley reached for another glass of champagne. The first two had been discreetly dumped into the potted arrangement of Oriental lilies. "Sea voyages are nothing to fear these days. Not when sailing on a sturdy Yankee schooner from my own fleet," he growled.

"The sea is not half so dangerous as French soil." The voice behind him was cool and mellifluous, like glacier water flowing over smooth stone. "What Monsieur Noilly means is that our city is said to have a seductive effect on women. There is something about the ethereal light, and the spirit of *l'amour* that makes them take bloom and spread their petals, so to speak."

"Hmmph. You must be one of those poxy new poets, who revels in writing romantic rubbish," replied the marquess with a slight sneer. Intuition had already told him who was speaking. But any doubts vanished as he turned and confronted Pierre Rochambert for the first time in the flesh.

Those golden eyes, that daggered smile. He had seen them far too many times in his mind's eye to be mistaken.

Noilly smothered a laugh with a cough.

"Allow me to introduce our host, Monsieur Daggett," said

Levalier. "Pierre, this is the American consul, who has just arrived here in France for talks on our Caribbean trade."

"Thomas Daggett," said Lynsley, with a small nod.

"Pierre Rochambert." The Frenchman responded with a more courtly bow.

Lynsley made a quick, dispassionate study of the figure before him. The picture he had in his head, assembled from a number of informants, proved to be highly accurate. A thin, almost effeminate face, framed by fair hair that fell in soft ringlets around his starched shirtpoints. A slender build, narrow-waisted, long-legged. A full, sensual mouth. A peek of perfect white teeth. A taste for expensive clothes.

The celestial blue color of his coat accentuated the man's cherubic looks, creating the illusion of a gilded face floating in a heavenly sky.

The Angel of Death.

So Rochambert had been dubbed by Allied intelligence services on account of his ruthless methods. The man was a cold-blooded killer, utterly lacking in conscience or compassion.

"Seeing as I have already had the pleasure of encountering your wife, Monsieur Daggett, I must agree with *mon ami* Guillaume that you are indeed a brave man," continued Rochambert. "Most men would consider Paris ... too dangerous."

"My wife is not some flighty schoolgirl," said Lynsley gruffly. "She is experienced in the ways of society, and I trust that she possesses the necessary poise and polish to conduct herself with the utmost propriety, whether at home or abroad."

The pompous speech brought a twitch of amusement to Lavalier's mouth.

"Then it appears you have nothing to worry about, Monsieur Daggett." Rochambert's voice held an edge of mockery.

Lynsley knew Napoleon's top assassin to be a man who

enjoyed cutting up an opponent with his tongue as well as his blade. *Forewarned was forearmed*, he thought with an inward smile. For now, he would set himself up as a stiff-rumped target. Contempt bred carelessness. Rochambert must be tempted to think it would be easy to move in and seduce Valencia. In his conceit, the Frenchman was likely to make a small slip, an errant stumble.

And then Lucifer would fall back to the hell where he belonged.

"I should think not," he said with a sniff. "Firm discipline, strict rules—a female is grateful for a husband's guidance ..."

Noilly started to smirk.

"Bonaparte should have applied his military genius a bit closer to home," finished Lynsley.

The attaché no longer looked so smug. "I daresay the Emperor needs no advice on marital tactics—"

A clink of crystal cut off the retort. "More champagne, Monsieur Daggett?" offered Levalier.

"Thank you," said Lynsley. "Damn difficult to get decent stuff at home, seeing as the British navy has your ports bottled up right and tight."

"If your American admirals had put up any fight," muttered Noilly. "The British might—"

"A toast, gentlemen." Levalier raised his glass. "To a quick defeat of our enemies."

"Aye, I'll drink to that," murmured the marquess.

Chapter Eleven

"What activities have you planned for the afternoon," asked Lynsley the next morning at breakfast.

"Shopping for bonnets with Madame Levalier and Madame Benoit," replied Valencia. "With what you give me to spend on fripperies, His Majesty could fit out a four-deck ship of the line."

"You will look far more elegant sailing down the streets of Paris," murmured Lynsley.

She blew out her cheeks. "It seems like such a waste of blunt. Not to speak of chip straw and ribbon."

"It is a small sacrifice to make, considering the stakes."

"I did not mean to whine," she replied. "I am simply unused to being so ... frivolous. Especially after all you have spent already."

He regarded her with a hooded gaze.

Inscrutable as always, she thought. How unfair. No man should be graced with such lovely, gold-tipped lashes.

"You don't care for fine clothing and costly jewels?"

murmured Lynsley after a moment. "I thought perhaps you had softened your objections to such feminine pleasures."

"I've little use for such things in my line of work," she replied somewhat sharply.

"Consider the indulgences as part of the job."

"I would rather be designing a way to penetrate Rochambert's residence than the trimmings for a poke brim bonnet," she muttered.

The marquess pushed back his plate and rose. "The Romany tribes have a saying—revenge is a dish best served cold."

"I've waited ten years," she said softly.

His jaw hardened. "Let me remind you again that this mission is not a personal vendetta, Valencia. If you cannot remain dispassionate—"

"Damn it, I know what my duty is." She, too, rose. "Have you any cause for complaint?"

"No, but I expect you to curb your impulsive tendencies while we are here in Paris," he said, suddenly raising his voice. "I'll not have you compromise my work."

Surprise rendered her mute for a moment.

"Word that we quarrel in private will be useful to our charade," he whispered.

Of course, she thought. Lynsley never lost his temper enough to miss an opportunity to further their chance of success.

It did not require much skill at acting to slap her serviette down upon the table and stalk from the room.

Valencia was still fuming as her carriage drew to a halt in front of Madame Fournier's chic little shop. But as she stepped down to the pavement, she smoothed her scowl into a smile. She would show him that she could match his stoic self-control, she vowed.

"Madame Daggett, how delightful that you could join us!" Madame Levalier looked up from a rainbow assortment of ribbons as the door opened. "Come, you must help me choose a band to match these sweet little cherries." She waved a thick cluster of artificial fruit. "Pierre is being such a tease, the naughty man ..."

Through the display of satin cabbage roses, Valencia caught sight of Rochambert.

"He is pressing me to pick chartreuse," continued Madame Levalier. "But I fear the color is *de trop*. What is your opinion?"

Valencia moved to her side. "You must show me the other choices."

Madame Levalier fanned a handful of colorful snippets across the countertop. "*Voila*! I simply can't decide!"

To Valencia, they all looked far too garish, but she took her time, pretending to give the matter serious consideration. "I vow, it is a difficult decision," she finally murmured. "But seeing as Monsieur Rochambert recommends the chartreuse, I think we must trust his eye."

"*Merci, madame.*" Rochambert flashed her a wink. "Are you always so agreeable?"

Her fingers stroked over the curls of satin. "I believe in yielding to one who possesses an expertise in a subject, be it art, or fashion, or ..." She deliberately let her words trail off.

A speculative gleam flickered through the fringe of his golden lashes. "Or anything that requires a certain specialized skill, madame?" Whispers of velvet and lace stirred as he glided through the draped display of fabrics.

"Within reason," she replied slowly.

"Ah. I should like to hear the American definition of the word."

However, a call from Mme. Benoit diverted any further flirtation. "La, Pierre, you must come here and settle the debate on which style of brim is most becoming. And do you prefer this shade of amaranthus to azure blue?"

Rochambert turned, but not before flashing Valencia another heavy-lidded look.

Valencia repressed a shudder. The man was as seductive as a snake. There was something flat and reptilian about his eyes ... but perhaps she was merely allowing her imagination to take flight. As Lynsley warned, she must stay focused on the mission and not let personal feelings color her judgment.

"Do let me show you the selection of bonnet shapes." Mme. Levalier took her arm and led her to another counter. "Mademoiselle. Cosette is the most renowned mantua maker in all of Paris, and I'm sure you will find a number of designs to your liking."

For the next quarter hour, Valencia poked through the piles of straw and felt, feigning an interest in all the variations of size, shape and styling. Why ladies made such a fuss over the dratted things was beyond her. She loved the feel of the sun and wind on her face, and the tug of the wind at her hair. Hats were a cursed nuisance, a confining constriction. However, she covered up her indifference by oohing and ahhing over the bunch, then selected the simplest one she could find.

"If I may be so bold, Madame Daggett, allow me to suggest these ribbons to go along with the chip straw bonnet you've chosen." Rochambert suddenly reappeared through the scrim of gauze and netting hanging across the aisle. "The pale peach color will look divine with your raven hair."

"How kind." She nodded to the salesgirl. "Please add the final trimmings as the gentleman suggests."

"Speaking of peaches," he went on in a silky murmur. "

Have you sampled the ice cream from the stalls on the boulevard des Italiennes?"

"No, I have not yet had the pleasure."

"They are a treat you should not miss." Rochambert offered his arm. "It is only a short stroll from here."

Valencia hesitated a fraction. "Won't the others think me rude to run off?"

He leaned in a little closer and lowered his voice even more. "Do you really care?"

Her hand slid lightly into the crook of his sleeve. "I trust you won't lead me *too* far astray."

"Oh, as to that, I make no promises, madame. You see, I'm not really a gentleman." The door shut behind them, setting off a tinkling of bells. "Does that frighten you?"

"Not particularly. You see, I am not really a lady."

A bark of laughter sounded. "You intrigue me, Madame Daggett. Tell me a little about yourself."

"As I mentioned before, my grandparents were Spanish and owned properties in the Caribbean islands. My mother lived on a sugar plantation in Hispanola. She married a prosperous trader from Charleston, in the American Carolinas, which is where I grew up." Valencia gave a mock shiver. "And now I live in New England."

"I have heard that Boston is quite a civilized city," he said.

"I could not say, seeing as we so rarely have a chance to visit it." She made sure that her pique was pronounced. "New Haven is a very dull place, whose only claim to fame is a college that attracts a rather dour, serious-minded set of young men as students."

Rochambert flashed a sympathetic smile. "It does sound quite dull." They paused by one of the street stalls while he purchased a dish of ice cream flavored with strawberries.

She shrugged. "Thomas has money. And he is ambitious. I don't plan on being stuck in such a provincial place forever."

"Indeed not." He gave a wave. "See, you are here in Paris. A city that is most definitely not provincial."

"The gaiety, the glamour." She gave a sigh. "It will not be easy to return to America when this is over."

"Who knows what the future may bring?"

"How very pragmatic, Monsieur Rochambert." Valencia licked a bit of the ice cream from her spoon. "So you are suggesting that we eat, drink and be merry today?"

"In these troubled times, it seems a wise philosophy to embrace," he said softly.

"And, mayhap, a dangerous one," she replied.

He, too, paused to taste the frozen confection. "Danger adds a certain spice to life. A steady diet of bland and boring fare is unpalatable for those who crave variety." Rochambert's gaze dropped and lingered overlong on her limping step. "You do not appear to be a lady who is afraid to take a risk, Madame Daggett."

Valencia took care to keep her voice noncommittal. "Perhaps my riding accident has soured me on the idea of acting impulsively."

"Perhaps. But in my experience, people who are by nature adventurous rarely change, even if they suffer a stumble or two."

"Dear me, Monsieur Rochambert. Put that way, you seem to mean that some of us never learn from our mistakes."

"*Au contraire, madame.* Let us just say that some of us understand that risks make the reward even sweeter."

"La, there you two are!" Her skirts kicking up a swirl of dust, Madame Benoit cut across the graveled walkway and hurried to catch up. "How very naughty of you to stray so far. Marie-Claire and I feared we had been quite abandoned."

"We were just turning back," said Rochambert smoothly.

"Madame Daggett was curious to see the cafes." To her he murmured, "Next time, you must allow me to take you to the Café Tortoni, which is a great favorite with the *haute monde.*"

Madame Benoit accepted the explanation without further chiding, but her smile remained somewhat sulky. Maneuvering with military precision, she forced Rochambert to offer his other arm.

"I should like to stop for a moment at Madame Moullier's shop and order a pair of gloves to match my new bonnet. Do escort me there, Pierre, so that I may have your opinion on what color of kidskin would best compliment this ribbon." She batted her lashes, along with a scrap of cerise silk. "La, I am sure that Madame Daggett won't mind returning the *corniche* and spoons to the ice cream vendor."

"Not at all," said Valencia.

Flashing a triumphant look, Madame Benoit drew Rochambert into a rapidfire discussion on the latest trends in fashion.

Valencia was happy to fall back a few steps, glad for the opportunity to make a more careful study of her adversary.

Pierre Rochambert. She had seen him often enough in her nightmares, but now was a chance to observe him in the flesh. He moved with a predator's grace, light on his feet and with an air of alertness about him, despite the smiles and superficial chatter. Such vigilance was second nature for one trained in the shadowy skills of their profession.

They were so alike. And yet so different.

The hitch in her gait was testimony to how ruthless he was with a blade. She did not begrudge the fact that he had tried to take her life. Those were the rules of the sordid game they both played.

Kill or be killed.

No, the truly chilling thing about the night of his attack was her certainty that Rochambert had deliberately tried to cripple her. He had meant to take his time in dispatching her. That fleeting flash of a death's head smile, cruel as curved steel, had betrayed just how much he had been looking forward to watching her suffer.

If not for the sudden appearance of the shore patrol, he would have taken great pleasure in making her death a slow and painful one.

Valencia gave an inward shudder. Not out of fear but out of loathing. She had killed several enemy agents, but always quickly, cleanly, and with a pang of remorse. She did it out of duty. He did it out of devilish delight. Thinking back over the long, bloodstained list of his victims, she decided this was one time when she would not hesitate for an instant to strike a mortal blow.

But first she must spot a weakness.

Every man had one. It was merely a matter of watching and waiting long enough to discern it.

Dropping back a discreet distance, she made a few more mental notes about his height, his reach, the length of his stride. The tiny details often divulged a telling flaw.

Her eyes suddenly narrowed.

The muscles flexed beneath his finely tailored clothing, and yet there was a hint of fleshiness softening the line of his shoulders. Rich food, fine wines, seductive strumpets—Rochambert was allowing himself to savor the decadent pleasures of Paris in between assignments. Was his edge just a touch duller, his reactions a fraction slower? No doubt he was supremely confident that no danger could reach him here, in the heart of the Empire.

A grave miscalculation on his part.

Gathering her skirts, Valencia veered off to rejoin Madame Levalier. She had learned through bitter experience that the most dangerous attacks came at unexpected times, and from unexpected angles. An agent who grew lax, even for an instant, did so at his—or her—own peril.

This time, she vowed, it would be her opponent who suffered the consequences.

As one of the assistant secretaries droned on about spice production in Martinique, Lynsley found his mind wandering from the tropics to the faubourg St. Germaine. Thankfully, he had the knack of appearing an attentive listener down to a fine art. Furrowed brow, thinned lips and steepled hands—they bespoke an intensity that few ever questioned.

This morning, however, he had no need to feign a frown or a tightness of his mouth. Though the first encounter with Rochambert had gone well, Lynsley was not ready to concede that his misgivings might have been exaggerated. True, Valencia had followed his orders with exquisite precision, wielding her looks and her flirtations with consummate skill. But Rochambert had not won his ruthless reputation on rakish charm alone.

The first skirmish might be hers, but the war was far from over.

The idea of Valencia crossing swords with the French assassin made his fingers twitch. It wasn't often that he was moved to contemplate murder with his bare hands.

"Do you agree, Monsieur Daggett?" asked Mersault.

Lynsley exhaled slowly, another useful trick he had learned over the years. "I will, of course, have to consider the matter more carefully, and review my own documents."

"Of course," said Levalier smoothly. "No need to rush a decision."

"Actually, my government prefers that I get this business wrapped up as soon as possible," said Lynsley.

"It would be a shame to deprive Madame Daggett of a

lengthy stay in Paris when she appears to be enjoying all the city has to offer," observed Mersault.

"My wife understands that in my line of work, duty must take precedent over pleasure."

The two Frenchman exchanged patronizing looks. No doubt wondering how a man could be so pitifully blind to human nature.

Ever the diplomat, Levalier made a polite murmur in response, then rose, signaling to the scribes and clerks that the formal meeting was over. "Did Madame enjoy the theatre and supper?"

"Very much," allowed Lynsley, as the subordinates gathered up their papers and left the room. "And she was thrilled by your wife's kind invitation to go shopping today with the ladies." He took the liberty of substituting his own adjective, seeing as Valencia's choice of words was unrepeatable in polite company.

"I am glad to hear it," replied the minister. "We must make sure that we introduce her to all the splendors that Paris has to offer. Even if it is a short stay, I should like it to be a memorable one for her."

"Indeed," murmured Mersault with a small smile.

Lynsley inclined his head. "How kind."

"Indeed, with that in mind, I have taken the liberty of arranging an excursion to the gardens of Malmaison for the day after the morrow," went on Lavalier. "Madame Daggett mentioned her interest in flowers, so I am sure she will find the grounds of great interest, even at this time of year. They are quite famous, especially for the variety of roses, and although our former empress is not in residence right now, the hothouses are filled with all manner of exotic specimens."

Valencia wielding a garden trowel? Lynsley repressed a snort of laughter. "Thank you. We shall be delighted to be part of your party. I am sure my wife will be in alt over the opportunity."

"Excellent. It's but a short drive from the city. We plan on leaving in the morning. That way, our group can tour the grounds, enjoy a picnic in one of the outdoor pavilions and return before dusk."

Lynsley flicked a mote of dust from his sleeve. "Is it to be a large group?"

"No more than a dozen or so," replied Levalier. "Though I may have difficulty limiting your wife's admirers to a manageable number. There are a great many gentlemen eager to make her acquaintance."

"Most of the guests will be people you have already met," offered Mersault. "Rochambert has already accepted, along with Captain Gillemot from the Home Guard."

"At least we gentlemen will have something more interesting than roses to discuss," said Lynsley.

"I shall endeavor to ensure that neither you nor your wife are bored," replied Levalier.

He and Mersault excused themselves and left together. Lynsley waited for a moment, then took his own leave, choosing a roundabout way to the main entrance in order to survey the layout of the building. It was always wise to know the ins and outs of a place. One never knew ...

The rapidfire tattoo of steps upon the marble tiles brought him to an abrupt halt.

"Monsieur Daggett."

Lynsley recognized the voice behind him as that of Georges Auberville. So far, the assistant Minister of Maritime Affairs had contributed little to the trade discussions, though surprisingly he had spoken up once or twice in favor of concessions to the Americans.

"I fear you have taken the wrong turn," continued

Auberville after pausing to catch his breath. "This is a more direct way to the street."

"Confounded corridors," muttered Lynsley, squinting through his spectacles at the long expanse of smooth white stone. "They all look alike?"

"Yes. Especially if you do not know the twists and turns."

A cryptic message? The minister seemed a little nervous, but perhaps he was reading more into man's mannerisms than was merited.

"Thank you for keeping me from going astray," said Lynsley. "Next time I shall bring a compass to keep me on course."

"This way, monsieur." Auberville backtracked past the copyroom and took a sharp left.

Lynsley's senses went on full alert. This route, he knew from a previous reconnaissance, was even more convoluted than the one he had chosen. However, for the moment, he followed along in silence, curious to know where all this was leading.

After descending a short flight of stairs, and turning again down what looked to be a deserted stretch of storage rooms, Auberville finally spoke up again. "Forgive the detour, Monsieur Daggett, but I feel it is my duty to warn you."

"Yes?" murmured Lynsley. He kept his voice neutral, though he was inwardly cursing. The last thing he needed was to become tangled in yet another knot of political intrigue. Were there factions within the Ministry? He would have to play this very carefully.

"It is a rather delicate matter." Auberville cleared his throat in some embarrassment. "Concerning your wife."

"Pray, do go on," he said evenly.

"Pierre Rochambert appears to have taken an interest in the lady. Have a care—he is a dangerous man."

"Rakes abound on both sides of the Atlantic," replied Lynsley. "It is not the first time a man has made eyes at my wife."

"You do not understand, Monsieur Daggett. Rochambert is a rake, yes. But more than that, he is … ruthless." Auberville's voice dropped to a whisper. "The rumors would make your hair stand on end. If I were you I would steer far clear of his social circle. He is not a man to be trifled with."

"Nor am I," said Lynsley slowly. "In building a shipping business, I have encountered a good many cutthroats and rapscallions. I'm not intimidated by men like Rochambert."

"Ah, but you should be. The fellow is a devil, but he has friends in very high places."

"I see." Lynsley considered the information. "Might I ask why you felt compelled to tell me this?"

The other man squared his shoulders. "I consider myself a gentleman, monsieur, and have a certain code of honor," he said with a sniff. "Rochambert thinks himself above the rules—any rules, be they legal or moral. I think it only fair that you know what you are up against."

"A sporting chance, as the English would say?"

"In a manner of speaking," said Auberville.

"I believe that your meaning needs no translation," answered Lynsley slowly.

"*Bon.* Then I will lead you back to the foyer." The minister resumed walking.

"Thank you," murmured Lynsley, falling in step beside him.

Auberville replied by picking up his pace. The echo of the sharp, staccato clicks echoed through the corridor. They did not speak again until the minister stopped short in shadows of an archway and gestured for the marquess to turn right up ahead.

"From here, you are on your own, monsieur."

Chapter Twelve

"Forgive me for missing supper, said Lynsley as he entered the library. "The meeting at the Ministry ran late, and then I decided to observe the pattern of evening traffic around Place St. Germaine."

Valencia looked up from the book she was reading. "Did you discover anything of note?"

"The Café Benoit serves a very forgettable claret," he replied dryly. "Aside from that, I consider several hours passed in watching the daily routine of the local residents time well spent. It is always a wise strategy to know the lay of the land." He moved to the sideboard and poured himself a glass of cognac. "How was your afternoon?"

"More interesting than I expected," said Valencia.

His brows arched in amusement. "So, have you found that you have a weakness for fancy plumage after all?"

"Such fripperies seem even more absurd after watching the others agonize over which shade of cerise to choose." She paused. "But it was worth the effort, seeing as Rochambert joined the shopping party for a short while. By the by, his taste in colors runs to rather gaudy shades of blues and greens."

"Our friend does appear to be quite a peacock." The marquess settled into one of the leather armchairs. As they had no social engagement scheduled for the evening, he had shed his coat and cravat. Untying the strings of his portfolio case, he slid out a sheaf of papers.

"He certainly struts around with his proverbial tailfeathers in the air," muttered Valencia. "Thinking that every female around him will be blinded by his beauty."

The swirl of the amber spirits momentarily obscured his expression. "Has he sought to single you out?"

She nodded. "I was treated to Italian ice cream and a not-so-subtle interrogation on my relationship with my husband."

"And?" he inquired.

"I've hinted that ours is a cold-hearted arrangement," replied Valencia. "You are a calculating prig, who married me for my family's trade connections. My own ambitions are just as pragmatic."

"Ah." He set his glass down. "That should prove useful."

She waited for him to elaborate.

Without further comment, Lynsley drew out one of the documents from his case and began reading.

She watched the firelight wink off his reading glasses, then returned to her study of the street plans of Paris. The old engravings provided page after page of exquisitely detailed maps showing the different quartiers.

Now, if only she could chart the inner workings of Lynsley's mind. She was completely lost when it came to following his thinking. So many twists and turns, so many hidden paths that trailed away into shadows.

The same could be said for her, she supposed. Her own feelings were a convoluted maze of contradictions. She should be glad that he seemed unconcerned about any risk to her from

Rochambert. It was what she had demanded—to be treated dispassionately, as simply another weapon to use against the assassin.

And yet a part of her was a bit disappointed that he hadn't expressed a tad more concern over the unexpected appearance of the enemy.

A blade cut two ways, she reminded herself. If she wished to live by the sword ...

A rude word punctuated the crackle of paper as Lynsley turned a page.

Peeking up, she saw him rubbing his fingers through the sidewhiskers that now curled well below his ears. "Do they itch?"

"Like the devil," he said. "Though it's not quite as bad as the time in Moscow, when I had to grow a full beard."

"Moscow?" Intrigued, Valencia put aside her own musings. Lynsley so very rarely offered any glimpse into his life, past or present. "Is Tsar Alexander as handsome as they say?"

"The Angel was barely more than a lad when I was there. I had dealing with his father, Tsar Paul I, whose looks and behavior were less than divine."

"Wasn't the father a bit of a mad monarch?"

"As commander-in-chief of the army, he once court-martialed a rat, and then had the animal executed. So I daresay that qualifies as queer in the attic," replied Lynsley dryly. "There is definitely something to be said for a democracy."

"Tsar Paul was assassinated, was he not?" She took a moment to recall her Academy history lessons. "Which handed the throne to Alexander, who was greatly favored over his father by the country's liberals and reformers."

Lynsley did not look up from his document. "So rumor has it."

"By whom?" she pressed.

"I believe it was said that his own Palace Guards smothered him with a pillow. But then, he had a tendency to fall into fits of apoplexy, so he may well have died of natural causes. The Russians tend to wax melodramatic about a great many things."

Sensing that the chances of getting a straight answer were virtually nil, Valencia refrained from further questions about the Russian ruler's untimely demise. Still, now that he had broached the subject, she was curious to hear about his other travels.

"What other exotic places have you visited?"

Lynsley scratched at his chin. "I've rather lost count. India, for one. Along with China and Japan.

"Japan is closed to all foreigners. On pain of death."

"So it is." He proceeded to give a detailed description of the cherry blossoms in springtime at the foot of Mount Fuji.

"You make it sound very beautiful," she murmured.

"It is a sacred place in their culture, one celebrated for centuries in poetry and painting. At dawn, with silence and mist shrouding the snow–capped peak, one can't help but feel a profound sense of peace."

This spiritual side added yet another complexity to Lynsley's character. Lud, the man had more facets than a fine cut gemstone. Intricate planes, crafted so subtly that many were invisible to the naked eye.

"Which likely didn't last long," she said after a moment. "Somehow I doubt you were there to admire the scenery."

As always, he artfully dodged the question of his clandestine activities.

"In contrast, the holy shrines of Jerusalem are surrounded by a cacophony of sounds and smells. Mullahs call followers of Islam to prayer, Jews kneel before their Wailing Wall and church bells summon the Christians to Mass. The smoke from sizzling meats swirls with the scent of Eastern spices ..."

Valencia set her book aside and inched forward in her seat. Such faraway places were only names or engravings on a printed page until now. Lynsley filled in the stark black and white with great, glorious brushstrokes of color.

"Constantinople," she murmured, mentioning the city that had always captured her imagination. "Have you been there?"

Lynsley didn't seem to mind this line of questioning. His face relaxed as he regaled her with descriptions of his exotic travels, from the Empire of the Turks to the jungle of the Mogul princes to the lacquered splendor of the Forbidden City, the legendary seat of the Chinese rulers. Perhaps the armchair journeys took his mind off the pressures of the current mission.

Whatever the reason, it was utterly fascinating. She could live to be a hundred and never grow bored of hearing about the world beyond her own sphere of war and death. It was little wonder that his descriptions of saffron silks and mulberry saris seemed so threaded with color and texture. Her life was cloaked in unrelenting black and white, its only softness the occasional shade of grey.

Sighing, Valencia drew her knees to her chest. Coals crackled, and the candles burned with a fire-gold light, kindling a mood that was cozy.

Comfortable.

It was all an illusion, of course, created out of deceptions and lies. Yet she *did* feel comfortable with Lynsley, something she would have dismissed as impossible just a few short weeks ago.

So the mission had accomplished something meaningful, though Whitehall would not see it that way. The gentlemen who made the life-and-death decisions did not give a damn about the human side of any assignment. They would gladly sacrifice her heart or her head—along with any other part of her anatomy—if it served their purpose.

Lynsley was different. Through the fringe of her lashes, she watched the play of light on his face. The austere chiseling of his long, lean features cut a sharp contrast to the subtle shadings of nuance in his eyes and his smile. *Flint and flesh.* Even at his most stern and solemn, the marquess never lost his essential humanity. He looked like a man capable of feeling pain and regret. Of feeling loss and longing.

Of feeling love?

Her heart gave a tiny hitch. Had Lynsley ever been in love?

"The beauty of Constantinople is seductive." His sigh stirred Valencia from her reveries. "I should have liked to spend more time exploring its treasures, but our group moved on to the deserts of Palestine ..."

She forced herself to pick up the thread of his narrative.

"Where I unwittingly offended a Bedouin sheik by eating with my left hand at his welcoming feast—the ultimate insult in Arabic culture," he went on. "The head of the British Mission offered him my head on a platter, but apparently the sheik preferred goat, rather than pig."

"I can't quite imagine you ever making a social faux pas," said Valencia. She tried to picture him as a callow young junior envoy, awkward and unsure, and did not succeed.

"Good Lord, more times than I care to count. Books and lectures can only teach so much. In the field, one tends to learn by trial and error."

"True." She thought back for a moment on some of her earliest assignments. "The same applied for our physical training. It's all very well to master a spinning back flip off of the Academy's practice wall, but if one doesn't factor in the seaweed and slime of a harbor breakwater, it throws the timing off. My first job was in Lyme Regis, and I was lucky to escape without breaking my neck. It took twenty stitches to close the gash in my scalp, but live and learn. I never made that mistake again."

A smile crept to her lips as she recalled her roommate's brush with death. "But that was nothing compared to Savannah's gaffe in bed with the Polish double agent in Cracow. Language class had not taught her the local dialect for intimate moments, and he soon saw through her charade. Fortunately she was more skilled with a stiletto than with her tongue."

Lynsley made a face. "Lord, if I had known any of this, my hair would no doubt be entirely grey."

Valencia laughed. "It wasn't really all that bad. We're well-schooled. When push comes to shove, we know how to improvise."

His mouth curved upward, but the corners were pinched and his gaze grew clouded.

Damn. This interlude was offering a rare glimpse of the man behind the stone sphinx mask. She did not want him to retreat into himself just yet.

"Like the time Geneva was sent to recover the jewels stolen from Lord Butterfield's home by his French mistress." Valencia continued her musing. "She came back with not only the earl's heirlooms, but with the diamond medallion reported missing by the Prussian ambassador. You allowed her to keep it, saying that like a Royal Navy captain, the Merlins ought to keep the prizes captured in battle."

"Her skills helped avert an embarrassing incident for the Prime Minister." Lynsley's expression lightened somewhat at the mention of the past mission. Unlike many, it had been high-lighted by a number of humorous scenes. "I saw no reason to return it to von Furtzen. I doubt he was the rightful owner, and besides, it looked much better on Geneva than on him."

Valencia exaggerated a sigh. "We were all green with envy. I had never seen anything like it. A clear, colorless stone, and yet it seemed to glow with a magical fire.

"In Greek, the diamond is called *adamas*—unconquerable force—since it defies flames and never becomes heated," mused the marquess. "The ancient philosopher, Pliny the Elder, believed it to be the most precious of all human possessions, fit only for kings. He thought the sole source was some mysterious mine in the middle of India."

Valencia leaned forward in her chair, intrigued by the change that came over his face when he spoke of such things. Telling stories seemed to lighten his mood. And he did it well, like so many things. His deep voice was rich and melodious, bringing the words come alive.

"Pliny wasn't far off the mark," he continued. "India had been mining the stones for centuries, and they were indeed reserved only for royalty. A few inferior specimens trickled out to the Romans, who wore them as talismans to ward off evil. But it wasn't until the 1600s that a Parisian dealer in precious stones named Jean-Baptiste Tavernier became the first European to visit the fortified city of Golconda."

"You make it sound ... romantic," she said.

"Tavernier did bring back a number of fabulous gems, including one from the Mogul Emperor, Aurangzeb, specially purchased for Louis XIV. Its rare size and color—a cool, smoky blue—made it the stuff of legend. From the Sun King, it passed to Marie Antoinette."

"Even *I* have heard of that stone. Wasn't it rumored to have been lost during the Revolution?" She propped her chin in her hand. "I wonder what became of it."

"I believe it is currently in the possession of the Prince Regent," murmured Lynsley.

"*Prinny* has it?" she exclaimed. "Good lord, how did *he*

contrive to get his hands on it? And how do *you* know about the affair?"

His lips twitched for an instant. "State secret, I'm afraid."

She realized her mouth was hanging open and shut it with a snap. "You are certainly privy to a wealth of interesting information."

"Much of it merely serendipitous," he said with a self-deprecating smile. "I tend to collect all sorts of odd nuggets during my travels. For example, when I was in Toledo, I discovered that the European and Arab philosophers of the Middle Ages had come up with their own fanciful theory as to where diamonds came from."

What female could resist *that* teaser? "Yes?" she demanded.

His brow waggled. "I thought you didn't care much for jewels?"

"I am always interested in expanding my field of knowledge," she said primly.

"Ah. A purely pedagogical reason. Very well, then, I shall proceed." His gaze once again gleamed with a teasing glitter. "Over the centuries, versions of the same tale have appeared in many writings, from the Eastern yarns of Sinbad the Sailor to the travels of Marco Polo. They all revolved around a mythical Valley of the Diamond, a forbidding place high in the mountains of India, where only the bravest adventurer would dare to venture. Pile upon pile of precious stones were said to lie on the valley's floor. However, they were guarded by giant serpents with heads and fangs so fearsome that any human looking on them would die of fright."

Valencia found herself shivering in spite of the glowing fire.

"So the only way to capture the treasure was to kill a sheep or cow, skin the carcass, and throw it into the chasms. The diamonds would then stick in the raw flesh—"

"How ghastly," she exclaimed.

Lynsley paused. "Shall I stop?"

"No, no, I'm dying to hear the rest."

He chuckled. "As you wish. The eagles who lived in the mountains would swoop down and bring the meat back to their eyrie. The diamond hunters would try to fight off the birds long enough to pick out the gems. However all was not lost if they failed in that skirmish."

"I shudder to ask."

"For the truly intrepid ..." He paused for dramatic effect. "There was always a chance to sneak up to the nest the next morning and go through the dung."

"Fie, you are making this up!" she exclaimed.

"I swear, I am not." Merriment swirled up from depths of his eyes. From there, it slowly spread across his face. "Even *I* would be hard-pressed to invent such a tale."

A strange sensation fluttered inside her ribcage. It made her feel a bit giddy to see him smile in such a way at her. It was as intimate as a caress, and suddenly the tickle was spreading the length of her limbs. He was a *very* attractive man, especially when he allowed his whimsical side to show. The ladies of London were said to be ruthless in their pursuit of eligible men. How was it that they had allowed him to stay single?

Perhaps they were blind as bats.

"Hah!" Valencia forced her eyes away from the whiskey gold strands of hair curling around his collar. "I am certain that you could charm the scales off of those serpents if need be."

There was a whisper of silence and a sidelong peek showed his gaze lingering for an instant on her face, her body.

Their banter tonight might almost pass as flirtation.

Her breath caught in her throat. She knew that many men thought her beautiful. She had received more than her share of compliments over the years—along with proposals, respectable and otherwise. But as she saw herself in an entirely different light, their admiration had never meant much to her.

But all of a sudden, she cared very much whether Lynsley thought her attractive.

Alluring.

Just this once, she wanted him to see her as a woman, not just one of his warriors.

Don't be a fool. The irony of such girlish dreams was piercing as sharpened steel. No doubt he saw her as a useful weapon in the fight against England's enemies, but the ability to lie, deceive, and murder did not paint a very pretty picture for a man to admire.

For gentlemen like Lynsley, the ideal female was a sweet, sheltered miss. A pattern card of polished manners and unsullied virtue.

An Innocent. Which she was decidedly not.

Valencia swallowed hard. Lord, she had lost her innocence long before meeting the marquess. The squalid streets, the grasping pimps, the hardscrabble struggle for food every day. For an orphan, life in the slums of London did not allow for much of a childhood. She couldn't remember a day when she had ever been free of the wary watchfulness needed to survive.

A stab of sadness cut to her core. She very rarely thought about what life might have been ...

The soft clink of crystal drew her eyes up. Through the swirl of the amber spirits, Lynsley was watching her with a quizzical look of concern.

"Is something wrong?" he asked quietly.

She shook her head. "No, nothing at all. I was simply reminded of something from long ago."

His expression remained solemn, serious.

Valencia quickly made light of the matter. "But my past

experiences do not make for anything nearly as entertaining as your stories. Indeed, most are rather forgettable."

"Yes, enough of reminiscing," murmured the marquess as he went back to his reading.

Despite the blazing coals, the room seemed a bit colder.

Right, she reminded herself. It was best never to lose sight of the fact that this was all about business. She found her place in the book of maps and resumed her study of the Paris streets.

Lynsley finished his cognac in a matter of minutes. "I think I will retire." He rose. "Good night."

Chapter Thirteen

"You need not feel compelled to rise with the sun. Ladies are supposed to sleep until noon." Lynsley set aside the plate of rolls and refilled his coffee as Valencia entered the breakfast room the next morning.

"I am tired of sleeping. And shopping," she said. "Lud, how do highborn ladies keep from expiring of boredom?"

"They feed on the gossip and cream cakes served up each day in the fancy drawing rooms of their friends," he replied

"Pastries." She gave a groan, and poured some tea for herself. "I swear, I shall soon be growing fat from all the rich food and lack of exercise."

He eyed her willowy figure over the top of his newspaper. "It does not appear to me that you are in any danger of snapping your stays. Besides," he added with a lift of his brow. "Frenchmen like their women voluptuous, so perhaps you ought to indulge in a few more custards."

Her cheeks turned a bit pink. "I thought our plans did not yet call for serving me up on a silver platter. So if you don't mind, I shall refrain from stuffing myself with croissants and crème caramels."

Lynsley stilled his twitching lips. He had not meant to make light of the danger. It was just that he enjoyed provoking a flare of fire in her face. "Don't worry, while you may present a feast for Rochambert's eyes, I don't intend to let you anywhere near his teeth," he replied.

Her sigh swirled with the steam rising from her cup. "That is the trouble. I am unused to being swaddled in silks and satins and forced to act like a lady. I am much more comfortable when it comes to taking action."

"You are doing your part, Valencia." He sympathized with her simmering frustration. He, too, was feeling the strain of their charade. But the mission could not be rushed. One false move and a consummate professional like Rochambert would sense it.

And they wouldn't get a second chance.

"We must be patient," he went on, trying not to sound like a prig. "We must learn more about Rochambert's habits and the lay of the land before we can think of making a move for the cipher."

Valencia crumbled a bit of toast between her fingers. Judging by the pile on her plate, she hadn't tasted a morsel of the baguette. "I understood your orders, sir," she said, her voice brittle as the toasted crust. "I am not about to run off half-cocked."

Was the past always to be a wedge between them?

For a time last night, there had seemed to be an understanding between them, a comfortable camaraderie that had banished the old conflicts. But whatever quicksilver spell had brought them together had dissolved in the blink of an eye.

Swallowing a sigh, he pushed back from the table. "Then I shall see you at luncheon."

"Where are you off to at this early hour?" she asked eyeing his buckskin breeches and boots. "Have you no meetings at the ministry this morning?"

"The talks have been put off until the morrow," replied Lynsley. "So I thought I would take a ride out through the Bois de Boulogne."

He had, in fact, been visiting the vast stretch of woodland and bridle paths nearly every day at dawn since their arrival. It was always prudent to have an escape route planned, and he had also found an isolated spot where he could exercise without fear of prying eyes observing his every move.

She bit her lip, the warring of pride and longing clearly writ on her face.

Asking for a favor did not come easily to her, he thought. She would eat nails before she begged to come along.

He strolled to the door before turning to ask, "Would you care to accompany me?"

"A breath of fresh air would be welcome," she replied, matching his nonchalant tone. However, she rose like a shot. "I shall just be a moment in dressing."

"I will have Bailin saddle your filly."

A half hour later, they passed through one of the ancient gates erected by King Henri III into the forestlands, followed at a discreet distance by his valet.

"A rather rough area, " she remarked, seeing several ragged figures slink back into the trees.

"Like many enclaves of the *ancien regime*, the Bois has fallen on hard times," said Lynsley. "However it has a long and storied history. In medieval times, it was the site of several monasteries, including the powerful Longchamp Abbey. Part of the forest was then sold to the Crown to create a royal hunting ground." He gestured to a wide, straight path cutting through a rustic field. "During the time of Louis XIV, a series of walkways were made, and it became a very fashionable place for strolling and celebrations."

She slanted a bemused look at him from beneath the curling

ostrich plumes of her hat. Her stylish new riding clothes—a deep green fitted habit with military frogging and fringed epaulets, topped off by a jaunty little shako—suited her striking looks to perfection. With the breeze ruffling her curls and the sunlight sparkling in her eyes, she looked like a glorious goddess of the forests.

Diana, the Huntress.

There were certainly times when she was prickly as a quiver of arrows.

It was his job to see that the huntress did not become the hunted.

A light laugh floated through the air. "A history lesson?"

"Sorry. I did not mean to bore you with dusty details."

"No, please go on. I like listening. You always know such fascinating things." Again, an odd sort of expression flitted over her features. "Is there *any* person or place about which you can't speak about intelligently?"

You. The word nearly slipped from his lips. In truth, she defied all attempts to define or describe with dispassionate logic. His powers of reason retreated when she was near, leaving him ...

Confused, conflicted.

And so, as usual, he took refuge behind a shield of steely self-control.

"A great many I should think," he replied lightly. "But the Bois is not one of them."

Her mouth took on a mischievous cant. "Do proceed."

Was she merely teasing him? Lynsley found he didn't care. It was good to see her lighthearted and laughing like a young girl. Reining in his horse, he cut across the grass to one of the side paths, a narrow way lined on either side by a thick hedge of bushes.

"Henri IV had 15,000 blackberry bushes planted here, in

hopes of raising silkworms,' he continued. "A plan that did not quite hatch."

"And so the place spun into decline?" she murmured.

He grinned. "Yes, during the Hundred Years War, it became the refuge of outlaws and cutthroats. Francis I, who built the Chateau de Madrid in 1526, restored its regal air."

"And the Sun King?" she asked.

"Louis XIV added his own touches of splendor, but he also wished to cut down the forest in order to build up his navy," he answered. "Luckily for England, that idea evaporated over time. However the Montgolfier brothers did launch their first hot air balloon from here." Lynsley looked around at the deserted paths and overgrown glades. "Unfortunately war has once again reduced the Bois to a haven for robbers and thugs. Proper Parisians don't often venture here."

"Ah. So is that why you bring along your valet? In case you have need of someone to defend you from such ruffians."

"A little respect for your elders," he growled, exaggerating a grimace. But despite making light of it, the comment pricked a little at his pride. At barely forty he still considered himself to be in the prime of life. "I've not yet grown so decrepit that I can't wield a weapon. I'll have you know I can still thrash any of the Merlins on the fencing field. Even Da Rimini admits that he is hard pressed to claim victory."

"Best a Merlin?" Her chin took a challenging tilt. "It would be interesting to test that assumption. My skills have not grown so rusty over the years that I can't still cut a creditable riposte."

"I will take your word for it," he said quickly, unwilling to have the air of easy camaraderie between them cut short by a crossing of verbal swords.

Valencia looked about to retort, then she, too, seemed to think better of it. Instead, she asked, "Why do you come here?"

"It seemed a logical place to look for a bolt hole, if ever we have to take flight. I've found several spots where we might take cover for a short time while deciding on a next move."

She looked around with a well-trained eye. "I see."

"And as I said, it's not frequented by the *haute monde*, so it's a perfect place to engage in vigorous exercise without drawing undue attention," went on Lynsley. "I've found a small clearing and stone cottage that makes an excellent private training ground. Bailin keeps watch on the bridle path, to warn of anyone approaching."

"Please don't let me disrupt your routine." Valencia tightened the reins to keep her mount from shying from the snap of a twig. "Perhaps I'll have a look around on my own.

"I would rather you didn't stray," he replied, hoping she wouldn't misinterpret his reasons.

The thud of hooves on the damp earth echoed his own mounting misgivings. Maybe it had been a mistake to ask her to come along. These intimate interludes seemed to ignite strange sparks between them, which all too often turned into a flare of fire. The morning was tranquil, a soft light dappling the budded branches of the trees and a gentle breeze stirring the meadow grasses. He did not wish to spoil the day with a fight.

"A good point. You are right to err on the side of caution," she allowed after some hesitation. "Then I'll just sit and watch, if you don't mind."

Valencia dismounted and took a seat on the ruins of a low wall that had once fenced in a small paddock area. The stone outbuilding facing her—a stable, she guessed—had long since lost its roof and doors, but the thick walls had withstood the ravages of time. Set between the two structures, a rectangular swath of dusty ground was well-shielded from the casual observer.

The marquess removed his coat and cravat, then methodically unfastened his shirt collar and rolled up his sleeves. Sunlight glinted off the golden hairs of his forearms, setting off the cording of sinew and muscle. Turning, he moved with a sure, silent step to the open archway where an iron cross bar was still set high in mortared stone.

Setting aside her shako, Valencia shaded her eyes, curious to observe what sort of training regime he had improvised. Whatever it was, the routine appeared effective.

Lynsley reached up and grabbed hold of bar, slowly pulling himself up until his chin touched the pitted metal. He held the position for a moment before dropping down, keeping his knees bent so his feet didn't touch the ground.

One ... two ... three ...

He repeated the exercise twenty five times before dropping back to earth.

No wonder his shoulders and arms were solid as steel, thought Valencia.

The marquess then proceeded through a series of exercises with two short iron rods. Lifting, spinning, swinging, he worked his biceps, his forearms and his wrists. A sequence of leg lunges came next, followed by several body stretches.

He turned, sweat glistening on his face, hair ruffling in the light breeze, His linen shirt was now damp and clinging to the contours of his torso.

Averting her eyes, Valencia was aware of a tingling sensation somewhere deep inside her that quickly spiraled out through her limbs. Lynsley was no longer looking like a perfectly polished patrician. He exuded a virile masculinity. An earthy, elemental attractiveness at odds with his carefully cultivated image as a paragon of propriety.

Again, she could not help from wondering why he wasn't married. It was puzzling. Provoking.

Never had she met a man so shrouded in secrets.

"A warm day," he remarked, uncorking a jug of water and taking a long swallow. "I trust you are not too uncomfortable?"

"Not at all," she replied, leaning back into the shade. Had he spotted the telltale flush of color? She repressed the urge to fan her cheeks.

Lynsley appeared not to notice her agitation. He picked up a length of rolled canvas that lay alongside the hamper of food and drinks that his valet had transported from town.

The soft *snick* of steel sounded as the cloth fell away to reveal a set of fencing foils.

Her brows rose. "Two?"

"Bailin knows the basic moves. We sometimes drill together. Solitary practice is all very well, but there is nothing quite like crossing swords with a real opponent."

"Quite right," she murmured.

The marquess turned his back and began to wipe the grit from the grip of his sword.

Impelled by some mystical, Merlin force, Valencia suddenly rose and took up the other one.

Swoosh. Light as a feather in her hand, the sliver of steel cut through the air with a lethal whisper.

Lynsley looked around. "Valencia, I think—"

His eyes widened as she started to undo the fastenings of her dress.

"Don't look so shocked, Thomas," she drawled. "I don't intend to fight bare-chested, like the Amazons. I wore a shirt and breeches beneath these cursed flounces."

"I should hope not," he said dryly, quickly recovering his composure. "They were reputed to have chopped off one breast in order to wield a bow and arrow more efficiently. A noble sacrifice on their part, but it would be a pity to destroy the perfect symmetry of your form."

Heat flushed her face as she kicked aside her skirts. "Though perhaps a flaunting of flesh would serve as a useful distraction. All is fair in love and war."

He gave a flashing salute. "So it is."

Forcing her eyes away from the tantalizing peek of tanned skin and tawny curls showing beneath his shirt, Valencia flexed her sword. Memories of her Merlin training took hold, and of their own accord, her feet slid and assumed the *en garde* stance.

"Come, I am ready for you to test my mettle," she said.

Lynsley set a hand on his hip. "The days of handing out grades are long gone, Valencia. You have nothing to prove to me."

"No? Perhaps not in the classroom, but surely you don't imagine that I can let a taunt to the honor of my sister Merlins pass without putting up a fight?" she challenged. "Besides, aren't you just a little curious as to how good a teacher Da Rimini really is?"

The corners of his mouth twitched ever so slightly. "Put that way, it would be ungentlemanly of me to refuse."

"And you are, of course, the consummate gentleman."

His steel kissed up against hers. "One acquires the skills early on, seeing as the training starts at birth."

"The lessons learned as a child are ingrained," she agreed. Drawing her blade upward, she reversed her position of attack, forcing him back a step. "They come naturally, without thinking."

"As opposed to ones we pick up later in life?"

"You would know better than I."

The marquess countered her move with effortless ease, his boots dancing over the uneven ground as if it were polished parquet.

"After all," she murmured, parrying his probing point. "You have far more experience in the real world."

Lynsley spun away from her riposte with deceptive grace. "You aren't a raw schoolgirl anymore, Valencia. I daresay you've seen more than your share of life's sordid realities."

She nearly missed the subtle flick of his wrist and the deadly quick thrust of his blade. *Damn.* Thank god her reflexes were still sharp. Darting back at the last instant, she managed to deflect the blow.

"I'm surprised that Da Rimini teaches a *botta dritta* as a defensive maneuver," remarked Lynsley. His light linen shirt clung to the contours of his shoulders, the lean, lithe stretch of his swordplay accentuating his tapered waist and snug buckskins. The soft leather looked molded to his muscular thighs, showing every—

No, she must keep her eyes on the blade of tempered steel.

"He didn't," she countered. "Rather, he taught us to improvise, to learn how to turn a weakness into a strength."

"Then perhaps the wily old wolf is worth the obscene salary he demands of me."

"That remains to be seen." Valencia whirled in midstep and tried to duck under his guard. Her *punta sopramano* slid wide of its mark. But only barely.

Lynsley flashed a grin as he pivoted away. "I see I must stay on my toes if I am to escape from this match unscathed."

Had the man any idea how attractive he was when he allowed himself more than a poker face? The hint of raw, animal emotion beneath the skin of refined reserve was devilishly distracting. An unfair advantage, she thought. He was wielding more than one weapon.

As the tempo picked up pace, they both fell silent, their swords cutting quicksilver slashes through the shimmering sunlight. Sweat glistened on their faces, and dampened their shirts.

Circling to her left, Valencia attacked with another

unorthodox combination, but the marquess evaded her strikes with maddening ease. Intent on creating an opening, she let fly with a flurry of thrusts.

Over, under, over under ...

Her leg buckled slightly as she widened her stance.

Lynsley stopped in his tracks and dropped his blade to offer a steadying hand.

Spinning out of reach, Valencia whipped up her weapon and pressed the blunted tip to his throat. "Don't be such a damned gentleman, Thomas. Show no mercy—you can be sure that Rochambert won't."

"Very well." His eyes darkened to a slate blue hue and took on a strange glint.

Dangerous? She wasn't quite sure why the word came to mind.

"We will score the first round for you," he went on. His sword cut a line in the dirt. "What say you to going two out of three?"

"Fair enough," she agreed. Their gazes locked as they met in the center of the enclosure and crossed blades. Standing toe to toe, watching the throb of pulse on his sun-bronzed throat, Valencia was acutely aware that the heat prickling along her spine was not entirely due to physical exertion.

"*En garde.*" From the ready position, Lynsley exploded in a whirl of lightning feints and slashes. She managed to beat off the first few attacks, but an angled thrust, swift and savage as the strike of a snake, knocked the sword from her grip.

He picked it up by the blade and offered her the hilt. "Or would you care to call it a draw?"

"Not a chance," she replied, trying not to wince as she rubbed at her wrist. "But you *are* good."

"So are you," he said softly.

Valencia had received many compliments from men but this

simple praise from Lynsley set her heart to fluttering against her ribcage. Like a wild bird seeking freedom. From what she did not quite dare to contemplate.

Masking her errant emotions with a shrug, she gave a flick of her swordpoint. "My footwork is not as good as it once was, but swimming helps keep my upper body strong and supple. That, and lifting beer barrels." A wry twist tugged at her lips. "Not to speak of throwing drunkards out on their arses."

The marquess repressed a laugh. "I don't imagine that many make trouble for you."

She grinned. "Not anymore."

"I see that *I* shall have to take great pains not to land on my arse." One by one, he wiped his hands on the backside of his breeches. "It would, you know, be very lowering to suffer such a grievous blow to my pride."

Her mouth went a bit dry watching his palms slide over the skintight leather. *Bloody hell.* She should *not* be staring at his lordly posterior. No matter how magnificent the musculature.

His brow quirked. "Ready?"

"Whenever you are," she said, fumbling for a moment to get a proper grip on the quillons of her sword.

Lynsley sketched a perfect *arrebatar* through the air before their blades kissed up against each other.

Valencia bit back a gasp, sure she could feel the heat of him sizzle along the steel. She slid sideways, keeping her steps slow and deliberate.

The marquess mirrored her moves.

The previous rounds had been marked by attacking athleticism. This time around, the match turned into a sinuous *pas de deux.* There was something supremely sensual about the dance of their blades, and the rhythm of their bodies moving in perfect harmony. As they reversed directions, his thigh grazed her.

Perhaps it was merely a quirk of light, but she could have sworn he winked as he whirled by.

She nearly laughed aloud. Her heart was racing, her pulse was pounding. The great gulps of air bubbled through her like fine champagne. A challenge seemed to spark a fire in her blood. In her very being.

A spinning parry brought them close together. So close she could inhale the intimate scent of sandalwood and sweat. So close she could see the smooth-shaven texture of his jaw and light dusting of tawny strands at the V of his shirt. The rapidfire rise and fall of his chest.

Valencia hesitated for a fraction of a second, tempted to reach out and run her fingers beneath the light linen. The contrasting textures—damp skin, coarse curls, smooth muscle— was awfully alluring ...

"Touché."

She dropped her arm with a muttered oath.

Lynsley fixed her with a penetrating look before commenting, "You lost your focus for an instant."

"As I said, I'm out of practice. The isle of Sark is not exactly teeming with skilled swordsmen." Looking for the excuse to turn away from his scrutiny, Valencia went to towel off her face. "My timing is off."

"You are still a formidable opponent."

Ha. Not against him.

Heaving a harried sigh, Valencia pulled the ribbon from her hair and shook out the tight plait, letting the dampened curls spill over her shoulders. "The Academy did not train us to be timid little sparrows. My feathers may be a bit dented, but on occasion I can still fly."

A sidelong look showed the marquess was watching her intently. His expression was inscrutable, as always. Yet strangely enough the smooth muscle of his jaw betrayed a tiny tic.

For some reason, she felt compelled to loosen the lacings of her shirt, letting it fall open to the swell of her bosom. Fanning her cheeks, she lifted her chin to catch the breeze. "Lud, it feels good to work up a sweat."

Lynsley was still staring.

That he found the view of interest touched off an even more erratic beat of her heart. It always seemed that he looked at her and saw only a hoyden hellion rather than a female of any grace or charm.

Not that she could blame him. Compared to the belles of the Mayfair ballrooms ...

His mouth slowly curled up at the corners. "A lady does not sweat, she only beads with moisture."

Valencia cut a last flourish with her sword, then set a hand on her hip. "But we both know I'm no lady, Thomas."

Lynsley didn't respond, save to set his sword down on the stone wall. Turning, he took hold of her blade and slid his hand up to the hilt. She let her fingers fall away.

"Have you kept up your practice with a pistol?" he inquired.

It was strange how he always changed the subject when things got too personal.

"Yes, my aim is still bang on the mark," she answered evenly, though she longed to shake him or slap him—anything to remove that look of cool composure from his face. "Running and riding present more of challenge these days. But I manage."

"I imagine you do." With painstaking precision, he began rewrapping the foils in the canvas.

Though he had moved only a few steps away, Valencia sensed him distancing himself to a remote retreat. *Lord Lynsley's Lair.*

Wherever that may be.

She gritted her teeth on seeing the change. In the blink of an eye, the marquess had transformed from a sweating, virile, vibrant man back to the stone sphinx. The quizzing teacher, ever tolerant of an unruly student.

She felt like stamping her foot in frustration. Or aiming a hard kick at his arse.

But before her temper could get the better of her, Lynsley drew out a knife from the hamper. "I trust your skills are still sharp with this weapon," he said. "In the confines of a city, we may be called on to use it."

She nodded.

He tossed her the weapon. "I've blunted the blade, so let us run through a few of the basic drills. Practice makes perfect."

After several attempts to get through his guard, Valencia stepped back and conceded defeat. "I thought I was good, but you are a master of hand-to hand combat." Indeed, he had deflected her attacks with maddening ease. After wiping her brow, she passed the weapon back to him. "I'm curious—how many men have you killed?"

"More than one," he replied tersely.

"Two? Three?" she prodded. "Were you attacked? Or did the mission demand that you dispatch the enemy?"

Shifting his hold on the hilt, he slowly spun the blade. "It's not something I care to talk about."

A part of her understood his reticence, yet a part of her rebelled at being shut out.

Her resentment must have shone on her face for he heaved a tight sigh. "Don't take it personally, Valencia. It's simply ..."

"Simply that you prefer to keep everyone at arm's length."

"Call it what you will," he said evenly. "Now if you will kindly step over here, I'll show you a trick that may prove useful in a pinch."

Valencia thought for an instant about challenging the order, but decided against it. She would only appear childish.

"It's a desperate, dangerous move, shown to me by a pirate

in Madagascar," continued Lynsley, once she had taken up a position by his side. "It should only be used as a last resort."

After he went through the moves in slow motion, she could see why. The sequence called for split second timing. One slip could be fatal.

"Show me again," she said, determined to get it right.

"Spin. Tuck. Roll." His words punctuated the second run-through. "Now you try."

Her attempt went smoothly until the last little twist. "Hell," she muttered rubbing at her bruised back. "If that had been for real, I would have ended up impaled on my own knife."

"Aye, that's the trick. But when done right, it will take an opponent completely by surprise." Lynsley retrieved the weapon. "You didn't do badly for a first try."

"Where did I go wrong?" she demanded.

"Hold your hand like so." His fingers closed around her wrist

"A tighter roll is key."

She got to her feet. "Damn. Let me try again."

Spin. Tuck. Roll. After several more attempts, she finally mastered the moves well enough to earn a nod of approval.

"Excellent," murmured the marquess. "Though I hope you are never called upon to try it." He checked his pocketwatch. "That's enough for today. We had better be getting back."

As if by unspoken agreement, they packed their gear and rode out of the Bois in silence. However, once the bridle paths gave way to the cobbled streets of the city, Valencia could not keep a rein on her tongue. Maybe it was the vigorous exercise, or maybe it was the recent rendezvous with Rochambert that her blood thrumming with impatience. Whatever the reason, she found herself pressing Lynsley about what progress he was making in their mission.

"Staying in practice is all very well," she remarked. "But

now that we have entrée into Rochambert's mansion, surely we can start planning to make a move for the secret weapon and its formula?"

"I've not forgotten why we are here." The last, lingering sense of camaraderie seemed to waft away in the breeze as he assumed a tone of formal command. "Or how much depends on our ability to get the job done. Like our drills, it's a matter of circling, watching, probing. Only when I am sure of his most vulnerable spot will I chance moving in for the kill."

"We know what his weakness is—it is women ..." Valencia hitched a breath. "Sir."

"It is one of them," he amended. "Whether it proves to be his fatal flaw remains to be seen."

Chapter Fourteen

"A garden party." Valencia glanced out through the windowpane as the carriage swung though the stone pillars and started up the tree-lined drive. Though she tried to keep her voice neutral, Lynsley thought he detected a faint note of reproach.

"Levalier says the grounds of Malmaison are the finest in all of France," he replied coolly, sensing that yet another day wasted in leisure pursuits was chafing at her patience.

"I was not being critical—"

"Yes, you were. You think me an old woman, overcautious to a fault." And damn him for a fool, he feared she might be right. A part of him worried that his concern for her safety was holding him back from doing his job.

A flush flared along the ridges of her cheekbones. "I am thinking nothing of the sort. However impressive your wide range of talents are, milord, they do not encompass mindreading."

That was for sure. For a brief, fleeting time, he had been under the illusion that the wounds of the past had healed. But since crossing swords in the Bois de Bologne, sunlight flashing over their steel and sweat, she had retreated behind the shield of old hostilities. He wondered now whether it had been a mistake to shed his air of reserve. Up close, his flaws were likely all too visible. Instead of the magisterial Head Merlin, he had shown himself to be a mere man.

A man who had found the clash exhilarating. The challenging gleam in her eye, the heated rasp of her breath, the taut flex of her thighs. He shut his eyes, trying not to think of the rapidfire rise and fall of her shapely breasts.

An experienced agent knew how to turn a weakness into a strength, he reminded himself.

The air was crackling with tension. Another glib comment would provoke a fight. And Rochambert, being the ruthless predator that he was, would smell blood.

"Actually, having passed some time with a Gypsy tribe in the Balkans, I've learned a little something about the art of divination," drawled Lynsley. He pressed his fingertips to his temples with a theatrical flourish. "I am sensing a stirring of anger."

"No, I am merely annoyed by your pompous, presumptuous tone," she countered. "If I were angry, you would be digging the tip of your elegant walking stick out from the depths of your arse."

Lynsley waited for a moment before replying. "Excellent. Well played. That should set the tone nicely for what I have in mind."

"You deliberately goaded me into a temper?" said Valencia through gritted teeth.

"No matter how good one is at acting, there is no substitute for the real thing. Right now, your dislike of me is apparent in a myriad of little ways."

"Like what?"

"Like the sparks in your eyes and the rigid set of your shoulders," he replied.

She muttered an oath and slouched back against the leather squabs. "And your mistrust of me is apparent in the cool contempt in your voice and the condescending curl of your smile."

Though he was feeling anything but cool, Lynsley answered with icy politeness. "You are mistaking pragmatism for personal feelings."

"And God knows, the high and mighty Lord Lynsley has none of those to speak of!"

"Dear me, we are beginning to sound like an old, married couple."

Valencia shut her mouth with an audible snap of teeth.

It was far better to have her furious than held in check by the oddly muted mood of the past day. Anger he could understand, and defiance. But subdued silence was so unlike her.

Or maybe it wasn't. A person could change beyond recognition in ten years.

Staring out at the stately elms, Lynsley caught his own blurred reflection in the glass. How did she see him? As a tyrannical teacher? A pompous prig? He had dared to show her a glimpse of his private self, and for a short time, he had sensed a new sort of bond growing between them.

But apparently, his instincts in regard to women were woefully rusty.

As for his own feelings ...

They were irrelevant, he reminded himself.

He took a moment to master the tiny twitching of his jaw muscle before turning back to business. "Now, perhaps we might convene a council of war without any further explosions?"

Valencia gave a curt nod.

"Contrary to what you believe, I am as anxious as you are to accomplish our goal as quickly as possible," began Lynsley. "But there are a number of reasons why we cannot rush our moves."

"You are in command, sir. You need not explain yourself," she said tersely.

"Ah, but I think I do," he said. "There can be no misunderstandings, Valencia. No misgivings. All jests about mind reading aside, we must be on the same page."

"I will follow orders to the letter. Sir." Had her voice been forged out of iron, it couldn't have been more rigid.

Heaving an inward sigh, Lynsley went on. "Before we can decide on a plan of action, we must be absolutely certain of success. You wonder why we cannot simply break into Rochambert's mansion after a single surveillance? Because we cannot know where the explosive might be hidden. I can hazard a guess, but if I am wrong, it would destroy our chance of success."

"I understand that," she said softly.

He ignored her response. "Secondly, we must be sure that the formula has not been passed on to the Ministry of War. From what we know of Rochambert's character, we can assume that he will want to take all the glory for capturing such a momentous prize. But we must be sure. And that will require a more intimate acquaintance with the man than we have now."

"You need not lecture me like a raw recruit."

"Ours is a complicated relationship—"

A wry laugh suddenly interrupted him. "*That* is putting it mildly," said Valencia, a small smile tugging at her lips. The movement, however tiny, seemed to break the tension between them. "I apologize for my earlier outburst. I—I suppose my nerves are a bit strained."

"Understandably so," he replied. "It can't be easy to flirt with that spawn of Satan."

Her lashes flickered in the dappled shadows. "Merlins aren't meant to have it easy. I would make love to the Devil Himself if that is what the job requires."

The idea of Valencia in bed with Rochambert sent a stab through his gut. Come hell or high water, he would see that it never came to that. "Right now, you need not sacrifice more than a smile or two. Just lead him on a little, and then we shall see where to go from there."

"I trust you had a pleasant drive." Levalier smiled as one of his footmen opened the carriage door and offered Valencia a hand down.

"Quite," she replied. "Thomas and I find everything about France so very interesting." She paused a fraction. "Though I fear we don't always agree on our impressions."

"Monsieur Daggett does seem rather serious," murmured the minister. "Does he never relax and enjoy the pleasures that life has to offer?"

Valencia stiffened her hand on his sleeve. "I suppose that would depend on how you define 'pleasure', monsieur. A rapid promotion to a position of power would no doubt bring a paroxysm of pleasure to my husband."

Levalier's brows gave a knowing waggle, indicating he hadn't missed the sarcasm in her voice. He reached out and plucked a lush bloom from one of the ornamental urns. "Americans must lean to stop and smell the roses," he said, offering her the flower with a wink. "Rush, rush, rush. They are always so impatient. And for what?"

"A good question, monsieur." She wondered whether Lynsley had been right in remarking that her body language spoke loudly about the state of her emotions. Levalier's speculative look seemed to say he had no trouble in reading the telltale signs of marital discord.

Though the flare of anger had died down, a lingering heat still burned her cheeks. She might be an open book, but Lynsley's moods were impossible to decipher. The man was an enigma. His mind a cipher, coded in some lordly logic that only he could unlock.

Out of the corner of her eye, Valencia saw the marquess veer off to join the group of men standing by the stone pergola. Levalier was more chivalrous in taking his leave, pressing a kiss to her gloved hand before leaving her to mingle with the ladies.

She listened with only half an ear to their twitterings about fashion and the latest tidbits of gossip. Her gaze kept returning to Lynsley. *Like a moth to a flame.* Though today, he had been ice rather than fire. It was strange—she imagined that most people would not think of him as a man of extremes. Indeed, his aura of unshakeable calm was rather intimidating.

And intriguing. At least to women. Valencia saw she was not the only lady whose gaze was surreptitiously following Lynsley. His charcoal coat and dove grey trousers stood out in stark contrast to the flamboyant finery of the Frenchmen. In profile, he looked harder, harsher.

Madame Noilly whispered something to her friend and both ladies tittered.

Did most ladies do nothing but scheme and speculate about sex? She bit back a scowl and watched Lynsley exchange words with Rochambert.

"Come, you must allow me to show you through the hothouse, Madame Daggett." Mersault materialized by her side. "It was built by Thibaut and Vignon and is one of the largest outside Kew Gardens. The length is over 150 feet."

Valencia eyed the immense glass structure. "Very impressive."

"It houses a superb collection of dahlias, amaryllis and mimosa, along with tropical fruits like tangerines." He opened the door, and drew her inside. "Along with Josephine's prized collection of roses."

The warm air was redolent with the scent of damp earth.

"And of course, there are prize specimens from all over the world. Much of the specimens from Baudin's expedition to Australia are here, much to the chagrin of our Museum of Natural History. But then, a husband must indulge his wife, and Napoleon was very good about allowing her to pursue her passion for botanicals."

"I have heard that he even allowed her to order plants from Lee & Kennedy, one of England's largest plant dealers."

"True. The English navy permitted her specimens to pass through the blockade, as a courtesy."

Valencia looked around at the profusion of lush blooms. "It is heartening to see that beauty can still bloom during times of war."

Mersault paused before a large bronze statue, it head crowned with vines of deep green foliage. "Josephine said Rousseau was her inspiration for gardening. But as we have seen over the last decade, nature in its primitive state can be both beautiful and wild."

"Man is not really noble savage?" she remarked, curious to hear his thoughts.

"I think very few people are motivated by noble sentiments, madame. What about you?"

"I would have to agree."

Further comment was forestalled by the approach of Madame Levalier and her friends. "Has Andre shown you the spectacular variety of roses yet?" asked Madame Noilly.

"We had not yet progressed that far," replied Valencia.

"Men! When it comes to certain things, they have no notion of what a lady really wants."

The next half hour passed in polite admiration of the various species. *Cuisse de nymphe emue, Beaute touchante, Belle Hebe, Rire niais*—Valencia was relieved when a servant finally appeared to summon them to the midday meal.

As the day was unseasonably warm, the luncheon was served outdoors in a large pavilion. A trestle table, set with gaily striped linens and potted flowers, was a colorful counterpoint to the bare trees and dormant hedges outside the canvas tenting. A hint of summertime sweetness wafted up from the hothouse fruits piled high around the silver centerpiece, a magnificent Louis XIV epergne.

Valencia sat between two young officers who took turns paying her florid compliments.

"You must try some of the wine," said Captain Hillaire. "Our Loire region is famous for its delightful whites."

She accepted a glass and sipped slowly. It was delicious, as was the food. The laughter all around grew louder as dish after dish of rich delicacies were passed, and the servants kept refilling her glass. *Careful*, she warned herself. It was important to keep her wits about her. A sidelong glance showed that Lynsley's wine glass sat untouched.

If the others noticed his sober demeanor, no one allowed it to dampen the spirits of the party. The mood was quite gay and relaxed when finally they all rose from the table.

"We must take a walk to see the folly overlooking the lake," announced Levalier. "It was designed in the classical Greek style, and boasts several exquisite columns from an Athenian temple."

"Is it not too difficult for the ladies?" asked Captain Gillemot after surveying the winding footpath.

"*Mais, non!*" exclaimed Madame Noilly. "I think we would all welcome a bit of exercise after such a repast."

"An excellent suggestion. Let's be off." Resuming his conversation with Levalier, Lynsley set off at a brisk match along the graveled path, forcing the minister to match his stride.

"Madame?" Noilly offered Valencia his arm.

"Thank you.

The path turned steeper and the footing grew a bit rougher, forcing Valencia and her escort to fall a few steps behind the rest of the group.

Glancing back, Lynsley barked a rebuke. "Do try to keep up, my dear. I am sure you do not wish to slow the group down."

"You go on," she said, releasing Noilly. "I shall continue at my own pace."

"But—"

"You may do as the lady says. I am in no hurry to stare at a pile of moldering marble." Rochambert took her arm.

"But as a connoisseur of art, aren't you curious to see such classical Greek treasures?" asked Valencia

"Not when I have a flesh and blood Venus so close at hand."

She stepped around an outcropping of granite, purposely brushing up against his leg "Do you always flirt so shamelessly with women?"

"I see no shame in showing an appreciation for beauty."

"How can a lady argue with that?" replied Valencia.

The bend twisted sharply, following the contour of the hill as its side steepened and angled away into rocky ravine. Loose stones made the path uneven, and she felt her leg twitch as she started up through the turn.

Up ahead, the path flattened out. Another few steps ...

But suddenly her half boots were slipping out from under her. Valencia flung herself back, trying to regain her balance.

"Madame!" Rochambert reached out, a fraction too late. She lost her footing and tumbled over the ledge.

Briars tore at her skirts as she bounced over the rough stones. Luckily, the ground leveled for a short stretch of grassy verge, and she was able to grab at the turf and arrest her fall. When finally she rolled to a stop, pain lanced through her bad leg, which was twisted under her weight.

"Madame!"

She tried to catch her breath and answer, but her bruised ribs protested even so slight a move.

Captain Gillemot was already scrambling down to where she lay. Lynsley followed but far more slowly.

"Mon Dieu, are you alright?" The officer knelt down and began chafing her hand. "Don't try to move. We can fashion a litter—"

"Don't be absurd." Lynsley cut him off with a curt laugh. "I'm sure she is fine. Just a little shaken up, isn't that right, my dear?" He reached out and lifted her none too gently to her feet. "Come, and walk it off."

She bit back a cry of pain. "Yes, of course."

The captain looked appalled.

"Now that the initial shock has worn off, I am quite fine," she assured him. Her face must have belied her words, for he shot the marquess a scathing look.

Both men helped her back up to path, where the rest of the group was milling in a state of shock.

"My poor dear!" exclaimed Madame Levalier.

"Let us go back immediately—" began her husband.

"We wouldn't hear of it—would we, Valencia?" objected Lynsley. "There is no need to ruin the excursion for everyone."

"No, of course not," she said tightly, not meeting Lynsley's gaze. Pain was shooting through her thigh. "It was clumsy of me. I will be just fine in a moment."

He turned and started off again.

She followed, dragging her step.

"Do try to keep up," he called from the crest of the rise.

The others were clearly disturbed by his unfeeling words. The ladies were now eying him with censorious looks, and from the men rose a few rumbled rebukes.

As if oblivious to the air of tension, Lynsley wheeled around and marched off.

Valencia forced a smile and waved the captain on as she passed a bench. "You go on with the others. I shall rest here and wait for your return, if you don't mind."

Chapter Fifteen

I t was Rochambert who circled back some moments later and sat down beside her. "Allow me to keep you company."

"It is really not necessary, she said through gritted teeth. "There are no wolves on the prowl in this park."

"No." He lit a cheroot and blew out a perfect ring of smoke. "Only *cochons*, it would seem."

"Thomas is not in the best of moods. His negotiations are not going as well as he planned, so I suppose that is why he is acting like a pig."

"You seem to be taking it in stride."

She bit back a laugh. "What choice does a wife have but to keep pace with her husband's whims."

Her companion eyed her through the scrim of smoke. "Yours is not a love match?"

Valencia exhaled sharply as she shifted against the slats. In her weakened state, she would have preferred not to engage the enemy. However, war allowed for no quarter.

"Oh, come, monsieur," she replied, concentrating on duty rather than the stabbing fire in her thigh. "Surely you do not imagine that the reasons for matrimony in America are any different from those here in the Old World. Alliances among the *haute monde*—be they in a democracy or a monarchy—are usually based on money, influence and power, not some flutter of the heart."

"Indeed." His smile revealed a flash of teeth. "I was simply not sure how much a lady wished to admit to the naked truth of life. So many of your fair sex are hopeless romantics."

"I prefer to take a more cynical view of the world. That way, I am rarely disappointed."

"We are alike in many ways, *madame*," he said in a husky murmur. "Tell me then, why the match with a prig like Daggett?"

Valencia considered the question, deliberately drawing out the silence before she answered. "My family has excellent connections with the Caribbean sugar trade, which have proved useful for Thomas. He has parlayed his cleverness into considerable wealth, and is likely to rise in importance in our country. I found it suited me to go along for the ride."

"I would have thought that you would have your choice of rich, influential men. They are, after all, the type who can afford to be attracted to beautiful women."

Valencia fixed him with a cool stare. "Indeed. But most of them want a perfect specimen, unflawed by an ungainly limp. The offers I received tended not to be respectable ones."

His eyes took on a speculative gleam.

"Time is not an ally for a woman," she went on. "So when Thomas was willing to overlook my infirmity and advanced years, I decided the prospect was to my advantage."

"You don't sound bitter."

"It is the law of the jungle. The strong have no mercy for the weak. Tears and tantrums would only be a waste of breath."

"You intrigue me, *madame*. It is rare to meet a lady who comprehends the true nature of the world."

She lowered her lashes, determined to fan his interest despite the fire searing through her twisted muscles. "And I appreciate the sympathetic ear, sir. You cannot know how very pleasant it is to be able converse with a like-minded spirit."

He sidled closer, joining their bodies from shoulder to thigh. "The rest of my anatomy is at your disposal—you have only to ask."

"Naughty man," she whispered, managing not to gag on the scent of his musky cologne.

To her relief, the return of the others interrupted the *tete a tete*.

"Feeling better, my dear?" called Lynsley.

"But of course." Valencia rose, somewhat unsteadily, and accepted his arm.

"Excellent. Levalier has just informed me that he has an important engagement in town, and I assured him we would not make him late." It was only then that he acknowledged Rochambert's presence. "Kind of you to keep my wife company, sir."

"The pleasure was all mine," replied the Frenchman. "Madame Daggett is a most interesting lady."

Lynsley turned away without answering him and set off at a brisk clip. "Don't dally, my dear."

Somehow, despite several stumbles, she managed to keep up. But every step was agony. Her scar burned from what felt like the assault of redhot pitchforks stabbing along the line of puckered flesh. Beneath her fluttering skirts, her undergarments were growing drenched with sweat.

Discipline. Don't give in pain. Valencia repeated the words like her long-ago yoga mantras, matching the silent cadence to her aching step. She was determined to match the marquess's sangfroid.

Lynsley would likely march from here to hell with both legs cut off at the knees.

Even with such thoughts prodding her on, it seemed like an eternity before they came to the courtyard where the carriages were waiting.

The marquess took his time in thanking their French hosts, while she managed a stoic smile in answers to their solicitous questions. Whether she could keep her leg from collapsing was a close call, but finally Lynsley finished his rounds and offered a hand up into their barouche.

Valencia climbed in blindly, her limbs seeming to move of their own accord. Half crawling, half falling, she slid onto the seat.

She heard his boot scrape against the iron rungs, followed by the rap of his walking stick, signaling the driver to spring the team.

As the whip cracked, Lynsley pulled the curtain closed, then quickly lifted her legs and lay her along the length of the leather.

Valencia couldn't hold back a cry of pain.

Dropping to his knees on the floorboards, he swept up her skirts, and suddenly his large, strong hands were skimming over her stockings. Ever so gently, he grasped her thigh.

The muscles spasmed under his touch.

"Damn, how bad is it?" he asked, slowly caressing his fingers over the scarred flesh.

"It hurts like hell," she rasped. "But nothing is broken."

A harsh oath slipped from his lips, and in the hazy half light, the lines of worry etched a web of black across his face. His hands kept kneaded her aching muscles.

"Sorry," she whispered. "That was careless of me." Every lurch of the wheels sent a jolt of fire through her injured limb. "I should have—"

"Hush." As Lynsley shifted his position, he touched his palm to her cheek. "We'll review strategy later. For now, just lie still."

Even had she wanted to disagree, Valencia hadn't the strength to argue. She closed her eyes again, using what little strength remained to fight back tears. No show of womanly weakness, she warned herself. The marquess expected no less.

Slowly but surely, the spasms subsided. His touch was gentle, yet firm and strong. Lud, he had wonderfully skillful hands. Pressing, probing, they seemed to sense intuitively just where to knead away the knots of tension. Through haze of pain, she was aware of his constant closeness. It was ... comforting.

"Better?"

"Much," she murmured. Curling on her side, she pressed her face against his chest. Through the starched linen, she could feel the warmth of his body and salty prickling of sweat. Strange, but his heart seemed to be beating even faster than hers.

And yet, its martial cadence was calming. *Thud, thud, thud.* The marquess's inner music. Listening to its steady drumming, she fell into a fitful doze.

As the carriage approached their residence, Lynsley eased himself up and smoothed her skirts back into place. "Valencia," he whispered.

Her eyes opened, and though it took a moment for them to snap into focus she quickly drew herself into a sitting position

"Sorry," he murmured, steadying her shoulders against the squabs. "I must play the unfeeling prig again in public." He brushed a tendril of hair from her face. "Can you endure the pain for another few minutes?"

Valencia nodded. "Of course I can."

Despite the quickness of her reply, she could not quite disguise the catch in her voice. A fleeting, fragile tremor. But he knew she would die before admitting she could not soldier on.

His jaw clenched. Is that what he had demanded of the Merlins? An unyielding, impossible dedication to duty. A notion of honor too lofty for any individual to live up to?

In ancient myth, Icarus had plunged back to earth on melted wings when he tried to soar too close to the sun.

Hating himself, and the whole sordid world of deception and lies, Lynsley held her close for another few moments. The scent of her new perfume, now edged with the sour tang of her suffering, stirred a welling of impotent rage in his chest. He wanted to lash out—to smash his fist again and again into some hard object.

Preferably Pierre Rochambert's face.

In the instant after Valencia's fall, their gazes had met and the Frenchman's half smile had been chilling to behold. A cold-blooded bend of his lips. And his eyes had been reptilian as well —utterly opaque and devoid of emotion.

A snake's eyes.

There was only one way to deal with a poisonous serpent. Cut off its head before it could strike again.

Lynsley gripped the brass door latch and drew a deep breath before throwing it open. One thing was now sure—one of them would be a dead man before this mission was over.

"Summon Guillaume and help *madame* from the carriage," he barked at the footman who came out to meet them. "She suffered a slip during our outing and needs assistance up to her room."

"*Oui, monsieur.*" The servant called for assistance as he scrambled to set the wooden steps in place.

"Do hurry," said Lynsley, punctuating his gruff growl by

tapping his boot impatiently on the cobblestones. "The air is growing damp and I don't wish to take a chill."

He forced his gaze to his gloves as Valencia, leaning heavily on the two footmen, slowly made her way up the marble landing. It took all of his considerable willpower to keep his hands from shoving aside the servants and sweeping her up in his own arms.

"Ring for *madame's* maid," he called to the new major domo. Tossing down his hat, he took his time in peeling the leather from his fingers. "The woman will know what to do."

"Shall I send one of the footmen for a physician, monsieur?" asked the man in some concern.

"Not necessary," replied Lynsley curtly. "Madame simply needs to lie down for a bit." He took up the letters lying on the silver salver and started up the stairs without a backward glance.

That should set the servants to gossiping about what a hard, unfeeling man the American consul was. The French, for all their faults, always behaved with great gallantry toward a lady.

Closing the door to his own bedchamber, Lynsley leaned back against the heavy oak and squeezed his eyes shut.

Damn. Damn. Damn.

He *must* find a way to get to Rochambert without using Valencia as bait. He had known it would be difficult, seeing her matching wits with her nemesis. But the full force of it had not hit him until now.

He realized his hands were shaking. *Fear or fury?* A little of both, he decided.

But logic must override all emotion. Ranting or raving accomplished nothing. It was far too late for dwelling on right and wrong. He must make the best of a bad situation.

The sounds of activity in the adjoining suite distracted him from his thoughts. He waited for the French servants to withdraw, before letting himself in Valencia's chamber.

"Order a hot bath," he snapped at her maid.

"Aye sir, I've done that," said Perkins. She had already helped Valencia to lie down on the bed. Her mud stained gown had been stripped off and replaced by a light lawn nightrail and duvet coverlet. Framed by the fringe of delicate lace, her face looked cold and pale as carved marble.

"Arnica salve will help with any inflammation," he said softly. "And a tincture of laudanum will ease the pain."

"I don't need opium." Valencia opened her eyes and tried to sit up, but the dullness in her eyes belied the assertion. "A strong draught of willowbark will be sufficient."

"For god's sake, Valencia, don't try to be a hero." Concern added a sharp edge to his voice. "Lie still and rest."

"I will send one of the servants to the apothecary," said Perkins in a low voice.

"Don't fuss over me, Thomas," added Valencia, mustering a show of her usual spirit. She drew in a deep breath. "You may leave me to Perkins. I assure you, I will be up and ready for duty in the morning."

"The hell you will."

Her jaw set. "It's just a twisted muscle. Trust me, I suffered through this sort of injury before and know how to handle it."

Lynsley hesitated, loath to sap her strength by arguing.

"It always seems bad at the beginning, but with a good night's rest I will be fine."

He turned to retreat to his room. "Let us do our best to avoid any more unfortunate accidents."

"It wasn't an accident," she replied. "I was pushed."

Chapter Sixteen

A flash of steel, quick as a cobra's strike ... she tried to spin away but her own movements seemed pitifully slow. The blade bit into her flesh, the pain of it hot and pulsing ...

Valencia awoke with a small cry, her limbs twisted in the bedsheets, her heart thudding hard against her ribs. Sweat dampened her hair and her nightrail was tangled around her knees.

"It's alright." A hand, cool and calming, touched her brow. "You were having a bad dream."

She struggled to sit up. *Damn.* The dream didn't usually lie. No matter how many times she refought the Frenchman, she always ended up lying in a spreading pool of her own blood, the piercing pain in her leg so fierce that it brought tears to her eyes.

Even though a warrior never wept.

The ache, however, was worse than normal tonight. The scar throbbed as she groped for the sheet twisted around her limb. She must have been thrashing in her sleep, hoping against all hope that this time a knight in shining armor might ride to her rescue—

"Here, let me help you." The deep, familiar voice cut through the haze of hurt. Lynsley gently unwound the knotted linen. "Feeling better?"

He was sitting in a chair by her bed, his chiseled features softened by the night shadows.

Caught by surprise, Valencia wasn't quick enough to hide behind her usual sarcastic anger. Her resolve was weak, her body bruised. *Fight back, Valkyrie!* The long-ago exhortation of the Academy fencing master rang in her ears. *No matter how badly you are injured, never show an opponent that you are hurting.*

But as she shifted and tried to regroup, every bone in her body screamed in protest. It felt as if she had been trampled by a regiment of Marshall Soult's cavalry.

A sound must have slipped from her lips, for Lynsley edged his chair closer and reached for her hand. His fingers curled with hers.

She stiffened at first touch, then slowly relaxed.

They sat for a few minutes, twined in a companionable silence.

"You have a goodly number of calluses for a fine gentleman," she said softly, aware of the pressure of his palm.

"Idle hands make for idle minds," he quipped. "As you have witnessed, it takes someone of my advanced years constant effort to keep in shape for the job." He cracked a small smile. "Besides, I should be bored to flinders lifting nothing more weighty than an eyebrow. Even if it means that my hands are more those of a ploughman than a patrician."

There was nothing roughshod about the way Lynsley smoothed the covers and retucked the sheet around her legs. "Lean back a little," he added. "The collar of your nightrail is twisted."

Valencia found herself suddenly seized by a longing to cling to his strong, capable hand. To take comfort from his closeness, to share his strength.

Lord, she had spent all her life standing on her own, never allowing a moment of weakness. Oh, how she wanted one now. He had stripped off his coat and his shoulders looks so solid and reassuring. A place of refuge, just a hair's breadth away.

Drawing away, she fell back against the pillows.

"A sip of laudanum?" he offered.

She shook her head.

"There's no shame in seeking relief from pain, Valencia. Fighting it only saps your strength."

Another oblique warning?

"I'm not trying to be a martyr, Thomas." Strange how easily his name came to her lips now. "I merely want to keep a clear head for the morrow. I know from past experience that opium affects me badly. My head remains muzzy for days."

"Then take another draught of willowbark. It will dull the edge, without any side effects." Lynsley mixed a bit of powder in a glass of water. "As for the morrow, you aren't going anywhere. And that's an order."

She drank the mixture without comment, then looked up to find him studying her face. It had started to rain, and the pelter of drops against the windowpanes echoed the erratic beat of her heart. Though the mizzle of moonlight had died away, the single candle caught the odd sparks in his gaze.

He cleared his throat with a cough. "I have been thinking about what you said earlier. You were pushed? By Rochambert?"

"I cannot say for sure," she answered. "Gillemot and Hillaire were close as well."

"Neither of them would have any reason to wish you harm. As for Rochambert ..." His lips thinned to a grim line. "I wonder what his motivations would be at this point."

"He remarked that he was curious as to what our feeling were for each other." Valencia hesitated before adding, 'Perhaps he merely wanted to see your reaction."

"Bloody bastard," muttered the marquess under his breath.

The vehemence took her by surprise.

"That's not exactly a revelation," she said dryly.

"No." His mouthed quirked. "I suppose not.

"Sorry I slipped up."

"Don't say that." His voice sharpened. "You've done well. Exceedingly well. Indeed, I confess that without you along on this mission, I should be hardpressed to find a way to get close to Rochambert."

Praise from Lynsley? Had the marquess added some other potent drug to her drink? All at once, Valencia was aware of a strange syrupy warmth spreading through her limbs. The aches ebbed from her muscles, the knots of tension unwound.

"Mmmmm." It must be the medicine kicking in, she decided. As she relaxed into a drowsy state of half sleep, her tongue loosened as well. Words she would never have dared say aloud seemed to have a mind of their own. "I—I always wanted your approval." She closed her eyes. "Mayhap that why I misbehaved so often. To get your attention, even if it was only to hear your scoldings."

Lynsley's chuckle was soft, soothing. "Was I such an ogre?"

"Ogre?" A sigh slipped from her lips. "Surely you were aware that all the girls were in love with you."

A dull flush crept over his face. He covered his embarrassment with a cough. It was rather endearing to see him so nonplussed.

"But we were, of course, under no illusions on that score," went on Valencia. "We, of all people, knew the realities of the world." Her mouth scrunched, recalling those long-ago days. "Still, even Merlins have girlish dreams."

He was silent for moment. "What of you, Valencia? What were your dreams?"

"Me?" She lifted her shoulders a fraction. "I never gave much thought to being aught but a Merlin." A draft from the rainswept breeze rattled the window casement. "I should have, of course. Even if I hadn't been injured, it is not a job one can do forever. One day I should have been forced to retire."

"As will I."

"You are hardly shuffling into your dotage," she remarked, cocking her head as she studied the planes of his face. "And it seems you haven't exhausted your formidable talents just yet." She hesitated before adding, "We all knew you were quite a daring operative before the Academy. The Madras mission is the stuff of legend."

He frowned and leaned back in his chair. "How do you know about Madras?"

"We added brandy to the Christmas punch one year and got Mrs. Merlin a bit in her cups. She told us some very interesting stories before the spirits wore off."

"That was an underhanded trick."

Valencia grinned. "Just practicing our lessons in devious deceptions."

"Hmmph." His attempt at sounding stern ended in a smothered chuckle. "Be that as it may, I've settled down considerably since then."

"I doubt most people would consider this foray to Paris a holiday excursion." She paused, feeling her mind turn even more muzzy as the painkiller spread through her limbs. Whether it was the drug or the darkness, her tongue loosened enough to venture a personal question "As for settling down, I can't help asking once again ... why haven't you married?"

He stiffened. "Once again, you are being impertinent."

"No, I am merely being curious. But it is clear you would rather not talk about it."

The silence stretched for some time. She thought he meant to ignore the question.

But strangely enough, after shifting in his chair, he replied, "I still have some years left in my dish. There is still time yet."

"That's another unfair advantage men have—you can breed well into old age."

He chuckled. "Please, not another lecture on biology. I am conversant with the mechanics of making an heir."

"So why haven't you?" she persisted. "In your world, a gentleman of wealth and title is expected to follow tradition."

"I rarely feel the need to bow to outside pressure." Lynsley crossed his legs and regarded the tip of his boot. "I suppose I haven't yet found the right lady."

Surprised by his candor, Valencia needed a moment to frame a reply. "Ah. You mean to say you are a romantic at heart?"

"Quite the opposite," he said gruffly. " I am a realist, not a romantic. Given my present profession, it would be highly unfair to ask a lady to wed. She would be expecting a very different sort of life than the one I lead." His expression turned meditative. "Gaiety. Glitter. Glamour. She would want all the trappings of prestige and privilege. And rightfully so. Not a husband who must be secretive about his life, often leaving without word of where is he off to, or when he might return."

"How noble." Valencia yawned. "But if she loved you, she wouldn't care about such superficial things."

His chair scraped over the carpet. "I should let you sleep."

She kept hold of his hand, loathe to let the camaraderie slip away. "Might you stay for just a bit longer. Just talking is ... nice."

Lynsley sat back down. "Very well."

Their gazes met and Valencia wondered whether she was simply imagining the strange swirl of blue. Light and dark, like the sea in storm.

"What's good for the gander is good for the goose," he said after a moment's of silence. "What of you, Valencia. Why have you never taken a husband?"

Her breath expelled in a sardonic sigh. "Like you, I'm a bit of a misfit in my world. Can you imagine me wed to a fisherman or a farmer?"

He didn't answer.

"Most men, no matter their station in life, want a wife who will manage their household and bear their children. The skills of a trained assassin are not high on the list." Not wanting to sound too bitter, she quickly tempered her tone with a light laugh. "I'm a bit too strong-willed to make any man a good wife. And a bit too old to change my ways. The Academy trained us to be self-reliant. I am quite happy as I am—free as a bird."

"Free as a bird," he repeated softly. "Are you happy, Valencia? Or have I been terribly selfish in thinking there is a honorable purpose in taking young girls and training them for a life of violence."

Valencia had never heard Lynsley sound uncertain. Her fingers tightened around his. "We did not exactly come from a world of sweetness and light, Thomas. Trust me, the stews are a far more vicious than any opponent you've ever asked a Merlin to face."

"That's too easy an excuse."

"Throughout our training, we are constantly given a choice. And many take advantage of the skills you give us to work in less demanding jobs. Those of us who go on to earn our wings do so because we believe in the same things you do."

Lynsley stared out at the fogged windowpanes. "At times, that is cold comfort."

Seeking to keep him from withdrawing into the darkness of Lord Lynsley's lair, she quickly asked, "Tell me more about the founding of the Academy."

"You know the story," he murmured. "A book I read early on inspired the idea."

"So you have said." Valencia mulled it over. "And yet, your commitment seems far more personal, far more ... passionate than a mere story."

He seemed to flinch. "Now it is you who are being romantic, Valencia. I was merely being pragmatic in trying to think of a way to counter the threat to our freedoms. Nothing more."

She didn't believe it, but much as she wished to press him further, her eyes slowly fluttered shut.

Lynsley sat back, watching the play of moonlight on her face as Valencia drifted off to sleep. She looked so achingly young with her hair loose and curling over the delicate lace of her nightrail. In repose, her expression was unguarded, a girlish smile curving her lips.

His throat tightened in regret and recrimination. She, and so many orphans like her, had never had a real youth. They had been robbed of their innocence early on. With no one to shield them from harm, they had been forced to confront the sordid realities of life. No child should experience that nightmare.

Had he been wrong to take them and given them a way to fight back against injustice and tyranny? Perhaps, like the street pimps and bawdy house matrons, he was just using them.

Despite all his high-minded principles, maybe he was no more than a pompous prig.

What a dirty, depressing thought.

It was not the first time he had brooded over such things. But Valencia's face—her courage and her heart shaping every curve and shadow—forced him to confront his own mixed feelings in a far more visceral way than his usual cerebral debates.

The marquess felt a twisting tension course through him. Oh yes, it was physical, this fight between conscience and duty. Right and wrong. Need and necessity.

Far too physical. Strange, it had been a long time since he felt such a simmering in his blood. He was no longer an impetuous youth. He had learned to keep desire under control.

What did he want?

Lynsley didn't dare admit it.

He rose, hands fisted at his sides. Reason told him to return to his own rooms, but some perverse power held him place. He reached out, his hand hovering a hair's breadth above her cheek. The candle flickered, its fading light playing over her features. He couldn't help himself—leaning closer Lynsley let his fingertip traced the thin scar just above her brow.

A memento of an Academy test of fencing skills. The day was still sharp in his memory. Her opponent's foil had lost its button during the bout and drawn blood. A good deal of blood, as he recalled. But Valencia, a rapier thin girl of fifteen at the time, had shrugged it off with a laugh.

A badge of honor, she had called it. Like the members of the Prussian dueling societies, who prided themselves on meeting any challenge with unflinching resolve, she had picked up her sword and insisted on continuing the match.

How many other nicks and cuts lay hidden beneath her lace?

Likely too many to count, he thought with a pang of regret. A sigh, soft as a zephyr, stirred the air as he brushed his lips to her hair. He would give an arm and leg to make her whole again. But he was no Merlin, no modern-day magical wizard with extraordinary powers.

He was just a man, with all too many human flaws.

His mouth hardened. Despite his own damnable weak-nesses, he vowed that he would come up with a way to keep her from further harm. Already an idea was taking form in his head ...

"Sweet dreams, Valkyrie," he whispered.

But as he turned for his own bed, Lynsley knew that for him, sleep would be a long time coming.

Chapter Seventeen

"I am tired of bed rest," muttered Valencia

"That may be, madam," replied her maid. "However, my orders from Mr. Daggett are quite specific. You are not to be allowed up and about until the morrow. Shall I bring you some hot chocolate and cakes?"

"No, thank you." Nothing could sweeten the situation. She felt like a schoolgirl of old, confined to quarters for some petty infraction. "Tyrant," she muttered under her breath.

"I am just doing what I am told," said Perkins.

"Not you. *Him*." Valencia scowled. "Kindly ask the master of the house if I might have a word with him."

"Yes, madam."

She sat up, fuming at the indignity of being treated like a child. *Orders be damned*. If he didn't show up soon, she would storm straight into the lion's den and confront him. Questioning his authority would come as no surprise.

The door opened with hardly a whisper. "You are feeling better, I hear," said Lynsley

"Quite," she snapped, belatedly realizing that her

bedsnarled hair and crinkled nightrail did not present a pretty picture.

He, on the other hand, was attired in an impeccable set of evening clothes, the faultless folds of his cravat framing his firm jaw and the elegant, aristocratic nose. His lips, however, betrayed a tiny twitch.

Which only set her nerves more on edge.

"I am glad to hear it," he replied. "By the morrow you should be strong enough to rise."

An unladylike word floated up from the tangle of linen and lace.

"It appears that *you* are not going to be spending the evening shackled to a bedpost."

His brow lifted. "As far as I know, such entertainments are not on the schedule. But in here Paris, the city of fleshly pleasures, I suppose anything is possible."

"You are on your way to a brothel?" she asked slowly.

He hesitated a fraction before answering. "Our party is gathering for supper at the Salon d'Etrangers and then going on to an evening of gambling at the Palais Royal. But Levalier did make mention of heading on to a certain establishment in rue de Rivoli afterwards."

The idea of Lynsley spending the night frolicking with a voluptuous whore did not improve Valencia's mood.

"Have a care not to catch the pox," she said sarcastically. "Perhaps you should ask your hosts for a condom—the French invented them."

"Thank you for your concern," he replied gravely. "I shall exercise caution, in case at some point in my life I should wish to procreate an heir."

"Enjoy your evening," she muttered, plumping up her pillows with a punch.

His face remained expressionless, but a hint of laughter

danced in his eyes. "As I said, by the morrow, you should be well enough recovered to be allowed out of bed."

"The only thing keeping me confined to quarters is your order," she retorted. "Perkins won't let me move a muscle without your approval." Flinging back the covers, she waggled her leg, uncaring that the movement exposed a good deal of flesh. "As you see, I am perfectly fit."

His gaze went opaque, shutting her out in the blink of an eye. *That dratted stone Sphinx face.* The statue had apparently tiptoed on its giant cat's paws from Luxor to Paris.

"I suppose we can relax the rules a bit for this evening," he said. "I shall inform Perkins that you are allowed to take a turn to the library if you so desire."

"How kind of you to give me your blessing, my lord," she said acidly. "Any other pronouncement from on high?"

"You need not wait up," he said calmly. "I will likely be late."

How easily he assumed that aristocratic air of bored arrogance. As if mind and body were in another world. It was ingrained, of course.

And infuriating.

When he looked like that, some demon deep within seized hold of her and she couldn't help wanting to provoke a fight. Anything to bring the blood to his cheeks.

"Or maybe you won't be home at all," she sneered. "After all, a brothel offers far more amenities than this mansion— warmed sheets, perfumed pillows, breakfast served in bed."

He turned without responding to her childish taunt. The door latch closed with a discreet click.

Valencia picked up the book by her bedside, restraining the urge to throw it at the polished panels.

But Merlins don't make a scene, she reminded herself.

Getting a grip on her wayward emotions, she drew a deep

breath and settled down to read. The library had yielded several books on travel to the Orient. But she soon found herself too restless to concentrate on tales from the Silk Road. The printed words seemed to twist and turn into a strange blur, as if challenging her to read between the lines.

She couldn't quite put a finger on it, but something was rubbing her wrong. Something more chilling that a flare of ill-temper. In the past, she had learned to trust her intuition. But her sense for impending danger was likely dull from disuse.

"Don't be a peagoose," she muttered aloud. Melodrama belonged on the pages of a novel. Only ink and paper heroines acted like idiots.

Snapping shut the volume, she rose and began to pace the perimeter of her room. The enforced bed rest had her itching for action, that was all. Her nerves were wound too tight. Another few strides ...

But try as she might, Valencia couldn't outrace a growing feeling of unease. A darkness seemed to shadow her steps. The hairs on the back of her neck were suddenly standing on end.

No doubt because they were desperately in need of a brush or comb. However, sarcasm didn't silence the stirring of intuition.

"Bloody hell." The whispered oath punctuated the heated debate taking place in her head.

Orders were orders, scolded Reason.

But Lynsley had not given her a direct order to remain in the residence, retorted Rebellion.

It was implied, reminded Reason

It was left unsaid, snapped Rebellion. *And a soldier was not dutybound to obey an unspoken command.*

She made her decision, damning the consequences.

It took only a few minutes to don her dark trousers and shirt. A hooded cloak hung in her dressing room, and beneath it sat a soft-soled pair of shoes. Moving quickly, she stole into Lynsley's bedchamber. The pistols he had purloined from the American consul were in the top dresser drawer. After adding a packet of extra powder and bullets to her pocket, she unlatched the casement window and stepped out to the window ledge.

Bathed in pearly starlight, the graceful spires and ornate rooftops of Paris looked sublimely beautiful. But beneath her feet lay a tangled web of dark streets, a reminder that a misstep could be deadly.

No matter how skilled, an agent in enemy territory could always use a back-up. Someone to watch his back.

She must not let her imagination run wild. Lynsley had far more experience than she did in foreign places. However, Valencia did not allow that fact to slow her down. Without a backward glance, she climbed down the copper drainpipe and traversed the alleyway.

Deciding that a hackney would draw too much attention, she hurried on foot through cobbled streets, keeping to the shadows. The rattle of metal and muskets helped her duck a patrol of soldiers. As for the other pedestrians, they paid her little heed in their own haste to complete their journeys unscathed. Even in the fancier parts of the city, Paris was dangerous after dark.

From her study of the maps, Valencia knew every passageway of the area by heart. After a small detour to avoid a group of brawling drunks, she had no trouble finding the right street.

With glittering lights ablaze in the shops and arcades, the Palais Royal stood out as a beacon of raucous activity amid its silent neighbors. Idlers loitered along its length, trading ribald taunts with ladybirds who paraded up and down the street, their plumage of mock diamonds and pearls waving brazenly in the night breeze.

Valencia climbed to a rooftop vantage point on one of the

warehouses facing the main entrance. It was, she decided, rather entertaining to watch the arrivals of the carriages. Men brimming with hubris descended for a date with the *vingt et rouge* tables in the gambling salon, while others hurried straight for the upper floors, which housed a nest of high-priced doves.

The amusement pinched from her mouth as those who had exhausted their luck at the *tapis vert* stumbled out in the throes of drink and despair. To chance everything on the turn of a card or the roll of dice was something she found hard to comprehend.

But then again, she, too, was a gambler—and playing for even greater odds.

On that sobering thought, Valencia spotted Lynsley strolling through the vaulted arcade with a group of gentlemen. His step was firm, his laughter controlled.

She doubted that the marquess ever took wild risks. Even when forced to play a high stakes game, he kept his head and did everything possible to make the odds in his favor.

A strumpet sidled up to Lynsley and rubbed herself up against his thigh. She was quite pretty, and he took a moment to look down at her décolletage—which even at a distance appeared to cut clear down to her navel. Then politely shook his head.

Valencia let out a breath. Only to draw a harsh gulp as the whore moved on to the man behind him. The marquess's movement revealed gold glimmer of hair.

So, Pierre Rochambert was part of the party.

Lynsley had failed to make mention of that. He had let her carp on about condoms and brothels, all the while knowing he would be spending an intimate evening with their enemy.

Damn his lovely, lordly eyes.

Did he think her too weak to help? Too inept?

Valencia sat for the next two hours, seething in silent frustration. The cold crept up through the rope soles of her shoes, curling her toes, numbing her legs. Would that it could dull the ache in her chest. Clenching her arms across her breasts, she hunched closer to the stone parapet. She wasn't sure whether to feel angry or hurt.

It would serve him right if she left him to fend for himself. Here she was freezing her arse, while he was likely warming his ...

By some perverse magic, Lynsley suddenly appeared, strolling out of the inner courtyard. Exiting the *Cour d'Honneur*, he waved off a hackney cab and began walking.

Valencia swore under her breath. He ought to know better than to venture anywhere on foot. Parisian streets were notoriously dangerous after dark.

The sense of foreboding was now like a sliver of ice skating down her spine.

Pushing back from the sooty stone, she crossed to the adjoining roof. As the marquess turned down the side street, she spotted a man stepping out from between two buildings, Tugging down the brim of his hat, he set off in the same direction.

It might be coincidence, but she was taking no chances.

Snaking through the chimneypots of slumbering shops. Valencia followed along, keeping her eye on the street below. Halfway down the block, the stranger was joined by two other shadowy shapes. Gangs of desperate men were rampant throughout the quartiers, many of them former aristocrats or priests reduced to robbery to survive.

Valencia allowed no more than a small twinge of pity. They were violent, vicious thieves, who would slit a man's throat for a *sou*.

The marquess seemed blithely unaware of the peril stalking his steps. His pace was leisurely, as if out for a Sunday stroll. Too much to drink? Or too sated with sex to be aware of his surroundings? He had never before appeared so careless.

She debated whether to call a warning, but decided against alerting the raggle-taggle ruffians on his trail.

Swinging up and over the ledge of a private townhouse, Valencia catwalked across the slate roof tiles and dropped lightly down to the top of a garden wall. Moving in a low crouch, she hurried along its length. She was now abreast of the three men. They had spread out across the cobblestones, in readiness to angle an attack on the unsuspecting figure ahead.

They moved swiftly, silently, eyes intent on their quarry. The only sounds echoing off the buildings was the soft slosh of the sewage stream and the yowl of an alleycat.

She gauged the distance and jumped.

Thump.

Rolling with a feral quickness, the ruffian slashed out with his knife but she easily dodged the blade. A hard knee to his groin drew a scream as he dropped headfirst into the ooze. She darted back as the second man spun around and aimed a kick at her head. Her hand caught his boot and jerked him off his feet. He fell with a bellowing curse. His pistol clattered to the cobblestones and fired. Smoke and sparks erupted as the bullet ricocheted off the brick, sending up a shower of shards.

"Bloody hell."

Valencia looked around to see that third attacker lay motionless at Lynsley's feet, his neck bent at an unnatural angle. Vaulting the body, the marquess rushed to her side.

"Dammit, we must be gone this instant." Swearing another oath, he grabbed her arm. "You can't be seen."

He looked around grimly. The shot had already set off several cries of alarm.

She seized his sleeve and pushed him into the sliver of space at their back. "Follow me." From her study of the maps, she had memorized the way back to their quartier through the maze of alleyways.

After coming out on the adjoining street, they raced on for some minutes through the sharp twists and turns, ducking low, squeezing sideways, scrambling at a dead run over walls of refuse. She didn't care to think what was squishing beneath her feet.

After a sprint across a deserted square and yet another darting traverse of a narrow lane, Lynsley finally showed signs of easing the pace. Hugging close to the crooked walls, he slowed to a walk, then suddenly stopped in a pool of shadows. Above the wheezing of her own lungs, she heard the growl of his breath scrape against the stone. He didn't sound winded at all. There was a rougher rasp to his tone.

Anger?

"Of all the bloody, *bloody*, reckless stunts ..."

Lynsley wasn't angry. He was absolutely furious.

"For the love of God, how dare you risk your neck and the mission like that?"

Her mouth dropped open, but she was too breathless to answer.

Just as well. Words might have goaded him to violence. As it was, his fury so palpable, she could feel it quivering in the air. Great waves, like stormtossed seas, buffeted her flushed face. In the next instant, it crested a rumbled oath. He grabbed her and shook her like a terrier toying with a rat.

"Bloody hell, what made you do such a damn foolish thing!"

"*You!*" cried Valencia without thinking. "In case you hadn't noticed, I was saving your damn neck, you ungrateful odious man." She tried to break free but to no avail. His grip was like an iron band around her wrists.

As she struggled, her hip hit up against the limestone wall.

She sucked in her breath at the sharp pain. Tears prickled her eyes, blurring her vision.

"Let. Me. Go."

But rather than accede to her demand, the marquess flattened against her, pinning her to the wall. Trapped between the mortared stones and his unyielding body, she reacted on pure instinct, lashing out with her knees, her elbows.

Lynsley gave a grunt, and then suddenly his mouth was covering hers in a bruising kiss.

Her lips parted to protest, but as his tongue slipped inside her, all coherent thought dissolved in a low, wordless sigh. Valencia felt her muscles melt. His heat was overpowering, a sweaty, savage masculinity that left her shaken to her very core.

"Don't *ever* do that again," he growled, his whiskered jaw abrading the sensitive skin of her neck. His hands speared through her tangled hair as he brushed his lips to her earlobe. His teeth nipped her flesh, sending a surge of conflicting sensations through her limbs.

She slumped a touch lower. Their eyes met, and through the haze of her own shock she saw that he, too, looked surprised as hell.

The sound of hobnailed boots shattered the silence. A patrol of soldiers was approaching.

"This way." Lynsley was the first to recover.

She followed along blindly, stumbling, speechless and near limp with shock.

When at last they emerged near a busy café, Lynsley waved down a passing hackney cab and shoved her inside. After calling a curt order to the driver, he followed suit and slumped back against the squabs.

. . .

Lynsley didn't trust himself to speak. *Didn't trust himself to think.* Sliding to the far side of the seat, he turned to stare out the window. But in the fogged glass, he caught only a self-mocking glimpse of his own brooding reflection.

It was the last thing on earth he wished to see. The guilt was great enough without seeing it writ plain on his face.

Bloody hell. Perhaps the sad truth was that he wasn't fit for active duty anymore. He had lost his head in the heat of the moment. Allowed fear to overwhelm reason. Seeing a blade flash so close to her flesh struck terror in his heart.

Even now, his body was still shaking.

Clenching his teeth in disgust, he quelled the urge to bury his head and in hands. Likely it was unrequited lust sending the spasms through his limbs. That momentary kiss had only ignited a far baser urge. Had the soldiers not saved him from perdition, he might have well have shucked off her breeches and taken her right up against the wall.

Damn him for a devil. Damn him for a fool.

As the hackney clattered through the maze of streets, Lynsley felt utterly lost. He was perilously close to losing command of the moment. Of the mission. Somehow he must master his mutinous mind and body.

Make them obey orders.

Duty, duty, duty ... The drumming of the wheels against the cobblestones finally skidded to a stop in front of their mansion. Thank god he given the servants instructions not to wait up. Surely his self-loathing was etched in every line of his face.

His key clicked open the lock, and he motioned Valencia to hurry inside. Her steps slowed and he heard her turn in the unlit foyer.

But before she could speak, Lynsley slid the door bolts home and stalked for the stairs, taking them two at a time.

Chapter Eighteen

amn, damn, damn the man.

Valencia flung off her cloak and yanked the ribbon from her plaited hair. He didn't fight fair. Most mortals would have screamed and shouted, but Lynsley simply retreated into his unassailable shell of reserve.

A bloody cover that was thicker and more impenetrable than a suit of armor.

One shoe hit the carpet, followed by the thud of the other. Peeling off her breeches and shirt, she threw them at the bedpost, where they caught and hung like flags of surrender.

Count to twenty, she told herself, recalling one of her first Academy lessons for cooling off.

One, two, three ...

Hell, all the numbers in the universe wouldn't add up to a rational response to Lynsley's *sang froid.* Cold blood? Ha, there had been nothing frigid about his sudden kiss.

She bit her lip, still tasting the sear of the moment.

Combat heats the blood to a boil—the pressure must burst out in strange, explosive ways.

Leave it at that, Valencia told herself. And yet, she couldn't.

She just couldn't. Stalking to the bed, she swore a savage oath and slammed her fist to duvet. Like the marquess, it shifted beneath her punch, the feathers refusing to offer any resistance. It was maddening. Mocking.

"No!" Valencia spun around, her temper flaring past the point of reason. "No, no, no." Enough of his patrician parries. This time, she would make him fight back.

Three quick strides, and without pause for thought, she threw open the connecting door.

The firelight caught Lynsley in the act of draining a glass of brandy.

"Go away, and that's an order." His voice was slightly slurred. "I'm in no mood for further fireworks."

She stepped over the threshold.

He turned away and sat down, swearing under his breath.

"Don't you dare ignore me, Thomas. We need to talk about this."

Lynsley looked up, his eyes overbright, and edged with a dangerous glitter she had never seen. "A lover's quarrel?" he said with biting cynicism. "Let us not carry the charade of man and wife too far, Valencia."

His tone, so at odds with his usual composure, goaded her to react with matching sarcasm. "I wouldn't dream of pretending that this match is anything but a marriage of convenience, a way for each of us to get what we want from this mission."

"Go away, Valencia," he repeated. "We will talk in the morning."

"Why?" she demanded.

Answering with a wordless grunt, Lynsley took a swig from the bottle. "Because I intend to drink myself into a stupor."

A single candle sat on the sideboard. She drew closer, like a moth mesmerized by the dancing flame.

"*Why?*" she demanded again. "Because I am repulsive?"

Pushed on by some uncontrollable urge, Valencia added, "Is that why you have never tried to bed me?"

"Don't. Do. This." he growled. She could hear his breathing grow more ragged. He recoiled from her, his face falling into shadow.

No. She would *not* let him withdraw into his Lair. "Do you find me ugly? Ungainly?"

The glass hit the wainscoting, shattering in a shower of tiny slivered shards.

Unrelenting, Valencia reached out. His dressing gown had come open, revealing a sliver of tanned flesh below the throbbing pulsepoint of his throat. The smell of spilled brandy and aroused male was overpowering. A dusting of curls, whiskey-gold in the flickering light, gleamed against his skin. Her fingers itched to thread through their finespun texture, to feel the contrast of coarse hair and smooth muscle.

Lynsley tried to knock her hand away.

She swayed, and had to brace her palm on his chest to keep her leg from buckling. Her own wrapper unraveled, baring her breasts.

Lynsley went utterly still. Not a sound, not a breath stirred between them. He might have been carved of stone, save for the sudden flicker of his gaze.

And then a groan wrenched from his throat.

Valencia looked down at the rumpled silk of his dressing gown. And felt her breath catch in her throat.

So—he was not impervious to carnal urges.

Driven by a devilish desire, she tore open the fabric and touched his rising desire.

"Oh, you wicked, wicked woman," he rasped.

She *was* wicked. Wanton. Willful. *And wild with need.* The passion she had thought long extinguished inside her burst back into flames.

"Tell me that you want me, Thomas," she whispered. Her teeth nipped the corner of his mouth. "Just a little?"

"God help me." Lynsley angled his face upward, the candlelight gilding his lashes in molten gold. For an instant, she saw longing in his eyes, the same fierce desire that swirled in her own veins. "I have never in my life wanted anything more."

His hands framed her face. The world held still for a brief instant and then he drew her down into a kiss.

"Thomas." Longing flooded through very fiber of her being.

His self-control seemed to melt at the tentative touch of their lips. "Val-kyrie," he whispered, his hold on her no longer gentle. His nails dug into her flesh, his mouth demanded that she yield to him.

Yes, yes, yes. Their tongues touched for the first time, and she nearly swooned as a purely primal jolt of pleasure shot through her. Mindless to all else but the need to feel his body impressed against hers, Valencia wriggled out of her wrapper and kicked it aside. Silk ripped in a ragged sigh as she pulled the dressing gown down from his shoulders. His hands left her for a fleeting moment, leaving them connected by only the deepening kiss.

It wasn't enough. Not nearly enough. She moaned against his mouth, having no coherent words to express her longing. Only his name seemed to have any shape.

"Thomas." Breaking away from his lips, she said it over and over again as her mouth traced the slant of his cheeks, the line of his jaw.

Lynsley pushed up from the leather chair, his arousal pressing against her thigh, and lifted her into his arms. Suddenly weightless, she felt herself spun through the air. A giddy laugh bubbled up in her throat and then burst free.

His voice joined hers, a low gutteral noise. Stripped away

was all semblance of the polished patrician. Raw need pulsed from every pore.

"Yes, yes, yes." Valencia urged him on with a nip to his shoulder.

He whirled for the bed, stumbling in his haste. Limbs tangled, they fell against the paneled door.

She laughed again, twisting against and wrapping her legs around his hips.

"Make love to me," Her voice hovered somewhere between a plea and a command. "Here. Now."

Lynsley had heard the words before, in countless terrible, taunting dreams. He held his breath for an instant, hardly daring to believe they were now real. And yet, her sun-bronzed skin was bucking against his body, her need as demanding and desperate as his own.

In his finespun fantasies, he had taken his time, kissing and caressing every lovely dip and curve of her body, drawing out the exquisite anticipation of joining their bodies in lovemaking.

"Oh, God." His mouth touched for a moment on her throat, the rapidfire beat of her heart pulsing against his lips. "I want you so badly, I think I might break apart into a thousand pieces."

"Not before you make me whole." She hitched herself higher, pressing her wet warmth against him. "I've waited half a lifetime—don't make me ask again."

Right or Wrong? Suddenly the arguments seemed meaningless. All that mattered was *Here and Now.*

With a clenched cry, he pulled her closer.

Valencia arched to meet him, and in the next instant they were joined as one.

You and Me. That was his last coherent thought. Time unraveled. A moment passed—or was it an eternity—and then he came apart, shattering into a glorious, glittering oblivion as she echoed his cry.

Tha-thump, tha-thump, tha-thump. Valencia drew in a deep breath as her body slowly came back to earth and the wild surging of her blood mellowed to a thrum of well-being. A sweet, sweet feeling that all was right in the universe. A gentle stirring of air tickled over her bared legs, its whisper the only sound in the room, save for the rapidfire pulse of their hearts beating in perfect rhythm.

Lynsley shifted and drew back a touch,

She tried to step sideways, but her leg buckled slightly.

Sweeping her into his arms, he carried her to the bed. The sensation was strange—she was used to being strong and standing up for herself. It made her feel delicate, fragile, precious. *Feminine.* All the things she was not.

But at that instant, Valencia found herself longing to be a lady. A *real* lady, not a iron-sharp warrior, with a birthright to be part of his exalted world.

Tugging down the coverlet. Lynsley lay her ever so gently on the sheets. In the flickering light of the candle, his eyes had deepened to a luminous ocean blue, subtle and shifting as the sea.

"Come to me, Thomas," she whispered, reaching up to thread a hand through his silky hair,

" Lucifer and all his legions couldn't keep me away," he answered. "But this time, I will try and be a gentlemen, not some ravening beast."

"I rather like to see you with your gentility stripped away," she murmured..

He responded with a husky laugh. "Down to the bare essentials."

"Mano a mano," she whispered.

"Hmmm." He teased a finger across her heated flesh, delving lower, lower.

"Thomas!" she gasped as a jolt of pure pleasure spiraled through her core.

A growled laugh.

Valencia couldn't hold back her response. "Yes, oh, yes."

"Not yet, sweeting."

Withdrawing his tantalizing touch, Lynsley began exploring every inch of her flesh. Their limbs slowly entwined, lips and hands touching, tasting, in a sweetly sublime feast of the senses.

The marquess had not been a monk. He was a skilled lover, gentle, yet passionate—a master of nuance and subtle play.

Pressing a gossamer-soft kiss to her knee, he started to feather his embrace upward.

Valencia tried to force his face away. "It is so ugly", she whispered, ashamed of her scar, and all that it stood for.

Lynsley's mouth touched the puckered skin, and tenderly traced the jagged contours. "It is not a flaw or a failure, Val, but rather a badge of honor."

His words made her want to weep.

"You are beautiful in both body and spirit."

"You have a silver tongue—" Her teasing tightened to a gasp as his kisses inched higher. His stubbled cheek scraped the sensitive skin of her inner thigh, sending shivers of pleasures through her. Their bodies came together, the friction of flesh against flesh igniting a frisson of fire in her core.

Valencia could bear it no longer and moved closer.

Closer. *Two as one.*

Moving in perfect harmony.

"Do you know what the French call an orgasm?" murmured Lynsley, once their hearts had ceased their wild pounding. "*Le petit mort*—the little death."

The little death. Valencia stared up at the ceiling and smiled. Oh, something elemental had died within her tonight—all the old anger and resentment. And something new has taken life. Something she dared not say aloud.

Love. She was in love with Lynsley. And always had been.

But he must never guess.

Holding back a sigh, she snuggled into the crook of his arm, and let herself be lulled to sleep by the gentle rise and fall of his breathing.

Valencia awoke a little later to find his beautiful eyes open and intent on her face.

"Val, I ... I am—"

She covered his mouth with her hand. "If you say you are sorry, I swear, I shall throttle you."

He laughed, his breath warm against her skin. "I'm not sorry," he said. "I am ... I am at a loss to describe my feelings."

"You? Speechless?"

"Bereft of words." A whisper of a smile played on his lips. "Bereft of sanity, of self-control."

"Is that so very bad, Thomas?" she asked hesitantly. "To allow yourself an interlude of personal passion once in a while?"

"Nay, Val. Not bad, but ... dangerous." His lips feathered against her brow, then he rolled on his back, facing up at the darkened ceiling. "You are like an ocean storm, an elemental force of wind and waves that I seem powerless to fight." He laced his hands behind his head. "Yet I must, else I shall be in danger of drowning in desire."

A dappling of moonlight, soft and silvery as spun silk, traced the outline of his profile. The chiseled cheekbones, the aquiline nose, the sculpted lips, now thinned in a half mocking curl—in such a light, his features were not merely austere, aristocratic. They blurred to a far more complex shape.

She knew every nuance of his expression by heart, but the momentary flicker of longing caused the breath to catch in her throat. "I'm not sorry. Not at all."

He turned to look at her, his eyes aswirl with intensity. Their depth seemed go on forever. Unfathomable in their beauty.

"I am not sorry either. Though God help me, I should be."

"Stop feeling guilty," she cried. "You are allowed to be human."

"I could say the same for you," he replied.

Her throat tightened. "You've never failed like I have."

"Oh, but I have. More times than I care to count." He pointed to the scar on his shoulder. "This happened in Italy. A French agent beat me badly, and left my superior with his throat cut. Blood from the severed artery was everywhere, soaking his shirt and mine. It took several minutes for him to die in my arms." Lynsley closed his eyes, as if it might shut out the memory. "So if anything, I bungled an assignment far worse than you can ever imagine, Valencia."

Her eyes softened. "I didn't know."

"No, why would you?"

"How did you deal with it—disappointing not only your compatriots but yourself."

"By getting up and trying again, no matter how much the wounds hurt," he said softly.

"It's damnably hard," she whispered.

"Aye, it is. You blame yourself, and yet you were the only one to suffer the consequences. I failed, and had to watch my closest friend and mentor bleed to death in my arms. Few people in our clandestine world of warfare escape unscathed."

"Oh, Thomas." Valencia drew him into her arms. "What a pair we are. Two scarred soldiers."

He rolled onto his back, dragging her on top of him. "For a duo of aging warriors, we aren't doing too badly."

She arched her back, sinfully aware of the wonderfully wanton sensations against her skin. Her hair spilling in wild tangles across her shoulders. Her legs straddling his hard, flat belly. Her laughter, slipping softly from her kiss-swollen lips.

"It seems we are still capable of rising to the occasion."

"I am not ready to stick my spoon in the wall quite yet," he quipped. "But as for a certain part of anatomy ..."

"Why Lord Lynsley, what a lewd and lascivious innuendo for a gentleman to make."

"Then I shall bite my tongue and let my hands do the talking."

Laughing, she stroked a fingertip along the chiseling of his ribs, drawing a deep groan. Perhaps it was distant thunder, warning of an impending storm. But despite the tempestuous emotions that swirled around them, Valencia felt lightning tingle through her limbs at his responding to her. At this moment, she felt them free from all else but the essence of their bond.

Two bodies, stripped of the doubts, the fears, the differences in rank that had kept them apart for so long. For against all reason. There was a powerful connection between them—it was elemental, impossible to define.

Impossible to deny.

Nothing had ever felt so right.

Lynsley hadn't allowed himself the luxury of mindless decadence since ... since just once, a long, long time ago. The memory still brought the bitter sting of bile to his throat.

Valencia didn't miss the tiny change in his expression. "Thomas?"

He tried to turn to the shadows.

"Tell me what's wrong."

He shook his head.

"You share your strength with me. Share your pain as well," she demanded.

He couldn't bring himself to move his lips.

"Tell me." Her tongue grazed over the grim line of his mouth.

A sweet taste of her essence seeped inside him. He licked his lower lip and groaned.

"Tell me."

Ruthless, ruthless woman. She wouldn't let him retreat.

Her arms came around him, holding him tightly. Like a child.

Lynsley suddenly realized tears were dappling his cheeks. Dear God—he was crying like a babe. "You asked me about the Academy." He managed to murmur. "Do you really wish to know why I started it? It isn't a pretty tale."

"Your secrets are safe with me. Surely you know that," whispered Valencia.

"It's not you I doubt, it is myself."

"Look at me." She bracketed his face with her hands, refusing him any quarter. "You think that I might be repulsed by anything you can say? Revolted."

"God knows, you should be."

"Never!" Her voice was fierce. "You are such a good man, it makes me weep."

"Don't." Lynsley tried to make light of things. "One wailing warrior is enough, else we might drown in salt water before we even set out to sea again. The experience is not one I care to repeat."

"A good try." said Valencia. "But I won't let you wiggle out of this. And go *there*."

"Where?"

"Lord Lynsley's Lair. That dark, dank cave. If you aren't careful, one day it will bury you alive."

"I ..."

"I think you should tell your story, and leave the judgment to me."

"Alright." A leap of faith. "Finding orphans for the Academy was not the first time I had ventured into the stews of St. Giles. I was sixteen, and had a friend ... he was several years older, and I was proud when he and some others invited me to accompany them to a brothel there. I had never lain with a woman, but ..."

"But at that age, it is viewed as a rite of passage," she mused. "A mark of being a man."

"A man," he repeated hollowly. "Oh yes, so it is." A pause. "We passed a place, an expensive establishment, despite the dirt, where men came for young girls. The door opened ..." His eyes shut. "A girl ran out, chased by a gentleman. A very high-born gentleman."

"You recognized him?" asked Valencia.

"Yes," answered Lynsley, his turning voice bleak. "A sancti-monious son of a bitch, known for his speeches in Parliament railing against the drunkenness and depravity of the poor." He sucked in a deep breath. "The bastard beat her, and I simply watched. Did nothing to help."

"Thomas, you were a boy."

"I was old enough to want to bury my own prick in some poor lass's body. I was old enough to know right from wrong. Yet I didn't lift a finger."

Reaching out a hand, she touched his cheek. "You coun-seled me to forgive myself. Now you must do the same."

"I ..."

Her stroking had suddenly turned far, far more intimate.

"Do we teach you that in the Academy?" he asked through a groan of pleasure.

"It's the class before Art History."

"Hmmph." The sound reverberated deep in his throat. "I may have to see about changing the curriculum."

"Why? Did I get a failing grade?" she teased.

"You are *too* well-schooled, Valkyrie," replied Lynsley. "You possess too many weapons ... it's not fair. No man can fight back."

"Discipline. Detachment. Devotion to duty."

He gave a harried chuckle. "Yes, but it is proving damnably difficult."

Valencia's laughter joined with his, but only for an instant. "Then we must take care that I am not a distraction."

"As well as the other way around." Essaying a light tone, Lynsley added, "So for the good of the mission, we had better lock away passion prepare ourselves for tomorrow."

"Right—discipline, detachment, devotion to duty," responded Valencia, repeating her earlier words. Slipping out from beneath the sheets, she gathered her wrapper from the floor.

"*A demain,* Thomas," she whispered before returning to her room.

Lynsley lay awake for a long while, the breeze from the window raising gooseflesh on his naked body. Taking up one of the pillows and clasping it to his chest, he was acutely aware that it was still warm and sweetly scented with her perfume. The lightness of verbena and the darker lushness of exotic spices.

Like a drowning man, he drew in deep lungfuls of air.

Nothing had changed, said the rational part of his brain.

But the rest of his body begged to disagree.

Everything had changed.

He shifted, the rumpled sheets, still damp with their love-making, sent a shiver along his spine.

She had touched him places he had thought too well guarded for anyone to reach. Oh, what hubris to think that he had made himself invincible. *Invulnerable.* For years he had believed that his defenses was impenetrable. Yet they had going up in smoke.

Fool.

He must somehow pile the ashes into some semblance of a wall, must somehow keep his personal feelings separate from the mission.

Always the mission.

It had, by necessity, come between them before. *As it would now.*

There was no other way. She understood it, as did he. Both of them were professionals. Both of them knew it was the right strategy to keep a distance from now on.

This fleeting tryst should cool his ardor. Maybe the attraction would burn out of its own accord. After all it had been banked for ten years, and wild conflagrations were by their very nature over in a flash—a burst of flame, then embers, then ashes and cold coals.

But his heart didn't believe it. She wasn't a passing fancy.

She never had been.

But like other tests of his willpower, he would find a way to come through the fire.

Chapter Nineteen

Steel slashed through the sunlight dappling the Sword Courtyard of Mrs. Merlin's Academy for Extraordinary Young Ladies, the swift thrusts and parries punctuated by the sharp ring of blade against blade.

"Well done," called the fencing instructor as he stepped back and signaled the end to the bout. "Next time, work on keeping your wrist a touch firmer on your ripostes, *bella*. But your footwork is vastly improved."

He cut a last flourish with his saber and pointed at the group of students standing close to the chalked circle. "I trust that the rest of you paid close attention to the techniques we demonstrated today. Tomorrow, I shall expect you all to match Verona's prowess." Cocking his hip, he flashed a grin. "Anyone needing private instruction may come to my quarters this evening. I shall be happy to show off the fine points of wielding a blade."

The student known as Verona made a rude noise.

"I heard that, *signorina*." Marco Moretti della Ghirardelli waggled his weapon. "Have a care that I don't hand out a demerit."

She stuck out her tongue, then turned and stripped off her padded doublet. "Rather a black mark on my record than your lecherous hands on my person, Mr. della Ghiradelli," she retorted with a saucy smile.

He laughed and shooed the group of girls on their way. "Hurry, or you will be late for Ballistics."

"The training is coming along nicely, Marco," murmured Mrs. Merlin as she watched the students file off to their next class.

"*Si.*" He wiped his brow. "She is good—damn good."

The headmistress nodded. "Yes, she is almost ready." A feathery sigh escaped her lips. "Another few weeks ..." Her voice trailed off.

Marco cocked an inquiring brow. "You have a mission in mind for her, *signora?*"

"Not anymore. Lord Lynsley decided it could not wait."

He frowned. "But none of the students has been sent on assignment."

"No." A long pause. "He went himself."

The fencing master muttered a rather colorful oath in Italian. "If His Lordship considered that the Merlins were not up for the job, he could have turned to me."

"The perils were prodigious," replied Mrs. Merlin. "And the stakes extraordinarily high." The wrinkles around her eyes deepened. "He did not wish to ask anyone else to face the dangers."

Marco swore again. "*Porca miseria,* he should not be risking his life in the field. The action ought to be left to someone like me, who is half his age."

"Don't let him hear you so." The headmistress allowed a faint smile. "The marquess does not consider himself quite past his prime."

"True," admitted Marco. "During our weekly training sessions, I am hard-pressed to best his skills with a saber or foil." He pulled a face. "And in the saddle, we run neck and neck."

There was a sliver of silence, broken only by the tapping of the fencing instructor's blade against his boot.

"Where is he?" Marco finally asked. "Somewhere on the Eastern front, trying to intercept the Emperor's retreat from Russia?"

"No, he's gone straight to the lion's den, as it were." Mrs. Merlin watched the sun playing hide and seek with scudding clouds for a moment before adding, "The City of Light—Paris."

"Paris!" Marco's dismay took on an even sharper edge. "What the devil is he after?"

Despite his outward air of cocksure swagger, Marco was a trusted member of the Merlins. The headmistress did not hesitate in giving a terse explanation of the mission.

"Let us hope that things are now going as planned," she added. "The trip got off to a stormy start."

"How so?" asked Marco.

"The marquess's sloop went down in a gale while crossing the Channel," she replied. "But by some miracle he survived and washed up ashore on the isle of Sark. From there, he somehow managed passage to Normandy. Last word I had, he had made it to Paris."

"How the devil does he plan to get close to Rochambert?" demanded Marco.

"By masquerading as an American consul for commerce." Her mouth curled up slightly at the corners. "The real envoy is apparently enjoying a prolonged stay in countryside of Normandy, courtesy of the marquess's network of operatives in that area."

"Any trouble so far?"

Mrs. Merlin lifted her shoulders in response. "As you know, communication is very dangerous from the heart of the enemy capital. His last message said only that he had arrived without incident, and we are not to expect further word."

Marco shifted his sword from hand to hand. "I suppose we must be satisfied with that."

Mrs. Merlin sighed. "I am no more happy about it than you are, Marco. However, we really have no choice but to trust that Lord Lynsley has not lost his edge."

"Si," he muttered.

But there was a mutinous gleam in his eye as he turned to put away his weapons.

Valencia dropped her gaze from the looking glass and fussed with the folds of her dress, pleating the textured silk to knife-edged precision. Perhaps she should have chosen the emerald jouquille instead ...

With a silent oath, she quickly untangled her fingers from the sash. Hell, she mustn't act like a nervous schoolgirl, about to face a difficult test. Lynsley was no longer her superior, he was her—

No. She must not think of him as that either. They were compatriots, allies in a formidable mission that demanded every ounce of their expertise. What had happened last night was perhaps inevitable when a man and a woman were thrown together in a powderkeg situation. Two strong-willed individuals rubbing together were bound to set off sparks.

Her mouth quirked. They were certainly old enough to act maturely about the matter. The marquess was not about to get down on bended knee and offer to do the honorable thing. Their profession had no conventional rules.

No future, save for surviving the moment.

That she had been in love with him for half of her life was a passion that had no place in their world. It must be locked back in the deepest recesses of her heart, so as not to interfere with the assignment. She must not make it difficult for Lynsley to order her into danger.

Her own schedule for the day presented little threat, mused Valencia as she entered the breakfast room. She was slated to attend an afternoon tea given by Madame Levalier, where the only weapons were likely to be teaspoons and butter knives. The boredom would be sharp, she thought wryly, but it was important to go through the motions of being a proper diplomatic wife.

"*Bonjour*, madame." One of the footmen offered a folded note along with her morning coffee. "Monsieur left this for you."

"Thank you," she replied. *Tactful Thomas*. Allowing the initial awkwardness to dissipate over the day was precisely the sort of thing he would think of.

Swallowing a sigh, Valencia opened the paper. She rather envied the fact that he could release any pent-up tension in the spins and sweat of his early morning exercises. For an instant, she was tempted to order a horse saddled and join him in the secluded spot, clearing the lingering languor from her limbs with the clash of steel.

But the crackle of foolscap quickly chased any such madcap desires from her head as she read over the note.

Bloody hell. What the devil was he up to?

Lynsley checked through the document folder once more, then tied the strings tight. That should whet Rochambert's appetite, he thought grimly. *Enough so to turn his jaws away from Valencia?*

Not for long. But even before last night, he had determined

that it was time to make a move. They could not continue this charade indefinitely.

He finished his coffee and angled his chair for a better view of the boulevard. Would Rochambert take the bait? The Frenchman might have spent the night at the brothel, or still be languishing in some other den of sin. In which case, he would have to find time later in the day to slip away from his ministry meetings.

"*Voila.*" The street urchin darted around the café tables and came to a halt in front of Lynsley. "I have your answer, monsieur. The man will see you."

"*Merci.*" The marquess placed a coin in the boy's grimy palm. Taking up his walking stick and case, he then paid his bill and proceeded up the street at a leisurely pace.

Would gaining access to Rochambert's private quarters help in the hunt for his objective? It was hard to say, but he had decided the change in tactics was worth the try. The prospect of winning more kudos from Napoleon might be as strong a lure for the Frenchman as the lust for Valencia's body.

To that end, Lynsley had gathered a few choice samples from Tobias Daggett's government documents. The chance to acquire American secrets should be compelling, especially ones concerning its intentions of Western expansion. All of Europe knew that Napoleon was very concerned about the vast territories bordering Mexico, now that Spain was under his thumb.

It was, mused Lynsley, a dirty trick to play on Mr. Madison. However, the American president was a clever man. He and his Congress had shown themselves able to defend the young republic against outside forces ...

The front door of the mansion opened and a liveried footman escorted him up the stairs.

Rochambert was waiting in his private study, clad in a brocade dressing gown and tasseled Turkish slippers. Raising a glass of brandy in salute, he asked, "A drink, Monsieur Daggett?"

Lynsley shook his head. "I am here for business, not pleasure," he growled.

"Do you never relax? I noticed that you did not linger long at the Palaise Royal last night, either," purred the Frenchman. He made a *tssskking* sound. "You Americans are far too serious. Or perhaps you find pleasure enough in the marriage bed." A lazy wink. "I must say, Madame Daggett is certainly a tasty-looking morsel."

He ignored the provocation. "I assume you read my note. Is your Emperor hungry for a look at what I have to offer?"

"That depends, Monsieur." Rochambert sat on the edge of his desk and appeared to be thinking it over. "Very well, I shall have a look."

Lynsley made a surreptitious survey of the surroundings as he untied his case and withdrew a sample document. "If you wish to know the innermost thoughts of the president and his cabinet, it is all here. But it will cost you." He named a high price. "The information is accurate, and can't be gotten anywhere else. So it should be worth a great deal to your Emperor."

Rochambert studied document for several long moments. "Naturally, I have a few questions." Looking up, the Frenchman was quick with a number of probing queries.

Smiling inwardly, Lynsley answered them all smoothly. As a master of interrogation techniques, he had anticipated every angle and had rehearsed the perfect replies.

Pursing his lips, Rochambert read over the document one last time, then set it down. He named a figure considerably less than the price demanded.

Lynsley made a counter offer.

Without replying, the Frenchman walked across the room

and opened a wall safe. Though muffled by soft leather, the chink of gold was audible as he sorted through its interior.

In the moments that Rochambert had his back turned, the marquess flicked a look around the room, making mental note of places where a valuable object might be hidden. However, his instincts told him the thing he sought was kept somewhere else.

"A down payment," said Rochambert as he returned and tossed down a purse. "I'll buy the rest when I see them, assuming they are of the same quality."

"Be assured that they are," said Lynsley.

"I will let you know when and where to bring them."

The marquess knew the haughty reply was a dismissal and turned away with further words. But as he reached the doorway, Rochambert added, "By the by, how is your wife feeling? Does she often take a *tumble?*"

The sneering sexual innuendo was crudely done. Still, Lynsley felt a welling of rage rise in his throat. However, he masked his emotions with a chill smile as he looked back at the Frenchman. "She is quite recovered, thank you. I have warned her again about the danger of not watching her step on unfamiliar ground. I believe she won't make the mistake again."

"And yet, some woman have trouble reining in their impulses." Rochambert spun his letter opener between his palms. "Madame Daggett appears to be a woman who can't resist a challenge."

Their gazes clashed, a silent shiver of steel against steel.

Lynsley didn't flinch. "Be assured, Rochambert. Certain things in my possession are available to the highest bidder. And certain things are not for sale at any price. Do I make myself clear?"

"Quite, monsieur." The Frenchman lifted his glass of brandy to his lips, a malicious gleam lighting his eye. "However, if something is offered for free ..."

The marquess left Rochambert's taunt to trail off in a soft laugh.

He who laughs last ... The Frenchman's hubris could be turned against him, of that Lynsley was sure. And that moment couldn't come too soon.

Valencia chuffed a sigh of relief as she climbed into the carriage. As she had feared, the afternoon had been a tedious bore. However, the time had not been wasted. Sumptuous cakes and confections had been served, and yet several of the ladies had been more hungry for gossip than sugar and buttercream. Between dainty bites they had asked probing questions about her and Lynsley—the discord had, of course, been noticed—and so she had been able to hint that the relationship was not all sweetness and spice. The whispers of strife would no doubt reach Rochambert's ears quickly ...

"And then be turned to our advantage," Valencia murmured aloud. Flexing her shoulders, she leaned back against the squabs. Waiting was becoming more and more difficult. "I am trained for action, not sitting around swathed in silks and satins."

Hurrying up the townhouse stairs, she inquired whether Lynsley had returned, and was quickly directed to the main parlor by the nervous-looking footman.

A bad sign, thought Valencia. The premonition was quickly confirmed by the marquess.

"Ah, there you are, my dear," said Lynsley in a low voice. He motioned her to join him by the windows overlooking the street, where the noise from the traffic would help hide their voices from any prying ears. Their private servants were already standing by his side, looking grim-faced.

"I was just explaining that we had an unsettling incident

happen here earlier this afternoon while Perkins and I were out running some errands for His Lordship," said Bailin. "Our steward went down to the wine cellar, and somehow the door snapped shut and tripped the lock, trapping him for nearly an hour before his absence was noticed.

Perkins gave a huff of skepticism. "And during that time, your bedchambers were searched. The other servants claim they were all engaged in various tasks and did not see any intruders."

"Aye," muttered Bailin. "My questions were met with Gallic shrugs. No one saw anything, or so they claim"

"Has the break-in been reported to the authorities?" asked Lynsley.

"Aye, sir. An inspector came by, but he spent most of his time interrogating me," answered his valet.

"I think we all know this is no random street crime," said Valencia slowly. "Though whether they are suspicious of us, or simply want to see what American secrets they can steal is uncertain."

The marquess stared out the window. "The longer we play at this charade, the more dangerous it becomes. We must make a move."

"And soon," added Valencia.

He nodded, his brow furrowing in thought as he contemplated the play of gold-flecked light on the limestone sill. "I shall have to think on what it should be."

"As to that," she said quickly. "I have an idea."

His gaze swung around—reluctantly, or so it seemed to her. "I have a feeling that I'm not going to like it."

"Probably not. But we all know that emotion can never be allowed to interfere with the planning of a mission."

A tiny muscle twitched as Lynsley tightened his jaw.

"Rochambert is hungry to get me into his bed. I think I should feed myself to his lust."

"And then?" asked Lynsley tersely.

"I shall either drug his wine or cut his throat, and then search his private quarters. I've heard whispers among the other ladies that he banishes his servants to the attics when he has a female guest. Apparently he has a taste for rough play."

"Absolutely not." The marquess's voice was no louder than a whisper but it carried an unmistakable note of command. "I've begun a game of my own with our quarry, tempting him with American secrets." He explained about offering to sell the captured documents. "That's where I was this morning. He'll want more, and soon. I have a feeling what we want is in the library, and once I have a chance to reconnoiter a bit more—"

"But you just said yourself that Rochambert will set the time and place for your next meeting. There is no guarantee when it will be arranged, or whether it will be at his mansion."

Silence.

"However, we do know that he will be at home the day after tomorrow—and that we will be dancing and dining in his elegant residence." Rochambert was hosting a fancy soiree, and they were among the invited guests. "It presents a perfect opportunity."

"You can't simply waltz into his arms," said Lynsley. "To have any chance of success, a plan would have to be choreographed down to the last little intricate step."

Valencia didn't bat an eye. "I assumed you would have it no other way." A discreet nod dismissed Bailin and Perkins. "So, here is what I have in mind ..."

A half hour later they were still in a verbal duel.

"There are too many unknowns," insisted Lynsley.

"A Merlin is trained to improvise," she countered. "Damnation, we shouldn't be fighting over this, Thomas. How many times have you reminded me that we must be dispassionate about making our decisions? It's our duty to do what is best for the mission."

"To hell with duty," he growled. "I cannot in good conscience let you try something so dangerous."

"If the roles were reversed, would you allow me to offer such an argument?"

His stone sphinx face betrayed a crack. "It's ... different."

"Why?" pressed Valencia, allowing him no quarter. "If you say it is because I am a female, I swear, I shall slice off your ... tongue."

A grudging laugh cut the tension between them. "God forbid. As head of the Merlins, I know better than to challenge your skill with a blade or bullets." Lynsley's twitching lips stilled. "Nonetheless, I must ask that you abide by your promise to follow my orders."

She shook her head. "Not when your sense of *noblesse oblige* is putting the mission in jeopardy. It is because of *me* that you are compromising your decisions. Guilt is coloring your judgment."

"You are fighting dirty," he whispered after a long moment.

"That is what Merlins are trained to do. Those are the principles that you taught us to believe in—sometimes it is necessary to sacrifice personal feelings for the higher good."

He turned to stare out up at the thickening clouds. Silhouetted against the storm grey hue, his profile was pale as carved marble. She had never seen him look so bleak. "I don't need my words thrown back in my face."

"Oh, but I think you do." Valencia hated herself for doing this. She knew how much he was hurting inside. "The mission, Thomas. That is why both of us are here."

"*If*—I repeat, *if*—I agree to this plan, you must in turn

promise to let me work out the details and agree to abide by my instructions."

"Yes, *sir*," she quipped.

He didn't smile. "I'm deadly serious, Valencia."

"So am I, Thomas. And together we will bury Rochambert in the deepest pit in Hell, where he belongs."

Chapter Twenty

Music drifted out from the ballroom, mingling with the lilt of laughter and the crystalline *clink* of champagne glasses. Gliding past a group of guests heading to the card room, Valencia crossed the corridor and entered the gallery displaying Rochambert's art collection, where she paused to admire a pair of ornately framed paintings. Candlelight flickered across the canvases, adding a sensuous golden glow to the rich color of the pigments.

"You like Fragonard?" asked Rochambert, as he came up behind her.

As Valencia had hoped, the Frenchman had followed her. The heavy velvet draperies had fallen back in place across the doorway, muting the sounds of the sumptuous buffet being served in the main dining salon.

"Very much," she answered. "I find the lushness of his figures appealing. As is their earthy enjoyment of the world around them." Cocking her head, she drew out her study of the painting for a moment longer before meeting his gaze. "American art is so flat and colorless in comparison. It must be their Calvinist background." She touched his sleeve. "They worship hard work and frugality. Enjoying the fruits of one's labors seems to be a cardinal sin."

"You make life in America sound very dull for a lady who appreciates art," said Rochambert. His gaze sharpened with a speculative glitter. *The predator on the prowl.* Scenting his prey was ripe for the taking. "Would you care to see the paintings in my private gallery? They are even more interesting for those who have a discerning eye."

She slid her hand to the crook of his elbow. "How can I resist such an offer?"

Rochambert led her into an alcove at the back of the ornate room, where a paneled door of polished oak was flanked by two gilded wall sconces. "Are you looking for something in particular from me, Madame Daggett?" he murmured in her ear.

"Why, an education on art," she replied archly. "You are said to be quite a connoisseur in the field."

A laugh rumbled deep in his throat. "I daresay my knowledge won't disappoint you."

"I was rather hoping you would say that." Valencia added a a sultry laugh as she watched him slip a keyring from his coat pocket.

How interesting. It requires two keys to open the double lock.

She felt a sudden tickling at the back of her neck that had nothing to do with the hand that was now teasing down the line of her spine.

Rochambert's art was unquestionably valuable. But enough so to require specially designed military hardware to guard against thieves? Valencia recognized the distinctive locking mechanism. Made by a small supplier in Marseilles, it was issued for use in highly sensitive areas such as a command headquarters, a cryptography copyroom ... a munitions warehouse.

Sparks flared as the Frenchman struck a flint and lit the branch of candles set on a stone pediment inside the door.

No—on second glance, she saw that it wasn't a pediment but an oversized penis, sculpted of pure white marble.

"Welcome to my private gallery room, Madame Daggett." He drew her inside. "As you see, I take pleasure in being surrounded by things of great beauty."

"Naughty man," she scolded, taking care to sound not the slightest bit outraged.

"Come, let me give you a tour of my treasures." Dropping all pretense of proper etiquette, he sidled closer, his touch growing bolder with every step. Already she could feel the flat of his hand creeping down her *derriere.* "Here are several of my most recent acquisitions. He pointed out a pair of nudes by Peter Paul Rubens. "What do you think?"

"They are magnificent. A feast for the eyes."

"But not as magnificent as you, *cherie.*" His lips nuzzled the nape of her neck. "Your breasts are even more luscious. When do I get a taste?"

Valencia dodged the question. "I see you have quite a collection of allegorical paintings here." She gazed up at the scene of Zeus shedding his disguise as a swan in order to ravage Leda. "The Greeks gods were certainly a randy lot."

"They possessed the power to take what they wanted. Why should they play by the rules of mere mortals?" said Rochambert.

"An interesting observation, monsieur." She moved on to the next canvas. "Do you see yourself as being above other men?"

"*Moi?*" The reflection from the gilt frame played over his face. "Like Napoleon, I believe that some men are destined to rise above their compatriots." He winked, setting off sparks from his gold-tipped lashes. "The ladies do call me *le beaux ange.*

The handsome angel.

"Because you transport them to heaven?" Turning, Valencia spied a marble plinth, half hidden in the shadows of a leering sculpted satyr. On it sat a brass box, decorated with an intricate interweaving of copper and silver latticework. The design was distinctly Arabic ...

Her heart skidded and lurched up against her ribs. *Steady, steady*, she warned herself.

"What an unusual pattern," she remarked. "It looks like something out of Aladdin's treasure cave. Or perhaps it's Pandora's Box. Shall we dare to have a look inside?"

"No need to bother. It's quite empty." Rochambert was quick to steer her away. "Indeed, it's just an old curio left over from a trip to Cairo. I have been meaning to have it moved to cellars." He leaned in to nibble at her earlobe.

Valencia allowed herself to be distracted.

"You have the most exquisite eyes," he murmured. "They are a compelling, shade of green—like liquid emeralds, shimmering with the depth of a seagreen ocean.

She slid a teasing hand around his neck, and let it trail down his spine to his derriere. "La, and you, sir, have a golden tongue. Tell me, are all Frenchman such lyrical poets as well as incorrigible flirts?"

"Oh, I think you will find that I am quite unique."

"You are very sure of yourself," she said, tapping a finger to his chin.

He caught it and slowly suckled its tip. "*Oui*, and with good reason."

"What a provocative answer." She rubbed her thigh against his, and then pulled away with a breathy sigh. "I should like to hear why, but alas, we had best return to the other guests. I wouldn't want to provoke my husband into making a scene."

"Should I be afraid of the old man calling me out? Sabers at dawn?" Rochambert's laugh was a low, leering scoff. "In a show of swordsmanship, Monsieur Daggett would not show to advantage."

Valencia hid her disgust with a flutter of her lashes. "You consider yourself quite a dashing blade?"

"The best on the Continent," he replied. "I have cut a rather large swath through the boudoirs of Europe."

"Leaving a trail of broken hearts, no doubt," she murmured. *Not to speak of severed throats and shattered limbs.*

His mouth pursed to a preening purse. "What can I say? Women seem to find me irresistible."

"Some might call that arrogance, Monsieur Rochambert."

"Perhaps." He stepped closer and captured his wrist. The feel of his bare flesh made her skin crawl. "But I assure you, *ma belle* Valencia, a night in my bed would be well worth it." The champagne sweetness of his breath was growing hot and heavy with lust. "The word 'pleasure' does not begin to describe what you would experience in my arms."

Indeed, it did not. For an instant, she saw naught but a scrawl of red letters spelling out 'revenge.' However, they disappeared in the blink of an eye.

Redemption. A chance to prove herself worthy of Lynsley's trust.

Yet it took all of her resolve not to recoil when Rochambert pulled her hand down and pressed it against his arousal.

Forcing a suggestive smile, she tittered. "You make quite a convincing case for yourself, monsieur—"

"Pierre," he interrupted. "Seeing as we can consider ourselves intimate friends."

"Pierre." Valencia mouthed it softly, hoping it sounded seductive, rather than as if she were spitting out a mouthful of rancid wine.

"The next time you say it, *ma cherie*, you shall be panting, pleading for me to pleasure you."

Teasing her palm along his length, she inched back. "Let us return to the main gallery I have an idea of how to deal with my husband."

Rochambert looked loath to delay his seduction, but gave a tight smile. "Do it quickly, *cherie*. I am not used to waiting for what I want."

Valencia gave him another teasing caress. "La, be assured you will soon get what you so richly deserve."

"I shall hold you to that promise," he said, stopping to seize her in a long and lush kiss.

As he pawed at her breasts, Valencia feigned a moan of pleasure—and eased the key from his coat pocket.

"Ah, there you are, m'dear." Lynsley stumbled slightly as he entered the private gallery. "My, my, m'dear, you've taken quite an interest in art lately." His words were badly slurred. "And it appears that French figurative painting has become a particular favorite."

"Really, Thomas. There is no need to make a scene," replied Valencia coolly. "Mr. Rochambert was merely showing me his collection of Baroque paintings."

"Ballocks," snarled Lynsley. "The man was all but mounting you in full view of anyone who cared to look into the room. I warn you, I won't allow your wanton behavior to ruin all I have worked for."

"Perhaps if your lovemaking was as finely honed as your greed, your wife would not have to look elsewhere for companionship." Rochambert cocked a malicious smile as he looked from the marquess to her. "By the by, did you know your husband is selling your country's secrets to me? So any lecture on honor from his lips isn't worth a dribble of spit."

With a roar of rage, Lynsley lunged for the Frenchman.

"Stop it!" Darting in between the two men, Valencia

grabbed the marquess by the shoulders and forced him back. "For God's sake, none of us wishes a sordid scandal."

"Quite right," said Rochambert. "A duel with a diplomat would displease the Emperor. So I shall refrain from handing you your prick on a platter, Monsieur Daggett."

Lynsley answered with a foul-mouthed curse, but made no move to resume his physical attack.

"Please, Pierre," she warned in an undertone.

"Pierre, is it now?" growled Lynsley. "Does the intimacy extend to letting the mongrel shove his paws up your skirts?"

Valencia tightened her grip on the marquess's lapels. "Do get a hold on your temper, Thomas," she counseled. "You know you are wont to overreact when you have too much to drink."

"Hmmph." He relaxed slightly.

"That's better." She patted his chest, coyly winding the tail of his cravat around her little finger. "Come, let me take you back to the supper table. I daresay a little *crème caramel* will sweeten your mood."

Lynsley's voice ratcheted up to a querulous whine. "I need another glass of champagne."

"Yes, yes, and I shall see that you have it." Slanting Rochambert an sidelong look, she mouthed the word "later" as she slipped her arm around Lynsley's waist.

His mouth curling in contempt, the Frenchman nodded.

"This way, darling." A harried sigh covered the whisper she breathed into his ear. "The key to the door is in your pocket. There's a brass box in here. I think it holds what we want"

Lynsley swayed against her. "Are you sure?" he asked in the same hushed tone.

Valencia hesitated a heartbeat before replying. "Yes." Raising her voice, she uttered a sharp oath. "Pierre, help me get him out of here, before he pukes all over your priceless Oriental carpet."

"Merde." Rochambert grabbed the marquess's other arm and hustled him none too gently toward the main door of the side salon. Lynsley hung like a dead weight between them, somehow managing to tangle legs with the Frenchman just as they reached the threshold.

Rochambert struggled to keep the marquess's flailing feet from soiling his immaculate fawn-colored trousers as they hustled Lynsley into the alcove of the *salle.* "One spot and you are a dead man, regardless of the Emperor's ire," he muttered, jerking Lynsley upright.

Valencia quickly nudged the private gallery door closed with her hip. She, too, could improvise. Lynsley's playacting was proving a powerful diversion. A last little maneuver on her part should keep the Frenchman distracted.

"I can try to hold him if you need to find your key." She knew that the La Chaze locks snapped shut on spring loaded mechanisms. "But please hurry. I fear he is drooling on my new satin slippers."

"Non, not necessary." The Frenchman grunted in disgust. ""Here, let me try to rouse him." A sharp slap punctuated his words. *"Alors,* Daggett. Listen carefully—to avoid an unpleasant scene, I suggest you depart by the side stairs. One of my servants will summon your carriage."

Lynsley's eyes fluttered open. "Leaving my wife to seek solace in your arms?" Wrenching free, he staggered sideways and threw a wobbly punch that missed Rochambert's chin by a mile. "You, sir, are a scoundrel. And you, madam, are a slut."

His shouts were beginning to attract the attention of the other guests. Several people were already gathering to observe the commotion.

"Daggett, you go too far—" warned Rochambert.

"As far as I'm concerned, I can't go far enough to escape from the two of you." Weaving an erratic path, he staggered out to the main corridor and disappeared into the darkness of the side stairwell..

"*Cochon*," muttered the Frenchman. "Your pig of a husband is playing a dangerous game, *cherie*. He has no idea who he is dealing with."

"I hope you will forgive me for allowing Thomas to spoil your soiree." Valencia pinched her voice to a note of sharp resentment. "He will sleep for two days, then wake and act as if nothing happened."

The anger in Rochambert's eyes flickered to a different sort of heat. "That gives you ample time to apologize for your husband's bad manners."

"I daresay I can come up with a show of suitable contrition." She flashed a sultry smile. "Send your guests home quickly and give the servants the rest of the night off."

Lynsley crouched in the shadows of the side portico, watching the guests file out to the waiting carriages. *So far, so good.* The plan of ending the party early seemed to be going as scheduled. But the idea of Valencia alone with a murderous miscreant had him counting the seconds.

To rush would be a grave mistake, he reminded himself. She was tough, and trained to handle any threat. *She was a Merlin.*

Still, his hands were shaking as he checked that the small equipment bag was strapped snugly to his back. He had stripped off his evening clothes and was now clad all in black— dark shirt, dark trousers, a loose jacket fitted with a number of hidden pockets. And weapons, of course.

Not that he wouldn't kill Rochambert with his bare hands if need be.

Flexing his fingers, he knotted a pirate style scarf around his head and tugged the silk low on his brow. Lordly scruples were under wraps from here on. Like a bloodthirsty buccaneer, he would give no quarter.

No mercy.

The front door of the mansion closed, and the faint scrape of a bar being slid into place signaled that the last of the party had taken their leave. Shaking out a thin coil of rope, Lynsley tossed the iron grappling hook up to the steeply pitched slates of the mansard roof. It caught in the decorative stonework, and after testing its hold, he rose, swift and silent as a hawk.

He had wedged a shim in the *salle de manger* window, preventing the brass lock from catching. A flick of his knife-point would allow him entry. From there, he had mapped out a route to the art gallery using his knowledge of the floorplan to take advantage of all the nooks and shadows. By now, he knew every square inch of the mansion by heart.

Including the master bedroom suite, replete with a bristling array of whips and chains.

No—he would not allow his mind to go there.

Valencia had unequivocal orders not to enter that room. Lynsley prayed that she would obey. She had given him her word, but in the heat of battle, resolve sometimes gave way to a far more primal emotion.

A thrust of his blade opened the latch.

After closing the casement, he ducked under the long table and cracked open the door. Silence shrouded the darkened corridor. A single sconce flickered at the far end, casting swirling patterns over the ornate carvings of staircase. The only other sign of life was a sliver of light showing from under the door of the main salon.

Lynsley forced himself to pass without a pause.

Timing was key. There was not a moment to lose. The plan called for Valencia to spend no more than half an hour alone with Rochambert before withdrawing to the appointed rendezvous spot.

But as an experienced agent, he knew all too well how plans could go awry.

"Ah, alone at last." Valencia perched a hip on the arm of the sofa. "Pour us a glass of cognac."

"I would rather taste your honeyed sweetness on my tongue." Threading a hand through her hair, Rochambert pulled back her head and covered her mouth with a bruising kiss. "And that is just the beginning of all the ways I shall take pleasure in your flesh." His voice was rough as he released her. "I've a book in my bedchamber from India. A manual of all the exotic positions a woman can use to satisfy a man."

"The *Kama Sutra*—oh, yes, I am familiar with it." Valencia watched his lips curl into a wolfish smile. " But what's the hurry? As you know, one of the little lessons in its pages is that anticipation adds to the climax."

"I have waited long enough," he rasped.

"A little longer won't kill you." She slipped free and danced to the sideboard. "Let us toast to the coming night."

"You like to tease?"

"Most men find the chase heats the blood." She poured a splash of spirits and lifted it to her lips. "Do you?"

Rochambert sauntered over and drained his drink in one gulp. "Oh yes, I enjoy the hunt." His hand flattened on her back and slide like a snake down her spine. "There is a powerful thrill in moving closer and closer, knowing that your quarry has no chance for escape."

"Some ladies might find the idea frightening." She sidled back with a saucy swoosh of her skirts. "What if I screamed?"

"My servants are trained to ignore any such noises." His

laugh quickly died to rumbled growl. "You see, I like it when a woman moans and begs. And in my bedchamber, I've a number of interesting implements to encourage such cries."

"It sounds intriguing." Valencia hid her disgust behind a titter. "Do tell me more."

As he launched into a lengthy boast of his sexual prowess, she listened with only half an ear, her mind working furiously to devise ways to draw out her teasing. She was well aware that she was walking on a razor's edge. Rochambert's lust was honed to the point of snapping. The smallest misstep would be fatal.

Her cut crystal glass cast a dancing of light over the gilded sideboard. A decade was a long time to be out of practice. Perhaps her skills had grown sluggish, hobbled by crippling memories of old mistakes. Even at her best, she had slipped at the critical moment.

Doubt could cut deeper than any knife. And yet, Lynsley had faith that she was up for the task. A small smile played on her lips. Perhaps it was time to leave the ghost of the past behind.

Spinning around, she began a flouncing walk around the perimeter of the room. "Why don't you go get your book and bring it here? We'll whet our appetite for the coming night with its pictures and another bottle of champagne."

Rochambert rose and followed her with a slow, stalking step. "I'm hungry enough already, *cherie*." He caught her wrist and turned her around.

"Just a tiny taste, now," she murmured, kissing the corner of his mouth. "Trust me, I have some very sweet ways of stimulating your senses."

His hand slipped down to her hip. "So far, I've had little to sink my teeth into.

"I promise, you not be disappointed."

Valencia was about to sidle away when he suddenly shoved

her against the wall, his forearm pinning her throat with crushing force. Before she could react, he yanked up her skirts, the ruffled silk skimming over her knees and her thigh. His nails dug into her scar, tracing its jagged length.

"Alors, what have we here? His fingers shifted, finding the slim stiletto held by her garter. "Enough of your coquettish games, *cherie*." Whipping the weapon from its sheath, Rochambert pressed the point to her jugular. "Who the devil are you?"

Chapter Twenty-One

lick. Click. Click. The tumblers of the brass box's lock yielded to Lynsley's probe with surprising ease. Rochambert had been confident that his secrets were safe enough within the guarded gallery.

Too confident.

He set aside his tools and slowly opened the lid. Hopefully, the Frenchman had grown lazy about other precautions as well. His own deliberate drunken staggers had already confirmed that Rochambert's whipcord muscles had gone a bit fleshy and the Frenchman's reflexes were just a hair slow. That was good, for he and Valencia would need every advantage they could get.

Valencia. Lynsley forced his breathing to remain tightly controlled as he unfolded the sheaf of parchment set atop the array of bottles. He must think of nothing but the mission and maintain an ice-cold resolve that nothing would be allowed to stand in the way of its success. But against all reason, against all will, Valencia had melted his reserve with her courage, her commitment, her passion. Her friendship. The memory of their bodies joined in lovemaking warmed him to the core.

Was love a weakness or a strength?

Lynsley stared at the scrawls of ink. That was up to him to decipher.

Smoothing out the sheets of paper, he set to work. The original notes, torn from a lined ledger and showing a smattering of telltale bloodstains, were a jumble of incomprehensible letters. A fresh set of foolscap showed that someone had been working on breaking the code. A Caesar shift had been tried and discarded, along with several other basic techniques.

He turned the page to find a Vigenere Square had been set up. So, Rochambert knew a thing or two about cryptography. Lynsley skimmed the variations and slowly smiled. But not quite enough to read between the lines. Taking up his pencil, he tried a few variations of his own. He had precious little time to devote to the process, yet understanding just what he had at his fingertips could be crucial. Knowledge was, after all, the ultimate weapon.

Deju vu.

Despite the cold tongue of steel pressed up against her throat, Valencia managed a calm reply. "Why, simply a lady who takes precautions. Of course I carry a knife. As you see, I've suffered the consequences of not being prepared to deal with an angry man."

"Who cut you?" he demanded.

"A ship captain in Martinique. He felt he hadn't received the services he had paid for."

Rochambert angled the blade a bit higher. "You lie nearly as well as I do, *cherie*. But as a master artist, I recognize my own work."

Valencia felt the razored edge cut a tiny nick in her flesh.

"Who are you?" he repeated.

She clenched her jaw.

"Silence? Yes, I remember that about you," he sneered. "Most women scream like a stuck pig when the blade bites into their flesh. But you—you never uttered a sound." The knifepoint slowly lifted and circled the tip of her left breast. "I always wondered how it was that a woman was my adversary that night. But lately, I have heard the strangest rumors. Rumors about a special flock of women warriors."

Slowly but surely, he sliced away a scrap of silk from her bodice. "The Merlins, eh? Well, I shall take pleasure in finally plucking your feathers."

She willed herself to keep a poker face.

"But first, I want to know exactly who you are working for. I want the name of the man who controls the clandestine operations for the British here in France." Rochambert paused, seeming to savor the thought. "The Emperor will pay a fortune for that information."

"The British?" Valencia shattered her silence with a harsh laugh. "The sodding pricks at Whitehall cast me off like soiled laundry when I was no longer any use to them. I have no love lost for *les Beefsteaks*. No, I work strictly for myself these days."

"*Oui?* And how does Daggett fit into the game?"

"There is no reason not to tell you. He really is my husband," she replied. It was worth a bluff. "After you left me crippled, I wasn't much use to the British anymore. So I went to the Caribbean, where I chanced to meet Daggett. He decided my skills might prove useful in helping him rise to a position of power in the American government, so we struck a bargain."

A flicker of uncertainty clouded his gaze. "Why come to me with the American documents?"

"Revenge of a sort," she admitted. "I knew, of course, that you were one of Napoleon's favorites, so it seemed logical that you would have the authority to take advantage of an opportune offer." She paused. "By the by, how did you know it was me?"

"Your eyes, *cherie*. Even obscured by the mists and your mask, their shape and spark were memorable." He bared his teeth in the same serpentine smile she had seen so many times in her nightmares.

"I see. A miscalculation on my part."

His mouth stretched wider. "Far more formidable people than you have tried to outwit me, *cherie*. None have succeeded. "But do go on. I am curious as to how you and Daggett meant to try it."

Valencia thought for a moment, then continued improvising. "Once you had paid handsomely for the secrets, the plan was for me to seduce you, then steal them back from your library while you slept. Thomas would then resell them to someone in the Ministry. Part of the deal would be a favorable trade agreement. And so, we would return to America with both money and a good deal of political coin to parlay into future profit."

"Very clever," said Rochambert. "In many ways, you are a woman after my own heart."

How very true. And if she had to crawl back from Hades to do it, she would see that it ceased to beat, thought Valencia. The Frenchman had caused enough evil. It was high time to stop him.

"But you would never have succeeded in getting at the documents. No one can get at my private—" A curse cut off his boast as he felt in his pocket and discovered that his keys were missing. "Why, you little bitch!"

She glanced at the clock. Had she given Lynsley enough leeway?

"You should have left well enough alone." Rochambert struck her, a hard blow to the face that knocked her to the carpet. "This time, I'll finish the job of mincing your flesh into pieces for pigeon pie."

She pretended to be stunned as he wrenched her to her feet. At this moment he was confident that he held the upper hand, for after all, this was the second time he had her at his mercy. But she was no longer the downy chick who had fought more with her body than her brains. Older and wiser, she would not make the mistake again of trying to best him with brute force.

She would have to prove herself more than a match in cunning and guile.

A frisson of doubt prickled along her scar. Failure was a palpable fear, searing a trail of fire against her flesh.

"Come," added Rochambert roughly. "Let us see just how far Daggett is willing to bargain in order to keep that pretty little throat in one piece."

Mention of the marquess gave her the strength to shove such trepidations aside. She had bested bitterness and the black abyss of self-loathing, all because Lynsley had believed in her and refused to allow her to disappear into the depths of despair.

While there was still a breath in her body, she would fight like the devil to prove worthy of his ... friendship.

The first imperative, decided Valencia, was to keep Rochambert guessing about the nature of her relationship with Lynsley. "You are much mistaken if you think he'll lift a finger to save my skin," she mumbled as he dragged her down the corridor. "My partner is ruled by pragmatism, not passion."

"I know a thing or two about lust, *cherie*," snarled Rochambert. "Monsieur Daggett—or whatever his real name—is not so detached from your fate as you claim. And not only that, I see something else in his eyes. He hates me, and I find myself wondering why."

"An act," she said.

He slapped her again. "I think not. But let us set the stage for a confrontation and see how the scene plays out."

. . .

Lynsley held the candle closer and adjusted the magnifying glass. The code was complex, but given his extensive experience with such puzzles, he was able to work out some of the basic text.

According to an ancient Chinese treatise on 'firedrug', the addition of certain other elements to the basic combination of charcoal, saltpeter and sulfur produces a potent chemical reaction ... He read on for a bit, his frown deepening with every word.

Bloody hell.

The technical terms were incomprehensible, but the gist of the data was frighteningly clear. Apparently the opinion of Lady Merton, his expert consultant on scientific matters, had been bang on the mark. While the Oxford professor he had asked dismissed the idea as absurd, she had said that a weapon of devastation was theoretically possible.

Lynsley opened his bag and began sorting out its contents. He could only pray that her expertise in chemistry was equally accurate.

The brass box containing the diabolical discovery was large and unwieldy. To neutralize the danger, he would have to proceed very carefully. One by one, he lifted the flasks of chemicals inside and gingerly rearranged the rows. The next step entailed combining—

The pounding in his ears was suddenly a good deal louder than his beating heart. Though reinforced with bands of iron, the gallery door shook with the fury of the Frenchman's fist.

"Open up, Daggett!"

Valencia voiced a different demand. "Don't do it! He—"

Her words stopped in mid-sentence.

Drawing a deep breath, Lynsley hurried through his last few measurements. *Steady, steady.* Just a moment or two longer.

"Daggett! I warn you. Open the door, or I shall start sliding your she-bitch under it, one bloody piece at a time."

"Hold your blade. I'm coming." The marquess checked the pockets of his jacket. Deep down inside he had always known it would come to this. *Mano a mano.* It wouldn't be easy to fool a professional like Rochambert, but he had a few tricks up his sleeve.

Crossing the carpet, Lynsley drew his pistol, then threw back the cylinders of the special lock and clicked open the latch. .

"Step back." Rochambert shouldered his way inside, using Valencia as a shield. He had her neck in a vise-like grip, and a stiletto poised a hair's breath from her pulse point. "Throw down your weapon, or I swear, I shall gut her like a fish."

Lynsley cocked the hammer. "Which will allow me to put a bullet through your brain."

The Frenchman was far too savvy to allow a clear shot. "Assuming I'm slow and your hand is steady." He darted back, dragging Valencia behind the leering bulk of the marble satyr.

He felt his breath catch. The move was as he expected, but it took all of his self-control to keep playing this razored-edged game. To his relief, Valencia was wise enough not to struggle.

"As you see, you are no match for me, Daggett. Now, if you wish to see your slut live an instant longer, you will throw down your weapon."

"Don't harm her. I'll do as you say." The marquess tossed the pistol on the floor.

"You see, I was right, *cherie.*" Candlelight caught the curling contempt on Rochambert's face as he slid out from behind the stone. "Your partner is thinking with his prick and not his brain. A fatal weakness for a man who fancies himself a match for a professional." The Frenchman made a show of tightening his hold on Valencia, forcing her spine to an acute arc. "Now throw down the knife, Daggett. Did you think I would not see it bulging in your pocket?"

The blade spun through the air, its point sinking into the parquet floor with a quivering flash of steel.

"Have you no respect for art?" sneered Rochambert." I don't like to see my possessions damaged."

"Neither do I," said Lynsley.

A bark of laughter. "*Alors*, you are not in a position to object."

The marquess slipped a flask from under his cuff. "No?"

Rochambert narrowed his eyes. "What's that?"

"Perhaps you would care to hazard a guess." Lynsley gave it a careless shake, setting the crimson liquid to a bubbling froth. "Hell, if I am going to die, it may as well be with a bang."

The Frenchman was no longer looking quite so smug. "You have no idea what you are doing, Daggett! *Arret—stop!*"

"On the contrary, I know *exactly* what I am doing. I am playing with fire. And I am prepared to burn us all to a crisp if you don't release the lady." Lynsley sensed his enemy's uncertainty.

And the first telltale signs of fear. Sweat was beading on Rochambert's brow, and his flared nostrils betrayed a quickening of his breath.

Would the man dare to risk an instant inferno?

"Stop." Rochambert drew the knife back a touch. "I am willing to talk."

Lynsley's own palms were damp as he stilled the glass vial. He was not only playing with fire, he was playing with Valencia's life. Forcing his eyes from the glittering blade, he waggled a last little taunting challenge. "Let her go and then the two of us will duel it out like men, eh? After all, it's me you want, not one of my Merlins. Think of what a feather in your cap it would be if you were able to hand over the Head Hawk, so to speak, to your master."

"Who are you?" demanded Rochambert.

"I will tell you exactly who I am—"

"Thomas, for God's sake, no!" exclaimed Valencia.

"It's quite alright, my dear. Monsieur Rochambert is not going to live long enough to pass on the information." A swirl of red spun in a slow vortex. "I am Lord Lynsley."

Rochambert appeared to be searching his memory to place the name. "Lynsley," he repeated, then laughed. "The aging aristocrat who pushes pencils around in the back warrens of Whitehall? *Sacre Coeur*, the English government must be truly desperate or demented to send a crippled female and dottering old dandy to cross swords with *moi*." His steel once again caressed Valencia's throat. "Pray tell, why would the Emperor give a rat's arse for your worthless carcass?"

"Because I am the Head of British Secret Intelligence," replied Lynsley. "The dottering old dandy who has foiled Napoleon's every attempt to parade his People's Army down Piccadilly. I imagine your Emperor might wish to pick my brain about the details of my operations."

Rochambert gnawed on his lower lip. "What sort of duel do you propose, Lord Lynsley? If I do as you ask and release the ladybird, you will hold every advantage. And please, do not insult my intelligence by offering your word as a gentleman to put the glass down."

"I daresay it would be a waste of breath. The reptilian mind can't comprehend the notion of honor." The marquess took some measure of satisfaction in seeing Rochambert's face mottle with rage. "What I had in mind was this. Shove the lady outside. Your special lock should ensure we are not interrupted."

Valencia's gasp was cut off by a rough jerk.

"Keep your mouth shut," ordered the Frenchman. His voice was sharper, shriller.

"Do as he says, Val. Don't try any pirate tricks." Lynsley locked eyes with her for a heartbeat, and saw a glimmer of understanding. "Trust me, and be ready to move quickly when Monsieur Rochambert releases you."

"So, you are suggesting that we fight hand-to-hand for possession of the explosive?"

"I'm not likely to risk blowing myself or the lady to Kingdom Come if I have any hope of winning."

"Let me consider it for a moment." As he spoke, Rochambert slid a step closer to the pistol. Another few inches ...

Now or never.

"Too late. Why don't we let the Almighty decide." Lynsley flung the vial at the Frenchman's head.

With a wordless cry, Rochambert let go of Valencia and grabbed for the glass.

She ducked and spun away into the shadows.

Lynsley threw himself forward, snatching up his knife as he tucked into a tight somersault. The Frenchman's slash grazed his scalp as he hit the floor. *Tuck. Twist. Turn.* A fraction off and he would be impaled on his own blade.

Rochambert struck again, quick as cobra. But the split second needed to catch the vial had given Lynsley the edge. He hit the other man's legs in a hard roll, and as Rochambert fell, he uncoiled his body, driving the knife upward into his enemy's gut.

A scream pieced the gloom and suddenly the hilt of his knife was slippery with blood.

Lynsley let his hand fall away.

"Thomas!" Valencia's cheek was wet against his, tears mingling with sweat and the scarlet spill of his flesh wound.

"It's naught but a scratch." He touched her throat and the

velvet softness of her skin nearly unmanned him. Burying his face in her hair, he whispered a kiss to the tangled curls. "It's over, my love."

Together they looked down at the fallen Rochambert.

The Frenchman's gold-tipped lashes fluttered open. As did his lips. However, the obscenity was dulled by the death rattle of his breathing.

Valencia averted her eyes.

"Yes, perhaps I shall see you in Hell. But whatever my sins, they pale in comparison with yours," replied Lynsley softly. He could muster no pity for a man who killed without remorse or regret. "Make your peace with the Devil, for I doubt that Heaven has any place for you."

"Oh, you and your doxie shall roast in flames too, Lord Lynsley." His fist clenched, the crackle of glass giving force to his last gasp. "Sooner than you think."

Chapter Twenty-Two

"*Merde*."

Valencia had not quite recovered from the shock of hearing Lynsley murmur the word 'love' when his oath rumbled in her ear.

"Dear God," she whispered, watching the crimson liquid spill across Rochambert's blood-soaked shirt. "Will it explode?"

"I added the neutralizing chemical, as the recipe spelled out, but ..."

A tongue of fire shot up from the torn linen, and then another.

"But I wouldn't stake my life on it." Lynsley grabbed her arm. "In any case, nothing will stop the stuff from bursting into spontaneous flame." Ducking beneath the plume of smoke, he headed for the door. The sickening stench of charred flesh was already overpowering.

"Thomas." Much as she longed to escape from the bilious black cloud, she held back. "The box—should we not finish what we came here for, once and for all?"

He touched a hand to his coat. "I have the papers." A glance at the rising flames. "The rest will take care of itself."

A shattering of glass punctuated his reply. Flying shards shredded the painted canvas on the wall behind their heads. "I never cared for Delacroix," he muttered, pulling her into the shelter of his arms."

"You are quite mad." She kissed his cheek. "And quite magnificent."

A lopsided grin gleamed through the ghostly light. "Not bad for an old man, eh? I must make a point of getting out of the office more often."

"Over my dead body."

"All joking aside ..." Lynsley fumbled with the locking mechanism as the *whoosh* of the flames rose to a roar. "We best hurry."

He heaved the door open just as a shuddering boom knocked them sprawling to the corridor floor.

"Stay low," sputtered Lynsley in between coughs. A noxious gas swirled with the smoke, creating a pale, poisonous pink cloud that blanketed the air. The wall sconces flared, then died out, leaving them in darkness. "And keep hold of me."

The heat quickly turned blistering. The wainscoting buckled and ignited in a shower of sparks. Covering her mouth with her skirts, Valencia choked down a welling of panic. Her eyes were slitted shut, and her lungs burned from the acrid fumes. Dizzy, disoriented, she clung to Lynsley's warm, strong hand. It was her lifeline, her hold on all that was good amid the crackling chaos of destruction.

"Just a bit farther," he called, as if sensing her faltering spirits.

It was strange how the connection between them had survived the pain and the struggles of the past. Through his callused palm, she felt the steady beat of his heart. Oh, how she loved his touch, his humor, his courage.

Indeed, she loved everything about him, even his infuriating stone sphinx stare.

Love. She dared not dwell on the word. The endearment had slipped from his lips in the heat of battle. An expression of friendship—it had no deeper meaning.

And that must be enough to carry her through this storm, and beyond. Lynsley had shared much of himself—his strength, his knowledge, his passion. But there was still a private place that he kept sealed to all but himself. A place with no fancy key of steel or iron. It would only open of its own accord.

"Unfasten the bolts!" From downstairs came a panicked cry and the pounding of running feet. "The mansion is ablaze."

Up ahead, the gilded banister winked in the wild light, its spiraling curve beckoning them to safety.

Lynsley rose to his knees.

She jerked him back, rolling to cover his body with hers as a beam came crashing down to the floor.

"Just who is saving whom," he quipped, quickly reversing their positions.

"It's a joint venture," she replied. His face was streaked with soot and his hair caked in cinders, but his eyes sparked with a clear blue intensity that eclipsed all else.

Lynsley. The light of her life.

A blinding flash exploded in the main salon. Looking over his shoulder, Valencia saw that the fire had spread quickly and was raging out of control. Silhouetted against the multicolored smoke, the shower of plaster flakes had an incongruous beauty, floating silent and serene amid the cacophony of snapping timbers.

"We can't go forward," muttered Lynsley. The carved moldings were starting to disintegrate, falling away in jagged chunks that rained ash and sparks over their heads.

"And we can't go back," she added. The corridor was blocked by a wall of flames.

He hesitated for an instant, then pulled her into the side parlor. "Our only chance of escape is the windows." He slammed the door shut before picking up a Chinoise sidechair and hurling it through the mullioned glass.

A blast of cold air funneled through the gaping hole. "You first!" he yelled over the rattle of the broken casements.

"No, you should—"

"That's a bloody order."

Much as she wished to object, Valencia realized this was no time to argue the fine points of honor. She scrambled up to the ledge and inched out along the narrow ledge of decorative limestone. The marquess kicked off his shoes and followed on her heels.

A crowd was milling in the cobbled streets below. A patrol of soldiers was trying to calm the confusion and organize a bucket brigade.

"It's useless," said Lynsley. "Nothing can extinguish this spark of Satan. It will burn itself out eventually—but not before destroying the entire street."

She watched a mother and three children fleeing from the adjoining building. "Heaven help the souls living here."

The fiery glow from the burning roof showed the anguish in his eyes. "I should have anticipated he would seek to inflict harm, even in death."

"Damnation, Thomas. Don't blame yourself. You did all in your power to prevent needless destruction."

The bleakness of his smile tore at her heart. "War is hell. Isn't that one of the pompous platitudes that I teach you at the Academy?"

She touched his sleeve. "Look, the cornice stonework appears to offer some sort of handholds. From there, we can climb down to the arched windows." She couldn't see past the jutting slates. "We must move. I can feel the heat seeping through the mortar."

Lynsley nodded. His eyes, however, remained locked on the flames licking out from the adjoining mansion.

Steeling her aching muscles, Valencia started off at a slow slide. The stretch of ledge was short, but the footing was treacherous. Narrow as a knifepoint, the ancient stone was crumbling in spots. The drifting smoke and gusting wind made it difficult to see—

Her injured leg, already weakened from the strain of her earlier exertions, suddenly gave way.

The scuff roused Lynsley to life. Reacting in a flash, he caught her around the waist and pulled her back against the wall.

"For the love of God, Val, don't you dare leave me now." His raspy murmur was rough as his soot-streaked jaw rubbed against her cheek, and yet strangely plaintive.

Love. That word again.

"Not after all we have been through together," he added.

Valencia held him tightly, steadying their foothold. The perch was precarious—an apt metaphor for their strange relationship, she thought wryly. Her laugh, no more than a breath of air, stirred his wind-tangled hair. "I'm afraid you are stuck with me for the duration of the mission. Merlins don't fly away from adversity. They rise to any challenge—isn't that what you teach us?"

"I don't think you have anything left to learn from me," whispered Lynsley. He hunched against her as a nearby window blew out in a welter of twisted metal and slivered glass. "Time to spread our wings."

The marquess slid into the lead, keeping a firm grasp on her hand. "Watch your step."

"I'm not some fragile piece of porcelain," she said lightly as they paused to catch their breath. "Like a jug of rum, I am still serviceable, even with a crack or two."

"Having had my lips on your spout, I would have to agree,"

"Why, Lord Lynsley! Another lewd remark?" Valencia knotted up her skirts and slipped her fingers into the chiseled detailing. "At this rate, your reputation as a paragon of propriety will soon go up in smoke."

He grinned through soot-smudged lips. "My reputation is likely blackened beyond repair. However, I am hoping you will keep it to yourself."

"Your dark secrets are safe with me, Thomas."

His reply, if he made one, was swallowed in the scorching wind. Hot and heavy as dragon's breath, its roar was deafening as she scrabbled her way down the side of the mansion. The building next door burst into flames, and sparks were spreading from roof to roof.

"Hold up." Lynsley joined her on the archway ledge. They were low enough to see the upturned faces of the crowd. People were pointing, their voices a cacophony of cries. A woman fainted and was hustled aside by a group of soldiers, who set to clearing a space on the trampled ground.

"You will have to jump!" called the captain, after having his men stretch a blanket between them as a safety net. "We will catch you."

"Bloody hell." Lynsley made a rapid assessment of the surroundings. "He's right. We have no choice. But it's rather like leaping out of the fire and into the frying pan. Our cover won't stand the heat of official questioning, and I don't really fancy finishing out the war in a French prison. That is, if they don't hang us for murder."

"We'll find a way to fly the cage," said Valencia, though the appearance of a second troop of soldiers did not auger well for their chances. "Once we're on the ground, I can fall into a lady-like swoon, and we can slip away in the confusion."

"It's worth a try," replied Lynsley. Shielding his face from the fire, he suddenly turned and edged closer to the open windows.

"Thomas!"

He pulled the sheaf of papers from his coat and threw them into the flames.

"T—the manuscript?" she asked as he returned to her side.

Lynsley watched the sheets swirl and sizzle into naught but ashes. "We can't be caught with such incriminating papers." He allowed a grim smile. "And in truth, I think it's for the best. The world does not need a weapon of such mass destruction."

"Madame! Monsieur! *Allez, allez!*"

He winked. "Ladies before gentlemen."

A groan hitched in his throat as the wind caught Valencia's skirts and twisted her in the mid-air. An instant later, she spun awkwardly into the waiting blanket, barely catching its corner.

A soldier scooped her into his arms as the captain waved Lynsley on. "Hurry, monsieur! Before it's too late."

Lynsley needed no urging. The wooden windowsill was crackling into a jumble of red-hot coals.

Valencia. He would jump through flaming hoops to reach her. Throughout this hellish ordeal, she had never lost her inner fire. Indomitable, in spite of her frailties. That was true courage —to soldier on through pain and self-doubt.

His feet hit the taut stretch of wool and he bounced up through the smoky air. The Academy taught resilience and resolve but she was no longer a student. Life outside the ivy walls had shaped her, sculpted her into who she was now. A woman of extraordinary grace and grit.

He cared deeply for all the girls he had taken under his wing. But Valencia ...

Lynsley landed hard, the force dropping him to his knees. "Where is madame?" he exclaimed, trying to pull free from the soldiers who took hold of his arms. "Let me go! I must see to my wife."

"The lady is safe," said the captain. "My men are ministering to her needs. In the meantime, monsieur, I would like to ask you some questions."

He coughed. "Please, can't it wait until I have some water, and assure myself that my wife did not injure herself in the fall. You know women—they are such emotional creatures. And ..." Improvising on the fly, he added, "mine is in a most delicate condition."

The officer looked a little embarrassed, torn between chivalry and duty. "I—I am sorry, monsieur, but my orders are quite clear. Until the source of the fire is determined, everyone seen leaving the mansion is to be kept under strict surveillance—"

"Quite right, Captain. But Monsieur Daggett is a distinguished diplomat. I can vouch for his credentials." Georges Auberville, one of the French diplomats they had met during the negotiations, elbowed his way through the line of guards, flashing an official document thick with ribbons and sealing wax. "As you see, I am from the Ministry of Foreign Affairs. He and his wife are to come with me. "

The officer studied the parchment for some moments before handing it back. "All seems in order. I suppose I must be guided by your authority." He ordered his men to make way. "Your wife is across the street, Monsieur Daggett. You both were extremely lucky to escape the blaze."

"Indeed," murmured the marquess.

"And accept my best wishes for the felicitous event. If the child is a girl, you may consider naming her Paris."

"Thank you," said Lynsley gravely. "Naming a female after a city? It is an interesting idea."

"Lady Daggett is with child?" asked Auberville in a low voice as they crossed the cobblestones.

"In negotiating with the captain, I may have taken some liberties in presenting the facts," he replied.

"I am glad to hear it," said the minister. "We may have to travel rough to get you out of this debacle."

Lynsley nodded, though for an instant the thought of him and Valencia as a family stirred a certain longing. However, it was Auberville who demanded his full attention at the present moment.

Friend or foe?

He ventured a cautious question. "Are you saying that the Ministry is already aware of this turn of events?"

Auberville gave a tense laugh. "*Mon Dieu*, let us hope not. But they will soon enough. We haven't much time to spirit you out of Paris."

"Actually, I've my own arrangements in place," he murmured. "But I would be grateful for assistance in getting to the rendezvous point."

"That is easy enough." The minister's face relaxed slightly. "I suspected that the Americans have other operatives in place. Mr. Madison and Mr. Armstrong are men who leave little to chance."

"You are allied with them?"

"I am. I believe the emperor is leading France on the road to ruin, and so I am dedicated to seeing that my country strive to be a true democracy, like the American republic."He dropped his voice even lower. "Is Rochambert dead?"

"Yes," replied Lynsley.

A flicker of satisfaction passed over Auberville's features. "*Bon.* That one was a right bastard. I am glad that Washington heeded my warning that his lust for blood might ruin our plans in Marseilles."

"As you say, Madison is a meticulous man." The marquess repressed a wry smile. Sometimes war made for strange bedfellows. "He likes to eliminate any obstacles that stand in the way of success."

"Indeed." Auberville slanted a sidelong look. "It was a stroke of brilliance to use you and your wife to draw Rochambert into a trap. I confess, you had me fooled for a while. You are more dangerous than you look, Monsieur Daggett."

"Appearances can be deceiving."

"Quite." Auberville flashed his document again, quickly quelling the objections of the officer standing guard over the makeshift medical tent. "Madame Daggett deserves a medal for having the bravery to serve as bait for that devil."

"I imagine our government will agree," said Lynsley. Spotting Valencia in the shadows, the marquess lengthened his stride. Her skirts were hiked up to allow a solicitous soldier to inspect a shapely stretch of leg. He did not have to call upon his acting skills to sound suitably upset. "Move aside, move aside. Are you hurt, my dear?"

"I think I have sprained my ankle," she said in a plaintive whine. "Oooooh, it *hurts.*"

"A cold compress—" began the soldier.

Lynsley shouldered him aside and gathered her in his arms. "I know damn well how to take care of my wife, sirrah! The first thing is to get her to more comfortable quarters."

"This way, monsieur!" The rest of the troops shuffled back as Auberville gave a brusque wave. "I have a carriage waiting close by."

Valencia's brow flicked up in question.

"Just play along," he murmured, brushing a kiss to her brow. "It appears we have a guardian angel."

She responded with a dramatic groan.

Auberville led the way to one of the side streets. "Let us hurry," he urged. "Before the Imperial Guard arrives to take charge of security. They are not so easy to bully as the local regiment."

"I am perfectly capable of walking," said Valencia.

Lynsley ignored her. "How far?"

"Just a few minutes more. The carriage is stationed by the Jardin de Luxumberg."

"Who else is involved," asked Auberville as they hurried down one of the side streets.

The marquess shook his head. "It's best you don't know."

"Ah. Yes, of course, you are right." Auberville, hurried ahead and opened the carriage door. "*Bon voyage*," he murmured, helping them up the iron rungs. "Do put in a good word for me in Washington."

Lynsley waved through the glass, then leaned back against the squabs and exhaled a long breath. It ended in a wry chuckle. "I do hope that Dieppe has a decent wine merchant."

"Wine?" Valencia grimaced. "The only *port* I wish to see is Dover."

His lips quirked. "I'll drink to that. But as we leave France, I should like to send President Madison and his cabinet a case of the finest French champagne."

Chapter Twenty-Three

Lynsley slipped through the door and shook the raindrops from his wide-brimmed hat.

"Any luck?" asked Valencia as she refastened the bolt.

"Yes, the merchant ship was there, just as I arranged with Jalet, and the captain was expecting us," he answered. "We sail for England on the morning tide."

"That is good news." She smiled, but the warmth did not quite reach her eyes.

Surely it was just a quirk of the candlelight, thought Lynsley as he shrugged off his caped overcoat. And yet, the snap of the wet wool stirred a strange mizzle between them. It felt as if a heaviness dampened the air.

They were both weary, he reminded himself. And the end of a mission was always bittersweet.

But as he hung the garment by the door, the chill of the rain clung to his palms. Perhaps she wished to have separate rooms. They would, after all, have to get used to sleeping alone.

Lynsley turned.. "Would you prefer your own quarters—"

Her lips touched his, stilling his halting words.

Closing his eyes, he drew her into his arms as reason gave way to need. A last burst of passion, sparked by desperation. A last flare of fire before their relationship burned down to cold ashes.

They were both old enough to know that life did not have fairy tale endings. One must grasp at happiness and hold on for dear life. It was all too fleeting. Like wind and sunlight and the very air that they breathed.

"Val," he murmured, deepening his kiss, savoring the sweetness as if it would have to last a lifetime.

A last wild intoxication before going back to his sober self.

She was exploring his body with the same desperate need. His cravat fell to the floor as the fastenings of his shirt yielded to her roving hands.

Steel and silk. He had never imagined a woman could be both hard and soft. The contrast, the contradiction was wildly sensual.

This valiant Valkyrie—a battle-hardened beauty, forged of fire and flame-gold honor. Oh, how he was in awe of her strength, her passions.

As for his own passions, he had surrendered any will to resist this temptation. Was it wrong? He had a lifetime to meditate his sins, if sin it was. Right now, the Devil himself could not pull him away.

"Val."

She tugged at the tabs of his trousers, and then her dressing gown slipped from her shoulders, slithering to the floor in a whisper of silk. An instant later his shirt followed suit.

He kicked off one shoe, then the other.

Thump, thump. As they bounced off the door, Valencia laughed, a low, husky sound that set his heart to skittering against his ribcage.

His trousers somehow caught on the tip of the bedpost, a flag draped in silent surrender of sanity.

Reason could go to hell.

They were now both nearly naked and stumbling for the bed.

Desperate desire sizzled through his blood. Be damned with Reason. He could spend the rest of his life devoted to discipline and detachment. But for this moment ...

For this moment, he wanted her so badly that he might shrivel up and die if he didn't bury himself in her warmth.

"Thomas," she whispered, her voice rough with need.

To the devil with rules and responsibility. All the things that normally regimented his life. For this last, fleeting interlude he would savor the sweetness of giving in to his heart's desire.

Valencia framed his face and pulled him close. Was it wrong to want one last blazing memory to warm her through the long nights?

The spark of his smile, luminous in the candlelight. The sherry-sweet color of his hair, glinting with silver. The strong, chiseled lines of his face. He was a noble in the best sense of the word. A man who had used privilege to serve rather than to take. Unselfish in every fiber of his being.

While she, on the other hand, would selfishly seize a last moment of sunshine before the black cloud darkened the horizon.

"Oh, Thomas," she whispered. His supremely sensual, capable hands were now sliding up the length of her legs. His touch turned tender against her scar, and as he murmured sweet endearments, Valencia felt her body melt with liquid desire. "Make love to me, Thomas."

He traced a kiss along her throat, muffling a low laugh. "I thought I was giving the orders here."

She pressed a palm to his cheek. "Actually, it was more of a request."

And a plea.

"Just so we understand who is in charge." He swept her up in his arms. "Make love to me, Val."

"Yes, sir."

"He's on the second floor, last door on the right," came a low whisper.

In answer came a muffled snick of steel.

"I'll go first," added Marco to his companion. "Remember, do not fire unless I give the order."

"Do you think the Frogs have Lord Lynsley captive?" Beneath the black silk bandana covering her hair, Verona's eyes gleamed with undisguised excitement."

"We shall soon see, *bella*." Marco drew his dagger and tested its edge on his thumb. "The barmaid said he was accompanied upstairs by another person, which makes me fear the worst. The marquess always works alone."

Verona exhaled sharply. "What are we waiting for? As we speak, he may be suffering god knows what sort of physical torture."

"*Si, si,* but we will soon put a stop to that." Marco signaled her to silence. "Follow me."

Lynsley lay tangled on the sheets, savoring the sweet euphoria of a mind and body utterly at peace. Their climax had come quickly, cresting in a white hot wave that had drowned out all other sounds and sensations. Now, he was drowsily aware of the ocean waters, lapping at the harbor quays beneath the window, and the silky tangle of Valencia's hair tickling the underside of his chin. Her cheek was resting on his chest, her breath a whisper of warmth on his skin, and her hand ...

Her clever little hand was rousing a devilish urge to repeat their lovemaking, though this time at a far more leisurely pace. He would lie still, savoring the blissful sensation for just a few moments longer—

A soft *snick* intruded on his reveries. The scrape of metal on metal.

In a flash, he rolled off the bed, taking Valencia with him. She had heard it too, for she was already on her feet and reaching for her knife. Lynsley signaled for silence as he tugged on his trousers.

She nodded, and moved noiselessly to a position by the door.

Damn. Surely the French had not sorted out the chaos of conflagration quickly enough to be on their trail. The Americans? Equally unlikely. Which left robbery.

His mouth quirked in a wry twitch. Pity the poor thief. If some local was looking to frighten a foreign couple into handing over their purse, the fellow was in for a rude awakening.

The sound came again. He glanced at Valencia, who motioned for him to open the door. She had pulled on his shirt, which covered her thighs. But with her loosened hair spilling over her shoulders and her eyes heavy-lidded with passion, she looked delightfully d*ishabille.*

He couldn't resist a grin and a wink. Lud, it was exhilarating to be with her. In bed, in battle, she was the perfect comrade.

Angling his pistol for a straight shot, Lynsley slowly eased back the catch on the lock. Outside the door, the floorboards creaked as a boot shifted ever so slightly.

"*Diavolo.*" The word was barely more than a breath of air.

Lynsley lowered his weapon a touch. "*Marco?*"

"*Si.* What do you need me to do, sir? Shall I blow the door off its hinges?"

"Not necessary." He opened it a crack. "As you see, there is no need for fireworks."

"*Santo Cielo.* We feared you were being held against your will, sir. The barmaid said you were not alone, and we worried that you might be under considerable duress."

"Actually, I was in bed, and quite comfortable until now." He opened the door a touch wider, only to see Marco's expression of concern twitch into one of bemusement. Given the rascal's prowess with ladies, Lynsley imagined the fencing master didn't need much of an imagination to guess that he hadn't been sleeping.

"Of course, I am delighted to discover that you are alive, sir." Marco craned his neck, trying to see inside the room.

Lynsley moved smoothly to block his view.

"Very alive," added the fencing master with a wink, his gaze moving down to the marquess's hastily assumed trousers with the buttons slotted into the wrong slots. "It's nice to know that a gentleman man of your senior status is still up for the rigors of a mission."

"Thank you for the vote of confidence." It was only now that Lynsley noticed the slim figure backing up Marco. "Now, may I ask what in the name of Hades the two of you are doing here?"

"Mounting a rescue mission," replied Marco with a small smirk. "We feared you might need assistance."

"As you see, you were mistaken." Seeing that the young Merlin was fighting back a grin, Lynsley mustered his most lordly look and fixed her with a pointed stare. "Do you find something amusing, Verona?"

"No, sir!" she replied, straightening to parade ground attention.

"I wouldn't think so," he said softly. "Indeed, if I were you—an unfledged Merlin away from the nest without leave—I would be too busy contemplating the seriousness of my transgression to be chortling over the private life of my superior."

Marco sobered as well. "The fault is all mine. I ordered her to accompany me. Any punishment—"

"Any punishment will be mine to mete out as I see fit," said Lynsley. He ran a hand through his hair, belated aware that great tufts of it were standing on end. Coupled with his naked chest, rumpled trousers and bare feet, he did not exactly cut a commanding presence.

The realization had him torn between maintaining a stern visage and cracking a schoolboy grin. "Now, if you don't mind, I would prefer not to attract any more attention. Consider yourselves dismissed."

Seeing that Verona's hand was about to snap up, Marco caught her wrist. "Dammit, don't salute, *cara*," he muttered.

Lynsley stilled the twitch of his lips. "I assume that as you managed to get here on your own, you will have no trouble returning."

"No, sir." Marco could not resist one last little stab of humor. "You are sure you wouldn't like an armed escort for the journey home, sir? Just in case any trouble should *arise*." He assumed an air of grave concern. "A man of your advanced years ought not be traveling alone."

"Marco ..." Lynsley leaned in a little closer to the fencing master. "You may take your blades and your banter and stick them where the sun doesn't shine."

The Italian swallowed a rumbled laugh. "I—"

Valencia stepped out from her vantage point, still clad only in his shirt. "You heard your commanding officer."

Marco stared in obvious admiration.

"*Andiamo*," she added, flicking her knife toward the darkened stairwell. "Lord Lynsley already has someone watching his arse."

It took a moment for Marco to master his mirth. "Come, Verona, I can see our talents are not needed after all." Backing off with the ashen-faced Merlin in tow, Marco blew an airy kiss. "*Ciao, amico*. Enjoy the rest of the night."

Valencia edged away from the doorway and set down her blade. "Weren't you a little hard on the girl, Thomas? She looked terrified of you, and of losing her place at the Academy."

"Verona?" Lynsley made a face. "I assure you, she doesn't find me at all intimidating. She is even more rebellious than you were, and takes a certain delight in seeing how far she can push me."

"Merlins are meant to fly in the face of authority," reminded Valencia.

"And I am meant to clip their wings from time to time." He closed the door and relocked the latch. "There is no harm in letting her stew a little over the possible consequences of her actions. It may also keep her from spreading the word of this little incident throughout the Academy. How very embarrassing to be caught with my trousers down."

"On the contrary." She pressed her palms to his shoulders. "I should think that a rumor of rakish scandal would only add to your storied reputation among the girls."

He gave a wry chuckle. "Maybe you have a point. As it is, I fear they see me as too ancient to wield a sword."

Valencia teased a hand down across his ribs, the flat hard planes of his stomach. "It seems to me that despite your encroaching old age, you still can muster a show of life."

She made him feel young, alive, gloriously aware of the

moment—the smell of her perfume, the fire-gold glow of the candles, the whisper of salt air stirring the curtains.

"When my country has need of me, I do try to rise to the occasion."

How sweet it was to banter with her. They were lovers, comrade-in arms. Most importantly they were friends.

"Dear me, the hardships you must endure for England." Her lips feathered against his ear. "Come back to bed, Thomas."

The sheets were still faintly warm, and scented with earthy essence of their passion. Valencia inhaled deep, the musk mingling with melancholy. Come morning, it would all quickly fade ...

No, she would not let such depressing thoughts cloud these last few precious hours.

Brushing back her tangled hair, she rolled onto her side, and watched Lynsley drape his trousers over the chair. The tallow candle had burned itself out, but the sky had cleared, and the pearly moonlight was just strong enough to limn the muscled curves of his buttocks and thighs.

How she loved the shape of him, and the sweet intimacy of observing him naked, engaged in the mundane task of straightening his clothes.

He suddenly turned and chuckled. "Are you watching my arse?"

"It's a lovely sight," she murmured.

"Throw me my shirt, if you please. An even lovelier sight is your glorious body."

Valencia eased the linen over her head, aware of his eyes following her every move. *To the devil with brooding*. She meant to squeeze every sinful, sensual sensation from these last fleeting seconds.

She gave a teasing wave of the cloth. "Come and get it."

"Is that an invitation?"

"I've decided it's my turn to issue orders." She crooked a finger. "March."

Lynsley slowly sauntered to the bedside, his sapphirine eyes never breaking contact with hers. There was something erotic about the connection. It was a palpable, pulsing prickling over her naked body.

"And now?" he asked

"And now, make love to me again. And again." *Until night gives way to dawn—for who knows what the new day will bring.*

Chapter Twenty-Four

Fog blanketed the harbor, muffling the cries of the gulls and the creak of the rigging. Lynsley turned from the misted windowpanes and finished dressing. The scent of the fresh starch was crisp against his just-shaven jaw. *New clothes for a new day.* Bailin had, as usual, been efficient in packing for their flight.

His shirt and cravat from the previous night were folded away at the bottom of his traveling valise. *Mementos of madness?* His hands clenched for an instant, recalling their desperate, delirious lovemaking.

Would her perfume linger in the linen? Could he keep them hidden in some private place, to sneak a sniff of *her* when solitude threatened to squeeze the air from his lungs?

A gust rattled the casement, stale with a stench of salty decay. Dawn was breaking. The tide was ebbing.

Time to go.

Valencia, her back to him, was slipping the final hairpins into her coiled curls. He moved around the bed, his gaze avoiding the tangled sheets, and tied off the last few fastenings of her gown. As he smoothed the collar into place, he pressed his lips to the nape of her neck. She tasted of salt and spice.

Neither of them spoke.

Taking up their bags, he shouldered the door open and shuffled down the stairs. A strange sense of sadness weighed his steps. It took a moment or two to realize he felt slightly ashamed of himself.

He wondered why. After all, he lived his life in a world of moral ambiguity. The lines between right and wrong were so easily blurred. His mouth pressed in a self-mocking grimace. Oh yes, the exalted Marquess of Lynsley was an acknowledged master of justifying his own actions. Noble ideals, righteous principles. All was fair in pursuit of the higher good.

But no matter how cleverly he twisted and turned, there was no getting around the fact that his actions last night had been terribly selfish.

What did Valencia think of their lovemaking?

The Academy—*his* Academy—taught the girls to view sex dispassionately. A basic human need, like eating and sleeping. Satisfying such urges had nothing to do with right or wrong—it was simply a fact of life. Had she bedded him in body only?

His jaw clenched, so hard he feared his teeth might crack.

There was no denying the chemistry between them. It was explosive—a fiery force far more powerful than the mad scientist's secret weapon. And like those unquenchable tongues of flame, the conflagration was impossible to extinguish, now that the elements had been unlocked from their containers and stirred together.

Its potent passion had left him singed to the very core.

But they had never talked about their feelings. He had discouraged any discussion of emotion. *One must be detached and dispassionate during a mission.* Now his own words were coming back to haunt him.

"Mr. Bingham?" A gravelly voice dragged him back to the moment

Lynsley turned, feeling even more like a stranger in his own skin.

The Lord of Lies. He forced a poker face to mask his inner turmoil. "Yes. I'm Bingham."

"Samuels. Quartermaster of the brig Sea Witch." The sailor wasted no time in pleasantries. "Please come along with me. We'll be ready to cast off within a quarter hour." He glanced at the two valises in Lynsley's hand. "Have you and your wife any other baggage?"

"No. The rest of our things will be shipped later," replied the marquess. In truth, the fancy gowns and elegant evening clothes would likely end up among the spoils of war, unless the American delegation managed to reclaim Tobias Daggett's possessions. A pity—Valencia had looked beautiful in the Parisian satins and silks that he had purchased.

"Good. We are crowded enough with cargo as it is," said Samuels. "This way."

Lynsley gestured for Valencia to go first. He brought up the rear as they cut through the tangle of cordage and fishing nets lining the docks, trying not to watch the sway of her hips. Trying not to imagine what lay beneath the layers of wool and lace. Impossible. The picture of her naked body would be indelibly imprinted in his mind's eye forever.

"Mr. Bingham." The captain of the brig stood at the head of the gangplank, consulting the manifest sheet. "We were beginning to wonder whether we would have to sail without you." A curt nod acknowledged Valencia. "Ma'am. I regret to say that your quarters are rather cramped. We are not in the habit of taking passengers."

"Thank you for making an exception," she replied. "Please

don't apologize. We are quite used to traveling under adverse conditions."

"Excellent." The captain eyed the pennant flapping atop the mizzen mast. "The wind is rising. It's best you go below while we get the ship underway."

Below. Locked in a dark, dank cubbyhole deep in the bowels of the ship. Lynsley felt his lips twitch in irony as he descended the ladder. The situation couldn't be more apt, considering his current state of mind.

Valencia watched Lynsley light the binnacled lamp and open his document case. The papers, already damp with salt, shuffled with a limp whisper. He placed pen and ink beside them on the narrow chart table.

"Whitehall will want a full report," he murmured. "Though I'll likely be accused of writing a horrid novel."

"I doubt anyone would dare accuse you of any such flight of fancy." She meant to use humor to defuse the tension in the air. But a strange, smoldering spark seemed to darken his eyes. A frown furrowed his brow as he looked down and began to sharpen his quill.

Valencia took a book from her reticule—she had purchased a copy of *Aesop's Fables* during the journey to the coast—and opened the pages. Her eyes, however, kept straying from the printing to his profile. It was hard to read his expression in the oily light. That solemn, serious Sphinx face. An outward calm etched in stone.

Hell. She knew he was not impervious to feelings. Thomas was a passionate man, fiercely tender, sweetly sensual, when he allowed his true self to show.

Yet he seemed almost embarrassed since waking. Had her own wild need shocked him. Disgusted him? How else to explain his oblique gaze. Why, he hadn't yet looked her full in the face.

She bit back an exasperated sigh. As they had passed by the harbor's edge, low tide had revealed a multitude of mollusks in the mud. Lynsley reminded her of a hermit crab, scuttling into the recesses of his shell.

A creature wholly unto itself.

Footsteps pounded across the deck overhead. Canvas cracked, sharp as the sound of cannonfire, and the hull lurched forward as the crew cast off the mooring lines. The final leg of the journey would last just a few more hours. The ship would divert to Dover, and from there, Lynsley would head to London. While she would seek passage back to the isle of Sark.

They both should feel a sense of great satisfaction. The job was done.

She sat in shadowed silence, the scratch of Lynsley's pen and the whisper of her pages the only stirring between them. Serpentine swirls of smoke clouded the airless cabin. A damp chill curled up from the bilge.

Her throat suddenly constricted, and she felt as if she couldn't breath.

Setting aside her book, she quietly slipped out the cabin door and made her way topside.

On the quarterdeck, the captain was busy barking orders to the helmsman, and aloft, the men were busy trimming the sails. The ship heeled as it headed out to open sea, leaving a trail of wind-whipped foam in its wake. Wishing to be alone, Valencia crept past the forecastle hatchway and found a sliver of deserted space near the bow of the ship. She laced her fingers in the shrouds and lifted her face to the gusting breeze. The ocean was choppy, its leaden hue mirrored the line of squalls hovering on the horizon. Salt spray stung her cheeks.

Or was it her own tears?

Merlins never cried, she reminded herself.

Never. Ever. They suffered pain and hardship in stoic silence.

But in the next instant a sob slipped from her lips as all her years of training came undone.

Valencia clung to the rail, her nails digging at the varnished oak to keep from sinking to the deck. And from there, to despair.

By the morrow, she would be headed home, back to her isolated island and lonely little cottage, surrounded by windswept rock, gnarled forest and farmland.

While Lynsley returned to London.

To a host of glittering balls and routs, a crowd of polished ladies and gentlemen. A world of wealth and privilege. There was so much there to keep him busy. The experiences they had shared would quickly fade, and become just another one of his adventurous tales.

And some day, a lady of his own class would convince him to do his duty to family and tradition. They would share a home, companionship ... and children.

Valencia hated her already.

"Valencia."

Strong hands were suddenly steadying her shoulders. She tried to spin away, but Lynsley enfolded her in his arms and hugged her close. *Too close.* The scent of bay rum and his male musk was overwhelming.

And suddenly all her Merlin training took flight, leaving her just a woman who had been foolish enough to fall head-over-heels in love.

"Valkyrie, what's wrong?"

What possible answer was there to give?

"Your leg—is it in pain?"

No, my heart is breaking into a thousand little pieces. Stifling her sobs in his shirt, she shook her head.

"Tell me."

Over and over, he asked, then finally fell silent and just held her tight, his hand stroking over her wind tangled hair. Oh, if only she could stay burrowed in his warmth, and never have to face reality. But no Merlin with a magic wand was going to sweep down from the heavens and grant such a wish.

"Sorry," she whispered, when at least her tears were spent.

"Valencia, please tell me what's wrong."

Again she shook her head..

Lynsley tilted her chin up. "You must. There should be no secrets between us."

"D—don't ask, Thomas. All I have is my pride. Strip that away and I am not sure I could bear it."

He framed her face, his broad palms full of warmth. "You have me, Val. I won't let you fall."

At his touch, his piercing gaze, she no longer cared about pride, about anything other than honesty

"Oh, Thomas, I shall strip away my defenses then. I was thinking of the future."

He seemed to hold his breath.

"Of sitting in my cottage, staring out at the empty seas. Of serving brandy and beer to my neighbors, then trudging home at night to a cold hearth and empty bed."

He pressed his fingertips to her cheek. "Valencia ..." he began.

"No, let me go on, while I have the courage to speak," she cried. "I was also thinking of you returning to London. To the glittering ballrooms, the gaiety, and the glamour. The ladies and all the luxuries of Town life. Your friends, your family. The social swirl will soon dull the memory of this interlude for you. But not for me."

Her voice cracked. "After the past, I thought I was tough enough to parry any attack. But love is far sharper than steel."

She saw a strange light flood his eyes.

"It cuts deeper than muscle and sinew. It cuts to the heart. You wish for there to be no secrets between us? Very well— I ... I love you. More than I can say. Not that it matters. I—"

Her halting words were cut off by his lips. A gentle kiss, a whisper of breath warm on her cheek.

"What you describe of my London life would not dull this interlude, it will only make your absence from my life sharper. My valiant Valkyrie, you think my heart is untouched? Like you, I have been staring at the sea, trying to imagine a world without you in it. All I see is an endless stretch of grey.

Her heart gave a lurch.

He smiled. "There is, you know, a simple solution—"

"I thought of it," she interrupted. "I was so desperate I considered suggesting it myself." Blinked the pearls of tears of her lashes. "It is so very tempting, Thomas. But I fear that becoming your mistress would end up making us both unhappy."

"Mistress?" He frowned, then slowly his lips quirked up. "I told you. I already have one mistress."

She gave an involuntary gasp.

"My work," he added quickly after pressing a kiss to her brow. "Valencia, I am not asking you to be my ladybird. I am asking you to be my wife."

"Impossible," she blurted out.

"Why?" he asked.

"You know damn well why. You are a powerful lord and I am a ... nameless nobody. Society would swoon to hear you have legshackled yourself to such a person. There will be too many questions, too many titters. Such nasty scandal would intrude on your work. As for your family, they will likely think you have gone stark, raving mad.

"You forget, I am very good at deflecting questions. You are the only one in the world who matters to me, Val. And since when have you known me to care about convention? Society can go to the devil." He hugged her close, enveloping her in his warmth. "We shall weather any gossip, my love, and Society will soon move on to fresh scandal."

Hope flared in her breast.

"There is just one thing."

Her heart skipped a beat.

"You will have to put up with my odd hours and sudden disappearances. I may be getting on in years, but I am not quite ready to retire."

"I think I can agree to that," she whispered. Slowly running a hand along the line of his jaw. "However, I must insist on a joint command. My training makes it difficult to submit to orders. Is that a problem?

"Is that a yes?"

It took less than a heartbeat to answer.

"Yes."

Thunder rumbled from the ominous clouds hovering on the horizon, drowning her murmur.

"Yes!" she shouted, tears mingling with raindrops. Sweet and salt. Holding him tightly, she watched the distant flashes of lightning illuminate the horizon. The future looked brighter than she had ever imagined.

Blinking away the droplets, she kissed him ...

A large wave shuddered the deck, throwing them up against the rail. "Damn," murmured Lynsley, his lips feathering against her damp hair. "Not another cursed ocean squall. I must say, I am getting heartily sick of turbulent seas."

"Not me. " Lifting her face to the wind and rain, Valencia let out a whoop of joy. "I shall always adore the sight of storm-clouds and wine dark seas."

"You must be drunk with love."

"I am!"

"Ah, well, in that case, kiss me again. And again." It was some moments before his lips raised from hers. "I suppose I can learn to like an Atlantic gale. Just so long as I always have you to bring me back to life."

Chapter Twenty-Five

Lynsley set his hat and gloves on the sidetable of Mrs. Merlin's private office.

"Excellent. I was hoping you would offer the usual refreshments," he said dryly, seeing the silver tray already arranged by the sofa. "The pastry chefs of Paris cannot match the skills of your cook, especially when it comes to strawberry tarts."

The headmistress peered at him over her glasses. "That was a close shave, Thomas. You were very lucky."

"Very lucky, indeed," he replied gravely.

As she smoothed at her dove grey skirts, her hands betrayed a slight flutter. "For a moment or two, you had me worried."

"I do apologize." He took a seat and crossed his legs. "So you sent out reinforcements to rescue me?"

"Hmmph." A tiny snort sounded. "That rascal Marco came up with the idea on his own. As for Verona ..."

"You may leave them to me," he murmured. "I have a suitable punishment in mind for them both."

Steam curled up as Mrs. Merlin poured a cup of tea and passed it over. "So Rochambert is dead?"

"Yes."

"And the weapon is safely in Whitehall's hands?"

"No. The fact is, no one has it. It was destroyed, along with the papers detailing its creation." He shrugged. "Bathurst is not overjoyed, but I cannot feel too disappointed. To my mind, we have enough ways of killing each other without adding a new dimension to our armaments."

"Amen to that." The headmistress sipped meditatively at her tea. "So, it seems everything turned out for the best, despite the rocky start." She took off her spectacles and pinched her nose. "You are certainly looking in fine fettle for a man who has gone through hell."

He smiled. "It was not all pain and suffering."

"If I didn't know better, I would say ..." She gave an owlish squint, then shook her head. "Never mind. Did you bring back anything else of interest from Paris?"

"Several bottles of excellent champagne. An embroidered waistcoat that my valet has already consigned to the ragbin." Lynsley tapped a finger to his chin. "Oh, and a wife."

Mrs. Merlin was starting to rise but sat down with a thud. "I beg your pardon?"

"Not exactly a wife," he amended. "A fiancée. However, we will be married on the morrow by special license. A small ceremony here in the country. I am hoping you will attend, Charlotte."

She took a moment to catch her breath. "I confess, this comes as somewhat of a shock. Not an unpleasant one, mind you. I have been wondering for some time whether you were growing too set in your ways. Like old age, old habits are hard to shake."

He grinned. "I think I have found a second youth."

"I am looking forward to meeting the lady," said the headmistress. "She must be a singular female to have swept you off your feet."

"That she is."

Mrs. Merlin carefully squared the papers on her blotter and lined the pens in a neat row before asking, "Is she French? It is not that I have any prejudice against such a match, but it might be a bit awkward, given your government responsibilities."

"No, my bride-to-be is English," replied Lynsley. "And actually, you know her, so I took the liberty of asking her to accompany me here this morning." He rose and went to the door. "Do come in, my dear."

Valencia entered the room and crooked a shy smile at the headmistress. "It has been a long time, Mrs. Merlin."

"Too long." The elderly lady moved with surprising speed to envelop her former student in a heartfelt hug. "Welcome home, Valencia," she murmured, a glint of tears winking from behind the lenses of her spectacles.

Lynsley cleared his throat with a cough. "Speaking of home, Valencia and I had a notion that maybe she could spend part of her time here. Perhaps teach a class or two, given the recently depleted ranks, we need to get the new master class of Merlins up to snuff in a hurry."

"True," agreed Mrs. Merlin. "I sense that Britain's need for our special warriors is only going to become more pressing as Napoleon seeks to make up for his set-backs in Russia.

"As you know, I have a small country estate close by, which would make the arrangement work quite well." He allowed a twitch of his lips. "Apparently my bride does not care for the idea of living in London as a titled lady of leisure."

Valencia smiled too. "I don't think I would make a very good Society wife. I need to be useful." She made a wry face. "And I can't quite picture myself making the rounds of morning calls, discussing the latest fashions and foibles of the *ton*."

"I think it a splendid suggestion," said the headmistress. "I can think of several subjects where your expertise and experience would be invaluable for the students."

"Perhaps a course on life after active duty." For a moment, Valencia's eyes sparkled with humor, then darkened to a deeper intensity. "It is something they all must face, and the transition is not always easy."

"Growing old gracefully?" suggested Lynsley.

"We could schedule it just before yoga class," murmured Valencia

His shoulders flexed. "It seems the schedule for the coming term is shaping up rather nicely." He winked. "Just so long as you are home in time to fix my supper."

Mrs. Merlin watched the play between them with an enigmatic smile. "A very good suggestion—the class, that is. Somehow I think your personal staff can manage to keep you fed, Thomas."

"You had had better not be expecting me to wait on you hand and foot," said Valencia.

The headmistress smothered a laugh in a shuffle of papers. "Speaking of the curriculum, Thomas, I do have several administrative matters we ought to go over, but perhaps you would rather put it off for a few days."

Lynsley pursed his lips. "Actually, we are leaving after the wedding for a visit to my brother's estate. So it would be best to deal with them now." He glanced at Valencia. "Do you mind, my dear?"

"Of course not." She rose. "In the meantime, I think I shall have a look around."

"Savannah heard that Lord Lynsley's carriage rolled through the front gates less than an hour ago. I wonder if we're really in for trouble, now that he's back." Verona made a face as she unrolled her fencing kit. "I don't dare hazard a guess. The marquess was certainly acting awfully ..."

"Horny?" suggested Marco with a waggle of his hips. "Who could blame him? Wherever he plucked up that ladybird, she certainly had a fine set of ... feathers."

"Ssshhhhhh." Verona kicked him in the shin. "Show a little respect for your superiors," she muttered. "I'm in enough trouble as it is. You are going to get me plucked of every privilege for the foreseeable future. Because of you and your damn rescue plan, I'm already stuck mucking out the stalls until the end of the month."

"I *did* say I would help."

"Aye. And quite a concession it was," snapped Verona. "I'm touched that you would deign to risk getting manure under your manicured nails."

"As well you should be, *bella*." Marco gave a flourishing wave. "These hands are precision instruments. They play a lady's charms like a fiddle."

"Trust me, they won't be pulling at *my* strings." She slid a chamois over the blade of her foil. "By the by, have you any idea who she is?"

"*She?*"

Verona whirled around at the wolfish growl.

"What *she* are you talking about?" asked the head fencing master. His lips curled in a lecherous leer. "

"Lord Lynsley's, er, female companion," she replied.

Marco was far less discreet. "*Si, si.* When we found him in France, he was sequestered with a tall, dark-haired beauty." The accompanying hand gestures were more than eloquent in explaining the circumstances. "But then, the marquess is said to be a master at forging strategic alliances. Apparently, old age hasn't blunted his skills."

Allegretto Da Rimini grinned. Like Marco, he was Italian, and in his prime the man known as Il *Lupino*—the Wolf— had been the most feared blade in all of Europe. Despite the slashes of silver at his temples, he was still a master of steel—and sexual innuendo.

But instead of making his usual lewd comment, his expression turned thoughtful. "Tall, dark-haired, you say ... Did she have emerald eyes and walk with a limp?"

Verona shook her head. "I couldn't tell."

Marco's gaze sharpened. "Why?"

Da Rimini shrugged. "Never mind." Unsheathing his saber, he ran a thumb along its edge. "Just an odd thought."

Seemingly loath to let the subject drop, Marco set a hand on his hip. "Talk about odd. You would have been astounded, *amico*, to see our lordly leader that night. The marquess is always so coolly elegant, with never a hair out of place, eh? Well, he had shed that air of reserve, along with his trousers ..."

The sound of voices made Valencia pause at the courtyard gate.

"*Dio Madre*, the perfume of passion was so thick in the air you could have cut it with a knife ..."

Ah. It seemed that the handsome young man—Marco?—was waxing poetic on their recent encounter in France.

"Which, I might add, Lynsley's ladybird held with a practiced hand," went on Marco. "It looked like she had a great deal of experience in handling a weapon." He grinned. "No wonder His Lordship was all afire to have us leave. The woman was hot ..."

She had picked up a fencing sword from the rack in the Weapon courtyard and with a flick of cold steel, she touched the rapier to his spine. "Talking out of school, *bambino*?"

Da Rimini looked around. "Well, I'll be damned."

"That goes without saying, you old wolf." Valencia smiled. "Aside from the benighted state of your soul, how are you?"

"As you see, trying to teach these young chicks to be as good as you were has turned my hair grey," he replied.

"You were a *Merlin?*" blurted out Verona.

"*Si*, the very best," said *Il Lupino* softly.

"That was a long time ago." Valencia turned to meet the student's wide-eyed gaze. "Thomas tells me you are the current queen of the roost."

"I—I ..." stammered Verona.

"She has a long way to go before she can soar to your heights," finished Da Rimini.

"I don't fly much anymore." Valencia touched a hand to her thigh. "These days, I live a rather down-to-earth life. I am happy to cede my place in the sky to a younger hawk."

Verona bit her lip. "I may not have my wings after His Lordship finishes his meeting with Mrs. Merlin."

"His Lordship is extremely patient with the headstrong hellions of his flock," said Valencia. "In my experience, he is understanding, and generous to a fault in granting a second chance."

"Understanding, my arse," growled Da Rimini. "Lynsley was a bloody idiot to let you leave the nest."

"It was my choice," she answered. "Thomas offered me terms. I did not care to accept them."

"Quite right, *cara*." Marco had been following the exchange with great interest. "The marquess may have pots of money, but I have youth on my side. If you are looking for a freelance position—"

"I suggest you sheath your tongue." It was Lynsley who stepped out from the shadows. "Unless you wish to be fishing your cods out of the courtyard cistern." He had changed from his formal dress into fencing garb—a loose linen shirt buckskin breeches, and soft leather boots. The breeze ruffled his hair and the pale blue silk kerchief knotted at his throat.

Valencia felt the air seize in her lungs. *Youth be damned.* No man was a match for the marquess. She loved every line in his face, every strand of silver-flecked hair curling at his temples. Every nuanced facet of his beautiful eyes. It was experience that gave them such depth and richness.

If the young man was lucky, he might some day measure up to his mentor. But for now ...

"Just a bit of good-natured teasing, milord." Marco grinned. "No offense meant, *cara*."

"None taken," murmured Valencia. "However, my services are not for hire."

Marco exaggerated a sigh. "So I see. I shall just have to be satisfied with, how you say, sour grapes."

Lynsley's sword cut through the air with a soft swoosh. "Like fine wine, I have improved with age."

A bark of laughter sounded from *Il Lupino*. "That is putting the pup in his place." He sauntered to the center of the fencing circle and drew a line in the hardpacked earth with the point of his saber. "What say you to going a round? For the past. And for the present." The fencing master pointed to the group of girls who had gathered at the far end of the pitch. "I should like my master class to see what heights they should aspire to."

She flexed her leg. "I'm not sure I'm still sharp enough to give you a fight."

Da Rimini tossed her a padded doublet and assumed the *en garde* position. "Old habits die hard, Valencia."

It was strange how life could come full circle. The angled light on the walls, the rough canvas quilting against her skin, the very ground beneath her boots brought back memories of her days at the Academy. She had come here as a wild and wary orphan, raging with anger at the world. And though she had learned so many life lessons within its walls, she had left with her body broken and her inner conflicts still unresolved.

And now? As she looked around, Valencia felt a profound sense of peace. Da Rimini was right—and wrong. Some things were impossible to change, and yet, she was living proof that one could learn from past mistakes.

She knew her strengths, forgave her weaknesses. But most of all, she understood what mattered most was heart, not steel. Forged in friendship, tested by trust, love was something worth fighting for.

Lynsley had made her whole again.

Her gaze met his, and warmth of his look curled her to her very core. No more questions. No more doubts. This was who she was meant to be.

"On second thought, Da Rimini, perhaps you ought to step aside and observe the action. The better to comment to the students." The marquess tested the torque of his weapon. "I wouldn't mind a match with the lady."

The fencing master yielded his place. "Have a care, *patron*. This could be embarrassing." He mimed a scissor-like snipping near his testicles. "My girls are trained to unman an opponent."

"I'm no longer a girl, *Lupino*," said Valencia. "Nor, for that matter, am I a lady."

A corner of Lynsley's mouth twitched up. "You will be by this time tomorrow."

Stepping in toe to toe, she set her sword against his. "Ready when you are."

"*Contrapassura*," called Lynsley, sliding slowly to his left.

She countered with a whirling *colpo mezano*.

Picking up the pace, he tested her reflexes with a series of lightning slashes.

"You haven't lost your touch," said Da Rimini gruffly.

In answer, she shifted the sword to her left hand and angled a quick feint before flipping it back to her right,

"*Bella, bella.*" In a louder voice, he added. "See how she holds her weapon, class? Firm, yet relaxed, the fingers applying just the right amount of pressure. Pay close attention, *signorinas!*" he waggled a finger "For you girls, fencing is like sex—you must keep control of the man's blade."

"And then, at the first opening, we should hit a man in the bollocks, right?" called one of the students. "That will sap all the steel from his sword."

Lynsley winced at the words. "Don't even think about it," he said to Valencia as he spun through a *mandritto*.

"*Il Lupino* has nothing to worry about!" called a voice from the rear ranks "I heard he lost his balls in a card game with a contessa and a cardinal in Milan."

"Ten demerits!" warned Da Rimini. "Ten demerits to the next little bird who insults my manhood."

Marco doubled over in mirth.

They fought on for another few minutes, neither gaining the upper hand. *Il Lupino* paced the perimeter, keeping up a running commentary. The master class stared, spellbound. Lynsley's training sessions had always taken place in private. They had never seen him display his prowess.

As word of the unusual duel spread like wildfire through the Academy, the classroom windows began to fill up with faces pressed to the mullioned glass. The third-year girls had all abandoned their archery practice and were perched on the top of the armory wall.

Da Rimini finally consulted his pocketwatch and rang the bell. "*Grazie* for the display, Valencia. With a little practice, you would be even better than in your student days." The fencing master turned to the marquess. "So *patron*, have you decided who will wear the trousers in your family?"

"Maybe we'll share," replied Lynsley with a straight face. He toweled the sweat from his brow. "Or perhaps we should go mano a mano for the privilege."

Valencia couldn't resist a mischievous smile. "You are sure you wish to risk a blow to your manly ... pride?"

"Oh, I think I am up for the challenge."

"Suit yourself." She looked down her nose at his sweat dampened linen and snug buckskins. "You will look quite silly walking down the corridors of Whitehall in your drawers."

"While you will look quite seductive lying in my bed with naught but a froth of lace on your legs."

The thought of sharing Lynsley's bed from now on stirred a lick of pure pleasure in her belly. "That is most ungentlemanly," she murmured, brushing close by him as she took up position in the center of the circle. "Trying to distract me is bending the rules of engagement."

"All's fair in love and war, remember?"

"I will keep that in mind." An instant before Da Rimini called *"en garde"*, she pivoted and flicked her sword down, swatting him across his bum with the blade.

"Touché"

The girls hooted and stomped their feet.

"First honors to the females." Lynsley inclined a courtly bow. "But unless senility has set in, I seem to recall that class bouts are two out of three." He angled a sidelong glance at the youthful faces. "No smirking, Verona. You are still on probation."

The young Merlin took cover behind Marco's broad shoulders.

"You are putting on quite a performance," said Valencia dryly as they resumed a starting stance. "I'm not sure the students will ever see you in the same lordly light as before."

"I thought you said I should appear human." His mouth

quirked. "And heavens knows, my dear, when I see your lovely limbs in action, I am all too aware of being a mere mortal man."

Their blades crossed with a velvet click.

"Now girls, watch closely!" announced Da Rimini. "It's not everyday that we have a chance to observe poetry in motion."

"*How do I love thee? Let me count the ways ...*" recited Lynsley in a voice that reached only her ears.

As Valencia bit back a laugh, the marquess moved with deceptive quickness. Even though she knew of his speed and agility, the feints and footwork took her off guard. His blade pricked one breast, then the other breast. "Tit for tat," he called, flashing a wicked grin.

"The cock shouldn't crow quite yet," she retorted, a remark that drew lusty laughter from Da Rimini and Musto. "The match is not yet over."

They broke cleanly for the third try.

Snick, snick, snick. The quicksilver clash of their swords was evenly matched. Parry, feint, riposte—the courtyard echoed with the ring of forged metal and flesh moving in perfect harmony.

A pas de deux—a glorious dance for two, choreographed to a symphony of steel.

Valencia spun, feeling light as a feather. This was home, the one place in the world where she was meant to be. Ducking low, she feinted and flashed a smile.

Their gazes met, and Lynsley winked. He hesitated for an instant, just long enough to let her next slash knock the weapon from his grip.

A raucous cheer went up as the girls applauded the victory.

He dropped to one knee. "It seems I have no choice but to surrender."

Valencia waggled her sword. "Why say you, girls? Shall we

make him run the perimeter of the grounds as punishment for the loss?"

His brow waggled. "At my age?"

"*Si, si*, have mercy on the old man," drawled Da Rimini. "He had better save his strength for his wedding night."

"You *are* going to marry him, aren't you, *cara*?" asked Marco. "Or are you and our saintly leader going to continue living in sin?"

"I have always thought piety vastly overrated," snickered Da Rimini. "I'd take up residence in the hottest corner of Hell if such a lady would share it with me."

"You can still change your mind, *cara*," added Marco. "I am at your service—"

"Marco, my friend," interrupted the marquess. "Unless you wish to contract your own nuptials as a *castrati*, you had better keep a respectful tongue when talking to my soon-to-be bride."

Lynsley remained kneeling as he slid his hand up the length of Valencia's sword. Pulling the hilt from her grip, he peeled off her leather gauntlet and pressed her palm to his lips. "Just so there's no misunderstanding, let me make my position clear to one and all."

Silence fell over the stones.

Valencia realized she was blushing like a schoolgirl.

"Valencia has done me the honor of consenting to be my wife."

A collective sigh fluttered up from the students.

"And as you see, I consider myself the most fortunate man in the world. I am humbled by her strength and her grace. She is ..." The marquess hesitated, as if searching for the perfect word. "She is ..."

"She is a Merlin!" called out a youthful voice.

"And a Merlin can bring any man to his knees!"

Rising along with another round of feminine cheers,

Lynsley swept her off her feet. "A Merlin," he murmured. "Since the day I met you, my love, you have had me under your spell."

Nearly blinded by the brilliant light in his eyes, Valencia had to blink. To her surprise, she discovered her lashes were wet with tears. "It must be ancient magic," she whispered.

"No, Valkyrie." Lynsley feathered a kiss to her brow. "It must be true love."

Their eyes met for a long moment, and then after a quick wink, he looked back to Da Rimini. "Why are you and your students still standing around? There's no time to waste in getting the fledglings ready to fly as true Merlins."

Also by Andrea Pickens

TRADITIONAL REGENCIES

INTREPID HEROINES

The Banished Bride

The Storybook Hero

Second Chances

A Stroke of Luck

A Lady of Letters

The Defiant Governess

Code of Honor

The Major's Mistake

The Hired Hero

Pistols At Dawn

DANGEROUS LIASIONS

A Diamond in the Rough

Sweeter than Sin

Devil May Care

REGENCY SPY/ADVENTURE/ROMANCES

MRS. MERLIN'S ACADEMY FOR EXTRAORDINARY YOUNG LADIES

The Spy Wore Silk

Seduced by a Spy

The Scarlet Spy

To Love a Spy

OTHER

Omnibus

Christmas by Candlelight

About the Author

I started creating books at the age of five, or so my mother tells me. And she has the proof—a neatly penciled story, the pages lavishly illustrated with full color crayon drawings of horses and bound with staples—to back up her claim. I have since moved on from Westerns to writing about Regency England (clearly I have a thing for Men In Boots!) a time and place that has captured my imagination ever since I opened the covers of Jane Austen's "Pride and Prejudice."

I have a BA and an MFA in Graphic Design from Yale University, where I studied book design (As you see, I've always had a left brain-right brain love affair with art and the printed word.) These days, when I'm not tethered to my keyboard I enjoy traveling to interesting destinations around the world—however, my favorite spot is London, where the esoteric museums, funky antique markets and used book stores offer a wealth of inspiration for my stories.